THE AWAKENING OF DAVID ROSE

A
"David Rose" Novel
by
Daryl Rothman

THE AWAKENING OF DAVID ROSE
David Rose – Book 1
Third Edition Copyright © 2019 by Daryl Rothman
Original 1st Edition Copyright © 2016 by Daryl Rothman

THIRD EDITION SOFTCOVER
ISBN: 1622535650
ISBN-13: 978-1-62253-565-1

Assistant Editor: Kirstin Anna Andrews
Senior Editor: Lane Diamond
Cover Artist: D. Robert Pease
Interior Designer: Lane Diamond

EVOLVED PUBLISHING™
www.EvolvedPub.com
Butler, Wisconsin, USA

Printed in Book Antiqua font.

BOOKS BY DARYL ROTHMAN

DAVID ROSE
Book 1: *The Awakening of David Rose*
Book 2: *David Rose and the Forbidden Tournament*
Book 3: *David Rose and the Days of Awe*

STAND-ALONE NOVELS
Gospel

DEDICATION

For David, Rachel, and Daniel,
whose bond continues to inspire this tale.

INTRODUCTION

"Death — the last sleep? No, it is the final awakening."
~ *Sir Walter Scott.*

"Failure or success seem to have been allotted to
men by their stars. But they retain the power of
wriggling, of fighting with their star or against it,
and in the whole universe the only really interesting
movement is this wriggle."
~ *E.M. Forster*

PROLOGUE
England: 5th Century A.D.

THE CASTLE FLARED INTO SIGHT WITH each cross-stitch of lightning, overlooking two of its favorite sons at war. The moon peeked occasionally from behind a patchwork of opaque clouds, as though afraid to pay witness. Curtains of rain raked through the countryside, rendering visibility poorer still. With each thunderbolt from the heavens, the knights set upon each other, their cries drowned by the reverberating clanging of steel.

Their horses stamped impatiently nearby, fog spiraling from their muzzles. Near the equines lay the knights' discarded shields, bearing the face of the beautiful maiden loved by both men. Rivulets flowed like tears from her likeness.

The knights circled, undeterred by the relentless downpour that rendered their theater a quagmire. The storm had swept in from the sea, which fomented and frothed beneath the sheer cliffs that lay not a mile from where the men now fought.

Their confrontation raged far longer than most duels, but one of them had—almost imperceptibly—seized the advantage, the force and angle of his strikes steadily weakening his foe. Like a predator sensing the kill, he intensified his assault with quick jabs of his weapon.

His adversary doggedly resisted, but continued his slow fade.

There would be no concession on this evening. Whoever would perish would extend the conflict until his last ounce of strength and last breath ebbed. So it must be. And so they fought.

***

Atop an adjacent hillside, a man watched. At moments, visibility became nil, but he persevered in his vigil. With each fleeting moment of illumination, he quickly assessed the developments unfolding between the two combatants he'd come to know so well. One warrior had dictated the pace and nearly executed a mortal blow on multiple occasions, but night now reigned, and the warrior's strength appeared duly diminished.

The game had begun to turn.

***

The faltering combatant let his heavy arms slump to his sides. A mistake, as his opponent hesitated ever so briefly, then exploded forward with a final thrust of his sword.

The vanquished warrior grunted and collapsed to his knees, his blade fallen at his feet. "Finish it!" he cried, his voice thick with hate.

The victor panted as he removed his helmet and gloves. His wild shock of brown hair fell around his stubbled face, and his cobalt eyes pierced the darkness as he shook his head and regarded his rival. "It didn't have to be this way, my friend."

The stricken warrior snarled with contempt. "It had to be this way," he hissed. "And no friend are you." His words trailed off into violent, bloody expectorations.

"We both loved her," shouted the victor. "But neither of us needed die in her name."

"Not just her. Do you so easily forget my brothers?"

"I pray forgiveness each day, but you know well that their deaths were an accident." A sky-blue glow began to shimmer around the edges of his blade.

"Lightkeeper," sneered the dying knight.

"A designation I never sought."

"Yet you gladly reap the rewards. But you are not the only one bestowed such powers." The fallen knight raised a trembling arm and gestured toward the frothing sea, beseeching. "Myrddin, hear me!" His cries echoed into the darkness, alighting on foul winds and carrying over the cliffs toward the churning waters and caves below.

The victorious knight shook his head in disbelief. "You seek reprieve in our wise and noble friend? These are powers even *he* cannot wield, unless he has by some miracle discovered the grail and held it secret from each of us, including our king. He will not intervene in this matter, and certainly not on your behalf."

"Your arrogance blinds you," gasped the stricken man. "You forget who sired our wise and noble friend... and you forget the times I have rescued him from the edge of death, thus currying favor of my own when the time should come. I curse the heavens that this be the result, but if there be a sympathetic soul in hell, I will beg such fortune that this not be the end."

The victor held his arms out to either side. "I have won this matter."

The fallen knight raised his head a final time. "So you think." His head slumped again, and his body pitched forward.

***

When a moment later the sky flashed white, the victorious knight saw his rival's eyes staring back at him, unblinking. An unearthly moan issued up from the sea below, and the knight stepped slowly backward and stared as vast fingers of darkness—darker than night itself—reached up and over the cliffside and spiraled forward in inky shadow. They enveloped the fallen warrior, whose chest heaved once as if in the throes of one final breath, and rolled back, disappearing into the depths from which they'd come.

The knight, summoning his last traces of strength, pursued them to the edge of the cliff. The downpour had at last abated, and he watched as the shadows slithered down the cliff face like black rivers. They emptied back into the sea and receded into the cave—his cave.

What dark union? What deal with the devil has in that tomb-like cavern been forged?

He knew not, and for this evening, it mattered not. Though wise men pontificated, mystics cajoled, and kings bargained for their very souls, when the last leaf had fallen, not one among them could claim enlightenment as to things eternal.

And so, for now, back to the sea.

He watched the waters lapping at the mouth of the cave, flowing in with the tide and ebbing out, a dark current. His eyes traced out toward the open sea, which breathed calmly now in the wake of the storm, vast and mysterious, and this only the scant bit visible to his mortal gaze. He looked and, in all he saw, knew there was infinitely more unseen: life and death, dark and light.

It rolled out before him in the ebb and flow of the waters, an endless bridge to shores and worlds and days unknown.

CHAPTER 1
Time

DAVID ROSE, ONE DAY SHY OF his fifteenth birthday, peered into the normally placid stream and tried to find himself. Rain had swollen its banks and the waters rose as if to meet him, but at first, he could not detect his reflection, probably on account of the darker than normal current and overcast skies. The stream snaked its way through the woods he crossed to get home after exiting the bus each afternoon after school.

Normally he skipped right over it, but that afternoon something had caught his eye, something shiny and large like a glistening trout. Even though he'd never seen a fish in there before, he couldn't reason what else it might possibly be. In any event, whatever it was had long since vanished.

He glanced at his watch before remembering the futility of doing so. The battery had died and the hands had stopped, and though he hadn't gotten it repaired, he nonetheless wore it dutifully. The rain fell harder now and the stream rose higher, and he turned to head further downstream in hopes of a narrower crossing. As he turned, he spotted a cluster of bright violet flowers coloring the ground near his feet.

He'd cut through these woods a thousand times but never once had noticed them. Today was apparently a day of firsts.

"Well, well, look what we've got here."

David's heart accelerated at the voice of one of the Gentry brothers, neighborhood bullies.

Technically freshmen like David, they'd been held back so many times that no one really knew their age. They played hooky more often than not, and whether they'd even gone to school on this day was anybody's guess. Probably not. They'd chased just about every kid in the neighborhood at one time or another, and beaten up more than a few. Their long, dirt-colored hair slicked across their foreheads from the now harder-falling rain, but not so completely as to mask the malice in their beady eyes. A cigarette—limp from the drizzle—dangled from the lips of one like an albino worm, flecks of ash dotting his tattered leather jacket. The other brother—despite the weather—wore a tank top, but did not seem the least bit cold.

David's eyes riveted now upon the pants pocket of each brother, and the unmistakable outlines of switchblades.

"Thought you were smarter than to come through here alone, Rose," said the tank-topped one.

David glanced quickly back toward the stream.

"No one here to save you," said the smoker. His eyes narrowed. "That watch," he said, peering at David's wrist. He extended his palm as though asking a simple favor.

"No." The word escaped David's lips involuntarily— it had clearly come from him, but it almost seemed as though it had come from a different him—a him *inside* of him. He had no time to ponder this. His stomach knotted as he watched both brothers reach into their pockets.

"No?" The one who'd extended his hand withdrew it now, his face awash with incredulity.

"You're definitely dumber than I thought." He flicked his wrist as though dealing a hand of cards.

David heard the unmistakable snap of an unfolding blade. Another *snap*: behind him, the other one had followed suit.

He was certain his mind had commanded his legs to start backing up, but for some unfathomable reason they did not obey. Now his head began to swim and his eyes, fixed upon the two switchblades, narrowed as the scene before him pitched, heaved, and clouded.

When the turbulence eased, the Gentry boys remained poised before him, except they weren't... them — not exactly. They had not so much disappeared as transformed. They now wore armor — *medieval armor* — and they no longer clutched their modest knives, wielding instead long, curving swords.

The smoker took a step toward him, and David jarred from his stupor. The hallucination faded, the Gentrys again became the Gentrys, and now the chase was on.

The drizzle had grown to a downpour, but he flew through the woods, past scraping branches and grabbing limbs, fueled by something more potent than mere adrenaline. He could feel the brothers close on his heels. The ground was a quagmire, and several times David's feet slipped and skidded, but he remained upright, and even managed somehow to increase his pace.

When finally he emerged from the edge of the woods, he came to a sliding halt near the water's edge and, heart pounding, whirled around. No sign of the Gentrys. He exhaled slowly but remained on high alert. Where he'd stopped, the stream gathered force before channeling into a raised, circular storm drain.

To his right a few paces, a gnarled tangle of overgrown roots and wayward tree limbs extended down from the edge of the forest and into the water. He stepped back a few paces, to allow himself ample momentum, as he'd never crossed this far downstream.

As he burst forward and went airborne, he managed to think — midair — *I'm not going to make it.*

He didn't. His lead foot landed on the opposite bank, but his trail leg splashed into the current. He pawed vainly at the muddy terrain, but his feet slipped from under him and he fell backwards into the freezing waters. The back of his head slammed into the concrete wall of the sewer drain, and he groaned.

It felt as though a small grenade had detonated in his skull. He massaged the egg on the back of his head with one hand, and braced his hands against the cold floor of the streambed with the other, then pushed up and stood. Shivering profusely, he stepped toward the muddy bank, but then paused.

He'd heard something inside the tunnel. "We have searched for you a long time," he thought it said, the sound unlike any he'd ever heard — mesmerizing.

He sloshed toward the entrance of the drain, gripped the walls, and poked his head inside. He heard a frantic splashing as whoever — or whatever — had made the sound scrambled quickly backwards. Water continued to flood into the dark tunnel. At first, David saw only blackness, but as his eyes adjusted, he thought he spied the faintest glimmer of eye-shine.

"Is someone there?" he called.

Nothing. Inside the tunnel, the water coursed and echoed like a whitewater river. Given the roar of the current, he likely would not be able to hear anything else.

And yet he did.

The waters slowed and grew tranquil, the rain stopped, and his body warmed. The sky cleared, showering him with the sun's warmth. It was, he thought, the most peaceful of moments.

"Master does not wish me to make contact with you just yet," the voice said.

David could hear soft splashing, like two little legs and feet lifting up and back down, inching closer in the water. "But The Great Assembling nears."

David closed his eyes and inhaled deeply.

The blow to the head. That has to be it.

He exhaled and slowly opened his eyes.

She was staring right at him, and she was beautiful.

Her golden hair fell in twisting curls from underneath a crown of small, white flowers. She wore a white, ruffled gown, yet somehow, neither gown nor hair nor flowers seemed saturated. Her skin was pale and unblemished, and her eyes glinted like emeralds.

David stared into them, transfixed, and felt himself falling into her. She slowly extended her arm, and he extended his, their hands touching at the edge of the tunnel, where the darkness met the light.

"Remember," she whispered.

His hand closed around hers and he shut his eyes.

A crackle of thunder sounded and he fell back, startled, into the once-more tumultuous current. The waters grew cold again, the skies went dark, and the rain pelted down. Everything roared loud and fast again. David scrambled to his feet but slipped and submerged once more. He grabbed for the edge of the tunnel with his left hand, but missed, and now he began to panic because his foot had caught on something near the opposite bank, and he could not for the moment free himself. The mass of roots and limbs acted as shackles, and he held his breath as the numbing water swept over him.

His lungs began to burn, and he thrashed about on the stone-cold streambed, but this served only to entangle him further. It occurred to him that of all the peculiar things that had transpired today, this would be the strangest of all: drowning near a sewer-drain in a stream, which on most days he could step across, life and freedom mere inches above his head.

He pushed up from the streambed with all his remaining strength, but the energy he'd exerted in this ordeal, combined with the numbing, powerful waters, rendered it impossible even to steady his hands upon the sifting soil. A strange peace began to overtake him, and deep inside he understood what this meant. It unnerved him more than the panic and the pain, both of which faded in its wake.

No. No. Not like this. Not here. Not now.

He fought back.

He struggled with all he had against the current and the tangle of roots and branches, thrashing like a fish on shore, but the more he did so, the worse things got. The burning in his chest had ended, and his body fell still, unburdened by the labors of heartbeat or breath. It occurred to him that he'd been submerged a terribly long time, and that time was up.

He saw himself floating away on strange currents toward strange shores, and smiled. Wherever his destination, it was surely better than where he now lay. As night fell along the unfamiliar horizon, he saw no more.

***

The pain in his shoulder paled compared to the wholly unsettling sensation of being awakened from a deep sleep. Bits of recognition dripped over him like water, which dripped over him as well, cold and jarring. Fragments of his senses meandered back to him, and his eyes fluttered against dawning light as a symphony of sounds rushed loudly into his ears. He tried to speak but his lungs seized up, and he coughed and choked and expelled what felt like gallons of water.

A hand rested on his back, gentle at first but then rougher, slapping him like a newborn baby. He coughed and choked and expelled more water, and when he was finally done, bent at the waist, panting and spitting. Then he finally looked up.

Robert.

Robert Fuller lived a few blocks away, and they'd been best friends since kindergarten. It seemed he was always helping David out of a jam. He explained that he'd managed to wade in, get a foothold, and pull David onto the slippery bank.

They both stood there, shivering and breathing hard.

"Thanks." David gasped for breath. "How did you know where to find me?"

"Went to your house. You weren't there, so I figured you might be taking the shortcut. What the hell happened?"

"Gentrys."

"Ah!" Robert nodded, having also had his own share of run-ins with the unruly brothers. "They tried to drown you? I didn't see them."

David gulped more air. "They chased me. They had knives. I lost them and ran down here, but slipped trying to cross, and I went under." He nodded back toward the coil of branches. "Got stuck on those."

Robert's eyes shot wide. "Damn, I must have gotten here right after you went under. Glad I got here when I did."

"Me too."

David considered telling his best friend all that had just happened—he usually told Robert everything—but then thought better of it. Fifteen-year-olds did not believe in shape-shifting bullies or mystical creatures. Robert would think him crazy... and maybe he'd be right.

He peered back toward the tunnel. The rain drummed down even harder, and with it the current roared, pouring into the tunnel and misting at the entrance.

No sign of... whatever she was.

Robert placed a hand on his elbow. "Are you okay?"

"I don't know." David gingerly traced the knot on the back of his head. "How did you spot me?"

Robert grabbed his wrist. "This, actually. It was reflecting out of the water really brightly."

The watch.

He lifted his wrist to his eyes. On a day—and in a year—when things seemed to grow stranger by the moment, this struck him as the strangest thing yet. The hands of the watch had once again begun to tick.

CHAPTER 2
Unending, Unbreakable

IT WAS DAVID'S BIRTHDAY, AND HE didn't know what to do.

Indecision had weighted him like an anchor lately. He knew what he *wanted* to do, but it would undoubtedly upset his dad, who already had enough to worry about. He hadn't told him what had happened yesterday. When he'd come through the door drenched to the bone, he simply said he'd slipped when jumping across the stream.

His head throbbed. It seemed as if life was happening around him, piling up.

After stewing about it all day at school, he decided to visit his mother. He would take Rachel, of course, after getting her from the bus stop. She was eight years younger than he was, and couldn't stay home by herself. Some days their dad left work early to be home for her, but today was David's day.

When he got to the bus stop, he eased onto the large, sloping stone that jutted from the swath of grass like an elephant's back. A yawn escaped him. He was always tired. Sleep once provided a refuge, but his demons had caught on and awaited him most evenings. His dreams were strange, insistent. The nightmare he'd awakened from that morning was the worst yet. Violent. Dark. Clanging steel, bloody images. The sense of being pursued—

hunted—from the depths of a faraway place. Just when it felt he'd be overtaken, a small but brilliant light had formed in the distance, accompanied by a gentle voice.

David.

"David."

His eyelids had resisted valiantly, but he'd forced them open and squinted against the shaft of sunlight filtering through his blinds.

A face materialized, appearing for the briefest of moments like an angel in the morning light. "Did you have another dream?"

"Yeah, but it's okay. I'm okay."

"Happy birthday," she'd said.

When her bus finally clattered down their lane and his sister—shouldering a backpack she could have fit inside—stepped down and spotted her brother on the elephant rock, she grinned broadly. "You're old now." She giggled.

She started toward their house, but David reached out and gently tugged her backpack.

"I'm going to take you somewhere today."

"Okay!" She snatched his hand. She'd always seemed to trust him implicitly.

It was just a few blocks to their destination, and along the way, Rachel recounted for her brother every possible detail she could remember from her day: the chicken nuggets at lunch that tasted like a shoe, the frog she'd found in the grass at recess but which Ellie Barton had frightened away—that nosy Ellie Barton!—and that annoying boy Billy Kinnet who, apart from being so annoying, was actually kinda cute.

"Oh!" His sister stopped mid-litany and tugged at his hand. "I made you a present." She wriggled out of her backpack, unzipped a side pocket, and withdrew a blue lanyard bracelet.

"I made it at art," Rachel said, brimming with excitement. "I told Mrs. Detwiler it was your birthday and that I wanted to make you something, and she asked me about you, and she said this would be a good thing to make. It's blue, your favorite color. Mrs. Detwiler says that color stands for etern... eterny... forever. Some word that means forever."

David smiled and tousled her hair. "Eternity."

Rachel nodded. "Yup. And the bracelet too. Mrs. Detwiler says the circle in the bracelet means an unending friendship, and the knots make it unbreakable."

"I love it," David said. "Thank you."

They resumed walking. This would be Rachel's first time visiting their mom. The possibility that dragging her along might be selfish of him, and even traumatic to her, gnawed at him, but if he saw it was getting to her, he could always turn back.

She had resumed her chatter about school and friends and birthdays, and had given no indication that she realized where they were going. Only when they passed through the black wrought-iron gates, which crimped forward at the top like claws, did she stop. Beyond the gates, acres of freshly manicured lawn rolled out beneath canopies of oak, and countless rows of headstones jutted from the earth like sprouting teeth.

Rachel's hand tightened around his, and her voice was so soft he almost didn't hear it. "Momma."

CHAPTER 3
Truth and Wishes

THEY WALKED GINGERLY PAST ROWS OF graves, as if being careful not to disturb anyone, but no one else seemed to be there. David navigated their route toward where he knew their mother's stone lay, keeping ahold of his sister's hand and glancing down every few moments to gauge how she was doing. Her eyes were wide and her bottom lip quivered a time or two, but the dam held; he could only describe her expression as uncommonly brave.

When they arrived at the headstone, however, and Rachel stood eye level with the inscription, her face fell as ashen as the stone itself.

David gently slid the backpack from her shoulders, set it on the ground, and scooped her up in his arms.

"How come you haven't taken me before?" she asked, still staring at the stone.

"I wanted to, but I didn't know if it would upset you, and you know Dad would be upset. He thinks you're too young. That's why he didn't have you come to the funeral."

"But it's my momma."

"I know. It's why I took you today."

She cocked her head and looked at him. "Why did you take me on your birthday?"

He shook his head. "I really don't know. Something was eating at me."

She giggled. "Eating at you?"

"Well, not really eating me." He grinned. "But a feeling—something inside that told me we needed to do this."

They looked at the stone.

> *Emmalie Elizabeth Rose*
> *August 14, 1973 – December 10, 2013*
> *Loving Mother, Wife, Daughter*
> *An Angelic Soul Called Home Too Soon*

Rachel laid her head on David's shoulder. "I miss Momma."

"I miss her too."

They stood silently, his sister's heartbeat palpable as her chest pressed against his, until the sound of approaching footsteps made him turn around.

A man with darting eyes and wild hair, which flared out beneath his ball cap like an overturned houseplant, gestured at him with a long shovel. "Whatcha kids doin' here?" His face and clothes were stained dark with dirt.

David shifted as his sister's arms tightened around his neck. "Visiting our mother," he replied.

The man's eyes softened immediately. "I'm sorry. It's just that sometimes we get kids in here horsing around, defacing stones and such, so I thought I better be sure."

They stared at each other for an uncomfortable few moments before the man's soiled, sunburned face lit with recognition. "Wait a dang minute! I know you. I seen you and your dad last year when...." His eyes moved to Rachel and his voice quieted. "At the service. I was on shift. You all seemed nice folk. Very sad thing, what happened." He nodded toward Rachel. "I don't remember this precious one."

"Our dad thought it would be too hard for her."

The man nodded. "Well, I can understand that, yes sir, I can."

Rachel lifted her head. "That man digs the holes where dead people go?"

David inhaled deeply. This conversation was not one he'd anticipated. "Yes."

"So he dug the hole where Momma's body is?"

"Yes, Rachel."

The man cleared his throat. "Well, no," he murmured. "Not really, of course."

David regarded him curiously. "What do you mean?"

The man rubbed the back of his neck, his gaze falling to the ground. "Well, I dug the hole, yes. I dig the holes. But you know there was no body, right? On account of how she... on account of what happened—the crash, the fire. There was no body."

David now felt his own pounding heart . It had been a closed casket, and he'd just assumed his father didn't want him to glimpse the remains of their mother after the fiery accident near Moreland Farms had claimed her life the previous winter.

"Ah, shoot." The man shook his head. "I ain't ought have said nuthin.' Just figured ya already knew." He removed his ball cap, the tangle of hair molded beneath it unpiling over his forehead, and nodded solemnly. "Apologies. I'll leave you to your business."

David watched him until he'd disappeared beyond some hills at the other end of the cemetery.

Rachel squirmed in his arms, and he set her down. She stepped toward their mother's headstone, regarded it momentarily, and turned back toward her brother, her face crinkled with the look of someone feverishly trying to work something out.

David braced.

"Did they make a mistake?"

His insides knotted. "Rachel—"

"With Momma. Did they make a mistake? If Momma's body isn't there, then she must be someplace else."

David stepped toward her, instinctively wanting to wrap her up in a hug and quiet these notions that would only cause her more pain, but she stepped back, closer to the stone. He didn't know what to do. She shouldn't have to deal with this at her age, and figuring out the best way to help her do so was something he never imagined he'd have to do either. He groaned as indecision welled within him again. How he responded in this moment might affect his sister for the rest of her life. He simply had to tell her the truth, painful as it might be. Letting her hang on to a kernel of false hope would only prove more hurtful for her.

And yet....

Yet? There is no yet.

There couldn't possibly be one, no matter what doubt had festered in him ever since that terrible night. No matter that none of it had ever made the slightest bit of sense to him.

They'd arrived home to find a note that read, simply: *Running out for milk.* This was so strange to David, not because his mom wasn't one to write notes, but because she *was*—always peppered with sentimental kernels of affection. *Love, Momma. See you later, alligator. Have a great day.* She left them notes — all of them, all of the time — in their lunches, on their pillows, and rarely without one of these greetings. On many evenings, Rachel clutched them to her chest while she slept. David remembered finding their mother one evening leaning in Rachel's doorway, watching her sleep. She'd said no matter what else, watching her little angel sleep made everything — at least for the moment — seem right with the world.

In all his life, David could not recall their mom running out at night for milk, much less in treacherous, icy conditions. He'd kept the note, folded up into a tiny square, buried beneath a tangle of socks in the top drawer of his bureau. These notions tortured him at times, but he always managed to push them back down. What use were they? She was dead, gone, and no amount of tormenting himself with questions of *why* would bring her back. But what the well-meaning man with the shovel had just shared with them had struck a chord — with his sister, clearly — and, inexplicable as it was, with him too.

"Maybe," Rachel said with the most solemn of expressions, "Momma is just lost."

"Rachel, no. It's just —"

"Do you think she's dead?"

Truth.

"I don't know."

What have you done?

She looked at him calmly, unfazed, as though his response had been the only logical one, the next piece of the puzzle she'd been working to assemble since the man with the shovel had said what he'd said. "Then make a wish. Everyone gets a wish on their birthday."

"Rachel, not that kind of wish...."

"Will you look for her? Will you at least try?"

David glanced at the far end of the cemetery, where the man with the shovel was digging another hole. With each word to his sister—whose world had been shattered by the loss of the person around whom it most revolved—it felt as though he were digging a deeper and deeper one himself.

"Sometimes," he said, "it just happens that way... that they don't find someone's body. I wish she were still alive too, but if she is, I have no idea where she is or what happened to her. I want her to be alive, but she probably isn't. I know that's hard to hear."

It was as if she hadn't. She grabbed his wrist, much like Robert had done, and looked up at him, her eyes alive with purpose. "Try."

A breeze whispered through the trees, coaxing a smattering of leaves from their branches. When he turned around, he grabbed his sister gently by the shoulders and crouched down so that they were at eye level. "Okay, but we can't tell Dad."

She looked at him a moment, then slowly nodded.

"Promise," he said.

"I promise."

He straightened up and stood beside her, facing the stone, and neither spoke for several moments. The breeze picked up, cooler this time. Rachel shivered but didn't complain, and David put an arm around her as the waning, tree-filtered sunlight glinted off his watch. His mom had given it to him on his fourteenth birthday. On the back, in minute cursive lettering, were inscribed the words: *Time is a Gift*. But time had turned out to be the cruelest of things, and one evening he'd yanked the watch from his wrist and, with a guttural cry, flung it against his bedroom wall. He'd immediately rushed over, scooped it up, and cradled it as one would a wounded bird. Its face was chipped and scuffed, the hands still, but he'd slid it back on and worn it faithfully since.

"We better get home," he said.

He helped her slip her backpack on again, and she grabbed his hand as they left their mother's grave and crossed back over the grounds, less gingerly this time, toward the exit. When they reached the gates, she tugged at his hand, and he stopped and looked down at her.

"You'll try to find her?"

He inhaled deeply and nodded.

"Promise," she said.

And he did.

CHAPTER 4
Lightkeeper

RACHEL FELT BAD ABOUT MAKING THE promise not to tell their dad, but a promise was a promise. Besides, their dad hadn't liked to talk a lot since that terrible night. He made sure they got to school, and he went to work, but after dinner most nights, he retreated into his study and closed the door. Unless they needed something, he usually didn't come out until bedtime—sometimes not even then—and on those evenings, David tucked her in and read her a story.

Sometimes, her dad sat and read only by the dull light of the small desk lamp, but one night she hadn't detected any light under the door. She eased it open and crept in to find him sitting in the dark, staring straight ahead, and when she'd touched his hand, she'd given him quite a start.

Sometimes, during the first few months after the accident, she'd heard muffled cries through the door. On one such occasion, she burst into the room and scrambled onto his lap, and he held her, and she cried with him until she fell asleep in his arms. Worse than any of those times, though, was the day she'd listened by the door and heard nothing, and she realized she'd heard nothing many nights in a row.

She came to hate that study. It seemed to have done something to the father she loved so much.

David had told her their dad just needed time, that he missed their mom so much, and sometimes grown-ups coped with things in strange ways, and this was their dad's way. She trusted her brother utterly and promised to try to be patient, but it occurred to her that in his own way, their dad seemed to be lost too. She'd determined in that moment that they needed to help both of their parents find their way home.

***

"It's time."

The words issued forth from the blackness at the far end of the room, but the man knew the voice and had grown accustomed to the darkness. Theirs was a world shrouded in shadow, and preserving it required an acceptance of things unseen.

"Are you certain?" He immediately regretted the inquiry.

For several moments, silence reigned, but then the man heard a click. A tiny orange-red ember appeared at the far end of the room, burning intensely and illuminating rich spirals of smoke before fading into a subdued glow.

"Am I certain?" The voice smoldered, and the flame flared again, like the eye of an angry dragon upon spotting a thief. "Dare not insult me. It is time: the year of assembling darkness."

"He is but a boy."

"He has reached the required age."

"The Lightkeeper?"

"The same."

The man's heart fluttered in his chest like a caged bird. "What of the woman?"

"His protector. She has been detained, as you are aware. A barrier removed."

"Why preserve her?"

A thick plume of smoke accompanied the latest flare. "Your education appears to be lacking. We abide by the rules of the game. The Guardian must be preserved until the Time of Sacrifice. Our attention may now be focused upon the boy."

"What are your orders?"

The glow from the back of the room intensified.

"We approach a razor's edge. Our movements must be equally sharp. When the moment comes, he will be at once his most vulnerable and most dangerous, but first he must be awakened. Now leave me. At last, our destiny is close at hand."

CHAPTER 5
By the Sword

SOMEWHERE IN THE FAR REACHES OF his consciousness, he registered Mr. Cheswick's voice, but David's mind—so easily distractible of late—had wandered off.

"David Rose."

"Yeah," he croaked.

A few chuckles sounded around him, so their history teacher put up a hand to quiet them and looked at David expectantly. "Do you know the answer?"

"Sorry. Can you repeat the question?"

More snickering.

"I asked if anyone knew of the Battle of the North Inch, Clan Chattan versus Clan Kay. You seemed to have your hand up."

David's face heated. He had no idea what Mr. Cheswick was referring to—had never even heard of it—but he cleared his throat, as there seemed no choice but to explain he didn't have his hand up.

"Medieval Scotland," he said instead. "Clan versus clan vendettas played out frequently. The Chattans saw the Kays as interlopers, and the hostilities escalated until finally it came down to trial by combat. They erected a makeshift battlefield and fought to the death. Even the king came to witness it. The Chattans prevailed."

Silence.

Mr. Cheswick studied him with a curious expression.

David's friend Chester McVee leaned forward in his wheelchair and leafed furiously through his textbook. Chester possessed an uncanny ability to remember the most microscopic details, and often concluded a discussion with "Q.E.D.," for *quod erat demonstrandum*, as though he'd just presented a geometric proof. His friends sometimes called him Sherlock, though he'd voiced a preference for Inspector Dupin of Edgar Allan Poe lore.

"You won't find it in there, Chester," said Mr. Cheswick, noting the boy's activity as well. "David must have been doing some of his own research. Well done, Mr. Rose."

David stared vacantly, then glanced quickly around the room as if hoping to spy whoever had really answered Mr. Cheswick's question. Maybe there was another David Rose, because it couldn't have been him.

Mr. Cheswick continued his lecture. "Many events throughout history have been decided by the sword—decided violently. Wars are the obvious example. In some cases, hostilities started with a single fight, an irreconcilable difference, a bitter dispute, a feud."

David surveyed the room, noting that most of his classmates appeared more attuned than usual. His attention stopped at the girl up two rows and one over: Amanda Keppinger. She was beautiful, with long, dark hair that touched her shoulders in the back, and kind, chestnut-colored eyes. She was tall, lanky, like many of the ninth-grade girls—taller than many of the ninth-grade boys. It was not the first time he'd lost himself gazing at her.

When the bell rang, he gathered his stuff and shuffled forward, still helplessly eyeing Amanda, who chatted with friends as they walked toward the door.

"Hey!"

David's attention snapped back and he looked down. He'd stepped on a classmate's foot, and the wrong classmate at that: Owen Gillespie, huge for a ninth-grader at about six-feet tall, and with a temper and reputation to boot.

"Sorry," David muttered, his heart pounding as Gillespie rose to his feet.

The remaining students stared wide-eyed at this sudden turn of events.

Gillespie shoved him, and he stumbled backward and thudded into the wall. His head snapped back, detonating a wave of pain in the base of his skull.

Mr. Cheswick scrambled out from around his desk, but before he could intercede, David flew back at Gillespie and shoved him in return.

Gillespie's anger seemed matched only by his shock. No one had ever stood up to him before.

"That's enough!" Mr. Cheswick stepped between the combatants and placed a hand on the chest of each. "Another fight, Owen?" He shook his head at Gillespie, then turned to David. "What's gotten into you, Rose?"

David remained silent. He did not for the life of him know.

***

The school mandated both boys visit the principal before classes that morning. They summoned Gillespie first, so David sat outside in the administrative area, awaiting his turn. When Dr. Lardman's office door finally opened and a smug-looking Gillespie strode out, David started to get up, but just then a tall man in a dark overcoat swept briskly into the waiting area, past Gillespie, and into the principal's office, closing the door behind him. David sighed and sank back in his chair, chin in his hands.

The office area was unremarkable: a clock; a few potted plants, which appeared desperate for water; and a poster that read, *Your PrinciPAL – if you earn it!* David couldn't help but think the latter would be better placed in an elementary school, and maybe not even there.

Mrs. Gittlebaum, a large, kind woman with billowy hair, which seemed to change color weekly, served as Dr. Lardman's assistant. She chuckled from behind her desk, then quickly put a hand to her mouth when she noticed David looking at her. "Oh, it's not you, sweetie. Just reading a funny message."

"It's okay."

Mrs. Gittlebaum returned to her computer, snickering every now and again, cupping a hand to her mouth each time.

David leaned back in his chair, closed his eyes, and inhaled deeply. He could make out, through the thin walls, some of the conversation occurring in Dr. Lardman's office.

"What more do you want?" he thought he heard the principal say. "I've hired the counselors you wanted."

A deep, muffled voice responded.

"Cheswick?" The principal sounded perplexed. "Harold Cheswick has taught here more than twenty years, and he's been doing what you asked."

The same voice responded again, more sharply.

A few moments later, the door swung open, and David straightened up from his rather obvious listening posture. The visitor exited the office as abruptly as he'd entered, and David never even caught a glimpse of his face. He registered only the sweep of the long, dark coat.

"Okay, sweetie." Mrs. Gittlebaum nodded at him. "He will see you now."

David stood and trudged toward the principal's office. He could hear Mrs. Gittlebaum, still chuckling at her emails as he closed the door behind him.

The principal motioned him toward a chair. "David Rose, please have a seat."

CHAPTER 6
Presque Vu

DAVID'S "PUNISHMENT," BEING HIS FIRST such offense, was to begin sessions with one of the school counselors that afternoon. He couldn't remember ever even seeing the counselors at all.

He tapped on the door, backpack slung over his shoulder, and after a moment, a kind-looking, well-dressed man of perhaps fifty years of age opened it.

"Master Rose." The man extended a hand. "Marcel Fontaine, school counselor. I've been looking forward to seeing you."

David shook his hand firmly, as his dad had taught him—back when his dad taught him such things. "Nice to meet you, Mr. Fontaine."

"A strong handshake." Mr. Fontaine looked at David as though they'd been lifelong friends. "And please, call me Marcel. I want you to know that, in our sessions, you may ask or say anything you wish. I will always be honest with you, and I hope you will be the same. All right?"

David found the informality a bit strange, but said, "All right."

"Would you fancy some fresh air?"

"Sure."

"Master Rose and I will be continuing our session while taking a little stroll," Marcel informed Ms. Gittlebaum as they walked past.

She smiled and returned to her screen.

It felt good to be outside—not cold, but just brisk enough to invigorate the senses. David inhaled deeply. Far across the field, some kids were playing kickball, but Marcel steered David in the opposite direction along the oak-lined walking path, which snaked around the fields.

After they'd walked silently a while, Marcel stopped and gestured toward the cemetery. "Do you know where our school got its name?"

"The Crossing? I never really thought about it."

"It's because of this." Marcel gestured with outstretched arms at the intersection of properties. "Some folks worried about building a school adjacent to a graveyard—thought it might upset the children, or even bring bad luck—but the school's founders saw it differently, a natural arrangement reflective of the cycle of life. It is an old graveyard, nearly three hundred years, built before the town even received its first charter. 'The Crossing.' Most literally, one crosses from one property to the other. More substantively, a crossing of worlds: one a world of vibrancy and youth, the other a place for souls passed on."

David raised an eyebrow as Marcel stepped off the path.

"It's all right," Marcel said. "Let us walk."

David left the path and walked toward Marcel, navigating the first few steps gingerly, as though crossing over hot coals. A line of headstones appeared almost immediately, the first of what looked to be hundreds, perhaps thousands, in a procession of rows that dotted the sloping, finely manicured landscape like ash-hued dominos. A small group of people gathered at the opposite end of the cemetery, and a few individuals visited gravesites. Here and there among the countless rows lay the sobering indentation of unfilled graves.

"Death," Marcel said quietly, "is but part of life."

They walked in silence for a few minutes, until Marcel stopped and turned to David. "Tell me about the woman in the tunnel."

David's eyes widened. "How," he asked in an unintentional whisper, "did you know?"

Marcel paused near a row of headstones. "It is my duty to know such things."

David closed his eyes as wildly opposed emotions pinballed off each other within him. "She was beautiful." His face grew hot, as though he'd just confessed a crush to Robert.

"That she is." A whimsical look lit Marcel's eyes. "And don't think she doesn't know it. Quite beguiling, that one, but not always the most obedient."

David opened and immediately narrowed his eyes. "Obedient?"

Marcel smiled. "Forgive me. That sounds worse than I intend it, but ours is a life of service, if not to a master, then to a calling. Malea is my charge in this lifetime."

David stared at him. *In this lifetime?*

Marcel chuckled. "If there is any keeping charge of a naiad." He glanced at David. "Ah, forgive me once more. Live as long as I have and you accumulate some bad habits. I doubt that the last two things I said to you made any sense."

David shook his head.

"And why would it?" Marcel acknowledged. "You are young, and you have not yet awakened."

David perked up at this last statement. A ray of hope strained through the massing clouds in his head. "Am I dreaming?"

Marcel regarded him evenly. "I'm afraid not."

David's heart sank.

"You are conscious, dear boy, but not yet awake — not in the manner of which I speak."

David staggered, as the hills seemed to pitch and roll before him.

Marcel stepped over to steady him. "There," he said softly. "Take a moment. Breathe."

David did.

"It sometimes seems woefully inadequate," Marcel said, "to attempt to explain something extraordinary in an ordinary manner. I have told you I will always be honest with you, and I will, but some things are better *felt* than merely heard." He gestured at a row of headstones. "I'm not one for theatrics, though a bit of it tends to come with the territory in our world."

David followed Marcel into the row. *Our world?*

Marcel pointed at a headstone. "Know him?"

David read the inscription silently.

> *Malcom Razimoff*
> *1928 – 2007*
> *Beloved Husband, Father, Brother, and Son*

He shook his head.

Marcel gestured at the next headstone.

> *Alexandria Bella Marconi*
> *1899 – 1965*
> *Dearest Wife*
> *Now with the Angels*

No. They moved to the next stone.

> *Sergeant James Chrissman*
> *1912 – 1945*
> *A Hero of Normandy*

Again, no. They moved to the next.

"Archibald Augustus Henry," David read, "1752–1812. Loved his family." He looked at Marcel, who watched him intently. "Met the founding fathers," he continued, his eyes still on Marcel. "Traveled to Philadelphia in 1788 to witness the ratification of the Constitution, the thrill of his lifetime. Encountered terrible storms on his way back home, became terribly ill and almost died, but never regretted a bit of it." David stopped, though more funneled into his head, flooding over him, into him. He slowly turned to read the rest of the inscription, certain the words he'd uttered weren't there, and looked back at Marcel, unconsciously raising a hand to the back of his head.

"It's not from your injury," Marcel assured him.

David felt drained—as though all the energy had gone out of him—yet emboldened, as if something else entirely had come in. He lurched forward, bracing himself on Mr. Henry's headstone.

Marcel placed a hand on his shoulder.

After a few moments, things slowed, and David straightened back up. "How did I do that? I don't know him."

Marcel regarded him solemnly. "Don't be so sure."

David shook his head, slowly at first, then more vehemently, as if doing so might shake off the cobwebs of uncertainty. "Past lives? Is that what you mean? No offense, but I don't believe in that sort of stuff."

"You wouldn't have reason to, until recently."

"Recently?"

"Meeting Malea may have been the most dramatic example, but it's hardly the only strange thing that's happened to you in the past year. Would that be fair to say?"

David nodded.

"In addition to that encounter, there have been other things, yes? Strange things: nightmares, visions, memories... that which you have just now demonstrated."

David looked down. Who *was* this man? *What* was this man? A therapist, obviously, studied and trained in the psychological realm. Perhaps all this was just parlor tricks, the cruel and inexplicable manipulation by an expert of a young, troubled kid.

But when he looked back up at Marcel, he saw nothing but kindness and patience in his eyes, and David didn't feel like a kid. He felt old, impossibly so, and in a way that seemed to align disarmingly well with everything Marcel had said.

"I don't know how I did that," he said. "Something just hit me, but it's more than that—something bigger. Like something on the tip of my tongue that I can't quite get to. Like déjà vu, I guess, but not really that either. I don't believe that all this has happened to me before. I don't remember knowing that guy."

Marcel smiled. "Always a quick learner, Master Rose. You are correct. Not *déjà vu... presque vu*, perhaps."

David rolled his eyes. "*That* I've never heard of."

"*Presque vu.* Tip of the tongue phenomenon, as you aptly put it. This has been happening more and more frequently for you, has it not?"

David nodded.

"In other forms as well, I imagine." Marcel's eyes now locked onto his. "Your dreams... are they vivid, yet agonizingly elusive? Just when it feels within your grasp, *poof*—gone like the wind? *Presque vu...* on the brink of an epiphany. I dare say you are on the brink of yours."

David met Marcel's gaze. "You said you would be honest with me. I don't understand these things. The things you're saying... the way you're saying them... they *sound* insane but they *feel* right, and it makes me think I've gone crazy."

Marcel listened with a look of admiration. "I did say that, didn't I? Well, I've been honest, in fact, but I suppose somewhat in dribs and drabs. I can understand how frustrating that feels, and I am sorry. I do not intend to make a game of this, but as I mentioned, some things are best experienced."

David toed at the ground with his sneakers and bit his lip. "So that's it then? That's what this is all about — past lives?"

"That is only the beginning."

"Beginning of what?" David very much wanted to know and very much didn't want to know.

"Too many think of it in terms of death, of lives gone by, of something ended. Yet when properly understood, it is merely an evolution, a continuation, an awakening into how life can — and must — be lived."

David looked down. His eyes widened as the grass near his feet flushed violet in a blossom of the same strange flowers that had appeared in the woods. Their brightness and color, though beautiful, seemed starkly mislaid in this gray and somber place.

"Amaranth," Marcel said, clearly unfazed by their appearance. "From the Greek, *amarantos*." He smiled. "Unfading. It is no coincidence that they spring up in your midst."

David closed his eyes. He couldn't help but like this man; nonetheless, he wished to be anywhere else at this moment. He thought of his mother. *"The eyes are the windows to your soul,"* she had been fond of saying.

He looked Marcel squarely in his. He did not—could not—believe the things this man was telling him, yet he harbored little doubt that Marcel himself believed them wholeheartedly.

"I don't know what to believe. It's been a hard time." His hand returned unconsciously to the back of his head. "There was more that day at the tunnel, in the stream. I almost drowned." He eyed Marcel nervously, anxious for his reaction, but the counselor couldn't have appeared more calm.

"As a matter of fact—" Marcel placed a hand on his shoulder as if to preemptively steady him. "—you did."

CHAPTER 7
A Light to Guide Her

DAVID WATCHED HIS DAD PRODDING AT pancakes on the griddle. He still hadn't told him any of what had been happening. He couldn't bring himself to cause him any more distress, and besides, where could he possibly begin? With Malea? The strange flowers? Almost drowning, and the strange but kind man who insisted that he had?

"I want lots of syrup." Rachel jabbed a small index finger in her brother's direction, as if to ensure no misunderstanding of her demands.

"Oh," their dad said, "I forgot to tell you that Donovan and Kathy are swinging by in a few minutes. He'll ride the bus with you."

David rolled his eyes at this news. Donovan McCourt was David's age; his mother Kathy had joined the same real estate office as David's dad nearly a year earlier, and they'd gotten pretty close. David resented it, resented *her*, even though Kathy seemed to be ever so gradually coaxing his dad from the shell into which he'd retreated. His dad actually smiled around her — a little bit, anyway — and that was more than he'd done in a long time.

If Rachel noticed the look on her brother's face, she didn't show it. Her attention turned gleefully to the plate of pancakes being presented to her. She clapped her hands, and as she started to say, "What about the syr—," her dad set it down beside her.

"Thank you, Daddy."

A knock sounded.

"Someone's here!" Rachel's long hair brushed over her breakfast plate as she twisted in her chair.

"Rachel." David got up from his chair and swept her hair back over her shoulders. "You're getting syrup in your hair." He grabbed a napkin and wiped as much of it off as he could.

"Syrup in my hair!" She giggled. "I'm silly!"

"Yes, you're silly." David shuffled to the front door to greet their guests.

Donovan was a tall, good-looking kid with a wavy crop of brown hair; his mother, an attractive, auburn-haired woman of about forty. When David opened the door and said hello, he thought he saw a most unpleasant look flicker over Kathy's face, and he involuntarily took a step backward. Then his dad arrived, and Kathy smiled and touched David's shoulder and said good morning with all the warmth in the world.

It must have been nothing.

"Come on in, guys," his dad said. "Donovan, I've got extra pancakes. Did you eat yet?"

"Thanks, I ate. David, you ready?"

"Yeah." David went to retrieve his backpack from the couch.

"Hey," his dad protested, "you didn't eat."

"I'm not hungry."

***

The front door thumped closed, and Rachel looked up as her father sighed.

Kathy smiled. "Kids... sometimes you want to kill them."

Rachel fixed her eyes on her. "Don't say that." She immediately returned contentedly to her pancakes, even casting an eye toward the unfinished portion on her brother's plate.

***

Rachel lay in bed and thought about her day. She'd come to realize her dad was wrong about some things. This was okay—she loved him just the same—but one of the things he was mistaken about was the lamp on her nightstand. Since the night Momma had gone, she'd insisted on sleeping with it on, and when her dad suggested it might be too bright and a nightlight might suffice, she'd shaken her head and insisted on the lamp.

It wasn't for her. It was for Momma, in case she was lost out there in the dark and needed a light to guide her home. Her dad was probably too sad to have thought of that, and probably distracted—by work, by worry, and maybe by Kathy and Donovan. Momma had loved everybody, and Rachel usually did too. Momma had taught her that there was something special and good inside of everyone, and usually she saw those things, just like Momma said, but sometimes now, she saw other things, felt them, and they weren't always good.

Like with Kathy and Donovan. Today wasn't the first time they'd come over. Kathy had sat in Momma's chair, and Rachel didn't understand why her dad had let her. It wasn't her place. There was something about them... Rachel wasn't sure what. It wasn't so much that she saw something bad; rather, she struggled to see anything at all.

Momma once told her something funny. She'd said Rachel was like a beacon, but Rachel was sure she'd said bacon. After they'd giggled about it for quite a while, Momma had said no, *beacon*, because she brought light to everyone around her. She'd thought about that a lot at school today, and her heart had welled with pride.

She didn't feel that way around Kathy and Donovan. Even when they were smiling—which they seemed to do a lot—they always seemed clouded in shadow, as if there were another Kathy and Donovan inside the smiling ones they saw.

She didn't want to think about them anymore—not tonight. It had been a good day, and now she was tired. Her eyes grew heavy, and she thought of Momma, and those were happy thoughts, and she was smiling as she drifted off to sleep.

She left the lamp on, as always.

CHAPTER 8
Old Soul

"ALL MEN'S SOULS ARE IMMORTAL," MR.
Cheswick said. "But the souls of the righteous are
immortal and divine."

David's mother had once called him an old soul.
He hadn't been entirely certain what she'd meant. He
didn't typically think about souls, but Mr. Cheswick's
words that morning jarred his memory.

He hadn't told anyone what had happened with
Marcel at the cemetery. He needed to make sense of it
himself. Alternating waves of doubt and belief washed
over him. Just a few days after that dizzying afternoon,
it all seemed far away and dreamlike, and his
skepticism was beginning to prevail.

"Socrates," Mr. Cheswick said now, evidently in
reference to his statement about souls. He seemed
particularly enthusiastic this morning. An unabashed
Green Bay Packers fan, he kept a triangular, yellow
foam cheesehead on his desk, which he was squeezing
like a stress ball. "The Trojan War is among the most
famous of battles that began with a bitter feud. And
has anyone heard of the Pig War? A confrontation in
1859 between the United States and the British Empire
over the San Juan Islands, which lie between
Vancouver Island and the North American mainland.
The pig was the only casualty of the war, thankfully."

Snorting sounded from the back of the class.

"A tad amusing, yes," Mr. Cheswick conceded. "But in most instances that is not the case. Many of you will one day take psychology courses, human behavior courses. Indeed, some of what we're going to focus on here, with these conflicts, with these feuds, gets at the heart of those things. It captures everything — passion, anger, love, loss — like good literature, in fact: compelling characters and compelling conflict, which somehow must be resolved, sometimes, as we'll see, with great violence and brutality."

David surveyed the class. The majority were sitting up straighter in their chairs, some leaning forward. Even the serial doodlers, such as Henry Blumquist in front of him, were demonstrating at least moderate interest. Chester McVee, to no surprise, was listening intently, taking diligent notes.

"Properly presented," Mr. Cheswick continued, accentuating his point with a raised index finger, "history is lived and breathed and comes alive. In this unit, you will not merely hear and read about these conflicts, but you will live them, experience them, act them out."

"Excellent." Harley Altman rubbed his hands together.

"We're talking cardboard and tin foil, Altman, nothing dangerous." Mr. Cheswick waggled a playfully admonishing finger. "You'll work in pairs to research the most noteworthy feuds in history. The online syllabus gives your instructions. As a team, you'll choose a battle or feud to focus on, and then you'll bring it to life by giving a report together and acting out the most compelling drama or conflict. Now... pick a partner."

David's heart began racing, and he inhaled deeply before turning to look at Amanda. She smiled at him, but while he took a moment to summon his nerve, Donovan leaned forward from his desk behind her and tapped her on the shoulder.

"What do you say," he asked her. "Partners?"

Amanda shot David a quick look, then turned back to Donovan and nodded. "Sure."

Resigned, David kicked Henry Blumquist in the foot.

Henry turned around, agitated by the interruption of his latest doodle. "What?"

"You better put those skills to good use. You're my partner."

"Whatever." Henry returned to his doodle.

David rapped his fingers on his desk impatiently while the rest of his classmates finished picking partners. After a couple minutes, he raised his hand.

Mr. Cheswick walked over to his desk. "Yes, David?"

"You mentioned the syllabus—I don't think I saw feuds on there last time I looked."

The odd expression that appeared on Mr. Cheswick's face was a stark contrast with the confident look he'd sported just moments earlier. "It's new," he said, then turned and walked back to his desk.

CHAPTER 9
A Gathering Storm

HENRY BLUMQUIST'S ARTISTIC SKILLS AND people skills were, David concluded, inversely related. It required persistent attempts to convince Henry to come over after school so they could work on their project, but once there, they achieved a rhythm. The topic energized David, as if something had begun to stir inside him, and he wanted to do well. He'd generated a few cool ideas for their presentation, and Henry—once he'd finally gotten to work—was cranking out some great sketches of McCoys battling Hatfields.

"That's awesome," David said.

Henry didn't answer, whether because of his headphones or poor social skills, David did not know. He didn't care. It was good work.

They continued another forty-five minutes, until Henry abruptly stopped working and packed up his stuff. "Gotta go."

David followed him downstairs to the front door. "See you."

As Henry crossed over their driveway and onto the sidewalk, Donovan and Kathy pulled in.

"Great," David muttered, but he waved and held the door open for them as they came inside.

"Hi, David." Kathy put a hand on his shoulder as she moved past him.

Donovan gave him a playful elbow.

"What's up?" David asked.

"Oh, didn't your father tell you?" Kathy asked. "We're all going to dinner tonight. Isn't that lovely?"

David bit his lip.

His dad came into the living room and greeted them, then asked David to help his sister get ready.

Donovan followed him out into the backyard, where Rachel sat spinning lazily on the tire swing.

"Push me!" she pleaded.

"Just for a minute." David bent down and grabbed the tire. "Dad says we gotta get ready to go eat. Now hold on."

She giggled in anticipation as her brother lifted the tire up and back, before releasing it and watching it arc back and forth, spinning wildly, Rachel's hair poofing up in the easy breeze with each revolution. She laughed gleefully with each pass, and when her momentum finally slowed, she begged, "Again, again!"

"Sorry," David explained. "We have to go now."

"Okay!" She leaped off the tire and ran toward the house. "See you later, Donovan."

"He's coming too."

She paused at the back door and looked back. "Fine," she said in her best *but I don't have to like it* voice.

"Don't mind her," David said.

Donovan had his hand on the tree trunk as he peered upward. "This would make an awesome treehouse. Rachel would like that, wouldn't she?"

David raised an eyebrow. "Yeah, probably."

"Cool. Maybe we can start working on it in the next few weeks."

David shrugged. "Sure."

Donovan smiled, and they stood silently a while as a low rumbling echoed in the distance. "They're getting close, huh?"

David furrowed his brow. "Who?"

"Your dad and my mom."

David bit his lip. "Well, they work together, is all."

Donovan eyed him curiously. "More than that, don't you think?"

A rapping sounded from the dining room window, which looked out on the backyard. Rachel made goofy faces through the glass.

David waved, then looked back at Donovan. "Not really. Just friends."

They locked eyes.

David's dad poked his head out the back door. "Hey, boys, better come in." He gestured skyward, where dark clouds had congregated. A golden stitch flared in the distant horizon. "Storm's coming."

CHAPTER 10
The Last of the Lightkeepers

OF ALL THAT HAD HAPPENED, OF all that Marcel had told him, one thing burned within David more than any other. Not the creatures in the woods, not his moments of inexplicable recollection, not even the mind-rattling idea that he was immortal—a notion that every rational fiber of his being still insisted was impossible. What remained foremost on his mind and in his heart was that which had preoccupied him for the past year—finding the truth about his mother. He had obeyed his dad's wishes and stopped speaking of "conspiracy theories," but he had never abandoned the belief that whatever happened to his mother, it was not as it seemed.

When he arrived that afternoon for his session with Marcel, Mrs. Gittlebaum smiled and motioned him through the counselor's open office door.

Marcel was scrawling notes at his desk. "Master Rose, attend to the door on your way in, if you would."

David pulled the door shut behind him and sank into the chair Marcel indicated.

"How have you been?" Marcel asked. "All things considered, of course."

David appreciated the disclaimer. There were many things to be considered. "Not bad."

"How is your family?"

"Hanging in there, I guess. It's what we do. My dad and Kathy seem to be getting closer though."

"Kathy?"

"Donovan's mom. They work together. She and Donovan stop by a lot."

"Ah." Marcel nodded. "I see. I take it this isn't the most welcomed development?"

David shrugged. "Especially for Rachel. She misses our mom. And there's' just...."

"Just?"

"It'll sound bad, because they *are* good to us, but I don't trust them — either of them. There's just... something about them." He sat back, folded his arms, and exhaled heavily.

Marcel leaned forward in his chair. "There are reasons our instincts alert us to things. Your protection of your sister is admirable. It is everything, in fact."

David appreciated the encouragement, but began to wonder when they would get to the other stuff — the *big* stuff. This strange but kind man had told him he was *immortal*. Sitting quietly in his office chatting about home life and instincts felt surreal.

After a moment, he said, "I haven't told anyone."

Marcel nodded. "That is probably for the best at this juncture, but I imagine it is a terrible burden."

David looked past Marcel out the window, across the schoolyard to the cemetery. "Why me? Is everyone immortal?"

Marcel smiled wistfully. "Leave it to Master Rose to open with the most elusive question of the cosmos. Alas, it is elusive for a reason. Perhaps everyone is immortal, in their way. We cannot truly know what happens after death." His expression grew solemn once more. "But we do know this: some souls are pursued through the centuries by mortal enemies from lifetimes ago — an eternal conflict simmering with unfathomable intensity, imprinted like forged metal. So powerful were these hatreds, they kindled a life of their own, enduring beyond their possessors' last breath."

David spoke quietly. "Even if this is all true, why does it matter? Couldn't I just go on living my life like before? No offense, but what if I don't believe this stuff?"

"It would be wholly understandable if you didn't, but there is no escaping the fact that there are those who do. Now that you have reached the required age—and in this, the year of the gathering darkness—they pose to you a grave danger."

David moved his tongue around his mouth, which suddenly felt very dry. "Why?"

"Nothing lasts forever, even in an immortal world." A pained expression spread over Marcel's features. "They believe that in order to accomplish their sinister aims, they must track down and destroy those remaining immortals who resisted the call to darkness."

David swallowed. *Did Marcel just say these people – whoever and whatever they are – intend to kill me?* "It sounds like something from a story."

Marcel smiled. "Doesn't it though? I only wish I could foretell the ending. Not to burden you any more than I already have, but I dare say you will have a hand in deciding it."

"How?"

"Your incipient soul—a critical concept for the immortals. You spoke of stories. Think of those that follow a theme of immortality. In almost all of them, the term refers to one's inability to die, but in reality, that is not the case at all. Everyone may die.

Immortality refers to an eternal state of rebirth. For the immortals, rebirth is eternal, unless their incipient soul is destroyed. Each immortal has sworn enemies dating back to their first lifetime. If an immortal is killed—in any lifetime—by an enemy from the days of his incipient soul, then his soul is vanquished along with it, never to be reborn again."

David's' stomach churned. *Why*, his mind screamed, *are you so worried about something you don't even believe?* He leaned forward and addressed Marcel again, just in case. "So the cycle ends, right? The person is then dead—really, finally dead." He sat up more fully in his chair, his shoulders squared.

"As a matter of fact, yes."

"Then I don't understand. Why is that such a bad thing? Doesn't that make them just like everyone else—just like non-immortals? They die, and either their soul goes to Heaven or Hell or nowhere, but they're just like everyone else?"

The faintest of grins danced across Marcel's face. "I should not by now be surprised at your wisdom, Master Rose. Yes, in that manner you are wholly correct—they become just like everyone else, and as with everyone else, not even the immortals or the ancients themselves truly know what happens next. But I'm afraid that is hardly the end of it. Our enemies desire something greater."

David's shoulders drooped. "What do they want?"

"Just as you have embarked upon a quest for truth, so too do they seek something: power, of a kind and to an extent the mortal world could hardly fathom."

"So all of this... it's all about power and hate?"

"No, that would be a dark world indeed. There are those throughout history who have resisted that calling, who believe more than hate endures in this world, and they have fought for that belief. The ancients believed that in this hidden world—within these invisible conflicts that persevere lifetime after lifetime—there are righteous souls, defenders of good, the world's last hope against evil. The ancients called them Lightkeepers."

"Am I one of them?"

"Yes, a rather important one, as it so happens."

David exhaled. "Why?"

"Those immortals—and their syndicates—who have embraced darkness would wield their powers to control the fate of mankind, to usher in an eternity of darkness. They intend to vanquish the last of these noble warriors." Marcel spoke quietly. "You, David Rose, are the last of the Lightkeepers." Marcel rose, went to his window, and gazed out. "And so you see, this matters very much, indeed."

David's chin slumped to his chest, and his eyes, which had grown heavy, fluttered shut. When he forced them open a few moments later, Marcel stood before him.

"I do not begrudge your lingering doubt, but there are those who, at this moment, intend your demise. Even should you choose to dismiss this hidden world of which I speak, if you wish to fulfill your quest for truth, to protect and reunite your family—if, my brave lad, you wish to live—you will at a minimum humor me, that I might do all in my power to help you."

CHAPTER 11
Brothers

HIS NIGHTMARES HAD GOTTEN SO BAD
that when his dad came into his room to wake him, he
exhaled in relief, even though it was early on a
Saturday, and even though his dad had come in to tell
him Donovan was there to see him.

"He wants to start working on the treehouse," his
dad said.

Ten minutes later, the boys stood in the backyard,
shielding their eyes against the sunrise as they
surveyed the white pine from which the tire swing
gently swayed. David's dad brought out the ladder,
along with shears and gloves and goggles, and
reminded the boys that before they did anything else,
they'd need to prune away excessive branches.

"*Careful* with those." He motioned to the shears.

David felt mildly embarrassed, but he smiled at
the show of concern from the man who had become so
detached in the past year.

"Your dad's a cool guy," Donovan said as they
slipped on their gloves and goggles and propped the
ladder up against the pine.

"Thanks," David said quietly.

Donovan looked at him. "Everything cool?"

David inhaled deeply. If he hadn't told his family
about all that had occurred, or Robert, or any of his
friends, he certainly wasn't about to let Donovan in on

the secret. But he could tell Donovan knew something was off, and since they'd be out there together at least a few hours, he figured he may as well be willing to chat. "Mostly, but...."

"But?"

"It gets tough sometimes with my mom gone... the way it happened. Rachel is so young."

Donovan tested the stability of the ladder, placed his right foot on the first rung, and nodded. "I'm sure it's tough. I had a tough time when my dad died, and I was older than Rachel."

Up until that moment, David hadn't known anything about Donovan's father. He considered asking how he'd died but thought better of it. Besides, Donovan was several rungs up the ladder now, so David stepped forward and grasped both sides of it firmly.

Donovan stopped about seven or eight feet up. "Okay, I better trim these."

David carefully extended the shears up to him.

Donovan started to prune some of the branches, and the ladder swayed slightly as he shifted his weight.

David quickly steadied him. "I got you."

They worked for a few hours. David had to admit they'd developed a pretty good rapport as the morning passed. They would pause occasionally to bundle up the extraneous branches. At one point, Donovan handed David one of the larger limbs and, retrieving a similar one himself, laughed and exclaimed, "On guard!" He thrust his branch toward David's midsection with surprising quickness, and without realizing what he was doing, David deflected it with his own, spun around, and went on the offensive.

Donovan parried his blows with equal dexterity, and they dueled another minute or so until their "swords" met at a mutual summit of their respective arcs and, with a resounding *crack*, severed in two.

David's dad poked his head out the back door. "Everything all right?"

The boys were bent over at the knees, breathing hard.

"Fine," David called. "Just messing around a bit."

His dad frowned slightly but then disappeared back inside, and they resumed their work.

Kathy brought them water a while later, seeming to do her best to fit in as if they were all one big happy family.

Rachel flitted out every so often to watch them. She would bombard her brother with a flurry of questions, but did not acknowledge Donovan.

"Sorry about that," David said after she'd gone inside. "She's just having a hard time."

"Understood. She's lucky to have you. You're a good brother. Maybe...."

David looked at him. "What?"

"Well, it sounds stupid, I guess, but I'm an only child. Maybe I can be like another brother for you guys."

They worked for quite a bit longer — until the sun perched high in the midday sky — pruning and taking measurements and discussing where and how to best construct the floor, walls, and roof.

"Hey," David said, as Donovan stretched out the tape measure. "I'd like that."

Donovan clicked the tape measure, and it snapped back into its casing. "Like what?"

"For you to be a brother."

Donovan smiled broadly. "That's awesome, man." He steadied the ladder as David descended. "I mean, brother." He gave David a playful elbow.

David smiled and gave him a shove in return, and they horsed around for a bit before resuming their work.

They worked through the day, pausing only for lunch and occasional breaks, until the sun began its slow fade and David's dad poked his head out the back door and called them to dinner. As they went inside, David paused at the door and turned to admire the progress they'd made. He'd been unsure about Donovan these last few months, but today had provided a new perspective.

They worked on the treehouse whenever possible in the following weeks. Any time David glanced out back and saw it, he was reminded of their growing friendship—something bright in a world that had grown dark for him in so many ways.

CHAPTER 12
Things Change

"YOU HAVE TO ASK HER."

David feigned surprise. "Who?" He had been petting Robert's dog, Bear, and when he stopped and looked at Robert, the canine snorted and rolled onto his back, belly exposed, and looked at David impatiently. David resumed petting him, and Bear emitted a low, happy growl, his left hind leg twitching in ticklish delight.

"You know what I'm talking about," Robert replied. "Amanda, the Valentine's Dance."

"Don't most people just go in groups?"

Robert shrugged. "I don't know. Maybe, but that's not the point. The point is, this is your chance to make a move."

David looked down and continued stroking the appreciative animal. As usual, his best friend was right, but David's stomach fluttered nervously at the thought of what he was proposing. "I don't know."

Robert stood up, stretched his arms above his head, and clapped his hands sharply. Bear rolled over and leaped to his feet, tail wagging. "Time for a walk, Bear."

They walked silently for several minutes.

"The worst you'll get is a no," Robert said. "And I'm not too sure she won't say yes. If you don't ask, the best you'll get is a 'what might have been.'"

"Thanks, Dr. Phil." David rolled his eyes, although he was appreciative.

They walked leisurely through the patch of land by the woods, and Bear kept his nose to the grass most of the time. At one point, a squirrel darted out in front of them, and it required all of Robert's strength to maintain hold of the leash. They veered back into the subdivision, and resumed the loop that would return them to Robert's house.

"I think we're going to the mall tonight," David said. "Do you wanna come?"

Robert looked at him. "Who's going? Your family?"

"Me and Donovan, actually. You should come. Probably just getting a bite and going to the game store or something."

Robert kicked at the ground with the toe of his sneaker. "Nah. It's okay. You guys go."

"You sure?" David asked, surprised. "Come on."

"I got a lot to do," Robert said quietly.

David frowned and started to reply, but something told him to let it go.

"Well," Robert said, as they arrived back at his driveway, "here we are."

David leaned down and gave Bear a final pat on the backside. "All right. I guess I better get going."

"See you." Robert gently tugged the leash, and Bear spun around and accompanied him back up the front lawn.

"See you." The temperature had fallen, and David jammed his hands in his pockets as he started down the street toward the woods, to head home.

***

There was a substitute for Mr. Cheswick that early December morning. He had a square head, a set jaw, and brown hair combed neatly over to one side. He introduced himself as Mr. Rendicott. When the presentations concluded, he complimented the class on their good work.

"Violence and feuds define history." He looked at David. "We're documenting some of the most famous ones, but history is consumed by countless examples, generations of families, governments, and cultures that, harboring ill will and vengeance, perpetrate violence as a means of settling matters—unfortunate but necessary business. We will finish the remaining presentations tomorrow, then come final exams, and we will resume the unit third quarter."

David furrowed his brow, but it was Amanda who spoke up. "Excuse me, but why would we continue on the unit? Don't we have other areas to get to?"

Mr. Rendicott's reply came swiftly. "Things change."

Amanda looked at him strangely.

"When will Mr. Cheswick be back?" David asked.

Mr. Rendicott walked over to David's desk and looked down at him. "I'm afraid it may be a while."

CHAPTER 13
Diamond Ring

DAVID'S DAD WAS PUTTING ON A tie. This wouldn't have been unusual save for the fact that he was putting it on in the evening, before heading out to dinner. He pulled the knot snug to his neck and adjusted his collar before finally noticing his son in the mirror. "What do you think?"

"About what?"

"This tie?"

David shrugged.

"Yeah." His dad smiled. "I used to count on your mom to dress me." The smile slowly faded into a faraway look.

"And now?"

His dad turned and looked at him, then sighed. "You're a perceptive kid. It would seem there are some things you want to ask me?"

David leaned against the doorframe, trying to appear casual, but he knew he needed to seize this chance to talk with his dad, because these moments had been few and far between. "I guess."

His dad nodded and turned back to the mirror, fidgeting again with his collar. "Shoot. I'm all ears."

"You're going to dinner with Kathy?"

"I am, but you knew that, yes?"

"I know. I guess what I mean is, why are you getting all dressed up?"

His dad, finally satisfied with — or at least resigned to — his appearance, turned back around. "No special reason. We're just going to a nice place."

Something twisted inside David, a twinge of wildly opposite emotions dueling within him. He should be happy that his dad had found a friend in Kathy, as he had in Donovan.

And yet....

"Daddy!" Rachel skipped into the room. "You said I could have hot dogs."

"Yes, I did — when I leave, in a few minutes. David will eat with you."

Quickly appeased as only a young child can be, Rachel smiled and tugged at her dad's tie. "I like your tie, Daddy. Can I take you for a walk?"

He smiled, and Rachel began skipping around the room, giggling. After the third pass, she wobbled precariously close to a bureau.

David gently grabbed her arm. "Slow down."

"Hey!"

"I don't want you to get hurt."

"I'm *not*."

Their dad walked over and patted her on the head. "Come on, baby." He slung a sport coat over his shoulder and turned off the light. "David's right. Go downstairs. I'll be right there. Hot dog time."

Rachel made a face at David before skittering from the room.

Once he could hear Rachel pattering around downstairs, David turned back to his dad. "Are you going to ask her to marry you?"

"What? Marry me? David, come on, just relax about all this. I need to get downstairs for Rachel."

David stood in the doorway. "I don't mean tonight, but eventually. Are you going to ask her? Please tell me the truth."

His dad put a hand on his shoulder. "I always do, and the truth is that I don't know. I guess it's possible. I know that's not easy for you to hear, but Kathy has meant a lot to me, to us. Donovan too. He's been like a brother to you, hasn't he? And you to him. We have wounds, each of us, and have been through a lot. I think we're helping each other heal." He looked his son in the eyes. "I will love and miss your mother for the rest of my life. She was my true love, but I think she'd want me to move on, in time, to find happiness, even as I mourn her for the rest of my days. I know this is hard, but whatever will be, I need your support. I need you to do whatever is best for the family, okay?"

David felt numb, as though he were watching the scene unfold from another vantage point. After a hazy moment, he saw himself nod slowly and, at length, shuffle away from his father's doorway.

***

Science was his favorite class, though this had little to do with the subject matter. It was the only class he shared with Amanda that... well, that Donovan didn't also attend. He felt bad thinking it, but girls liked Donovan, and what wasn't to like? Donovan liked Amanda, and who could blame him? David considered it an accomplishment that he had, over the past several weeks, struck up a rapport with her. It consisted mainly of friendly greetings and occasional exchanges about whatever topic they were covering in class, but it was *something*.

He had showered, combed his hair, and dressed a little more nicely than usual this morning, taking a page from his dad's book from the night before. His stomach had knotted all night, and he didn't know if or how much he'd actually slept. Kids were already starting to invite dates to the dance, and this morning, he was going to take Robert's advice and ask Amanda.

His conviction to do so took a blow when Amanda walked into class accompanied by Donovan. They were joking around and laughing, and they even gave each other a hug before Donovan headed off to his class. David looked down, flustered, but perked back up a moment later when Amanda appeared at his desk.

"Hey, David." She took a seat near his. "How are you?"

It took him an uncomfortably long moment to conjure a response. "I'm good. How are you?"

She smiled, and his heart raced.

Their teacher, Mr. Delson, strolled in, dropped some folders onto his desk, and started scrawling on the chalkboard. The bell rang, and a few stragglers scurried in and found desks at the back of the room.

David took a fluttering breath and leaned toward Amanda. "Can I ask you something?"

She leaned back toward him, attentive.

"I was wondering," he said quietly, "if you wanted to go to the Valentine's Dance with me. I mean, I can't dance or anything, but I thought it could be fun, you know, just to go and hang out, you know... with you."

An odd expression spread across Amanda's face. "Oh, I... um... I... goodness, I actually thought you knew. You guys seem so close."

David looked at her quizzically.

"*Donovan*. He already asked me, a few days ago. I just assumed he told you."

David shook his head, his mouth suddenly gone dry.

Amanda put a hand on his shoulder. "I'm sorry, but you should come anyway. Ask another girl, or come with some friends, or come with us. People will just all be hanging out, you know?"

He nodded.

She smiled weakly at him. "Timing is everything, huh?"

He looked at her, uncertain how to respond.

"I was waiting for *you* to ask me, but you never did. Well, until now."

Mr. Delson was lecturing at the front of the room, but David's mind only vaguely registered the topic — something about eclipses. On March twentieth, Mr. Delson said, the moon would for a short time completely obscure the sun.

David's mind wandered.

He gazed around the classroom, referred to by many as The Dungeon, owing to the haphazard arrangement of desks and tables and laboratory equipment, some of which looked as though it had been salvaged from a medieval lair. You had to be careful navigating the room. You didn't want to collide with anyone or anything, particularly if you were carrying a test tube or working with a Bunsen burner.

"Unfortunately," Mr. Delson said now, "the eclipse won't be visible here. Unless you spend your spring break in Europe or a few other places around the globe, you'll miss out, which is too bad, because it's quite a phenomenon. Even the brightest skies fade into total shadow. Animals sometimes lose their bearings and act strangely. People report it is a powerful experience."

David cast a quick glance toward Amanda, wishing he could fade into shadow too. He never should have asked.

"Powerful as the eclipse is," Mr. Delson said, "something else astounding occurs along with it—the diamond ring effect. Glimmering beads of the sun's surface form around the disc of the moon's shadow, and when for a brief moment only one bead remains, it glows brilliantly, like a diamond ring—a beacon of light in a vast sea of darkness."

CHAPTER 14
A Chance to Win

"WE'RE BUILDING A TREEHOUSE."

It was the first thing David could think to say. Marcel had asked him again about his relationship with Donovan, which seemed slightly odd to David, given the far more pressing topics at hand, but odd things were becoming more commonplace by the day.

"That sounds like quite a project," Marcel said. "And one which requires a good deal of cooperation. I take it the two of you are getting on well together?"

"I guess."

Marcel leaned forward over his desk. "That hardly sounds convincing."

"He asked Amanda to the dance first."

"Ah, a girl. Can you tell me about her?"

David's lips curled into a sheepish grin. "She's great. I mean, you know, she's nice and all."

"I have no doubt she is."

"She's just cool, really nice. She just seems — I don't know — different. Usually you think you can't talk to a girl like her." He looked down, certain he must be beet red.

"She sounds like a special young lady. I am sorry about the dance."

"Thanks. The thing is... she said she would have gone with me, if I had asked her sooner."

"And this makes it even tougher?"

David raised an eyebrow. "Well, yeah. Knowing that if I hadn't waited so long.... Robert kept telling me to ask her."

Marcel jotted something on his notepad. "Robert is a good friend, but again, I remind you that *you* are an intelligent and insightful young man. Let's pursue this question just a moment longer. Are you certain what Amanda told you makes matters worse?"

David glanced out the office window, where he noticed the first few snowflakes of the season beginning to flutter down. "I guess it means she likes me — at least as a friend."

"It is sometimes a painful lesson, particularly for one so young, and yet, you are a bit of an old soul, if I may say so, and that is a good thing. I think you will understand this, and even more so as time goes on. Love, joy, the beauty of a kindred connection with another soul is never, in the end, about *possessing* them. We may *desire* them, *want* them for a girlfriend, a wife, a partner — or to attend a dance with us — but that connection, that place in another's heart we may be fortunate enough to earn, that is something which endures for eternity. If I may be so bold, from where I sit, you enjoy the better position in this matter."

"I do?"

"He takes her to the dance, but it would seem you have been the one to capture that place in her heart."

David felt his smile returning. "I want to tell her." He looked at Marcel anxiously.

A twinkle of surprise flickered across Marcel's face, but then he smiled too. "You are free to do as you wish. I might simply ask you to be sure of your motivations."

David nodded. "It's not because I like her. It's because I trust her. I don't know how, but I do. Maybe she'll think I'm crazy—sometimes I still think that—but it's something I need to do."

"Then you shall do what you must." Marcel checked his watch. "And once more, our time runs out too soon. I must wish you a good day, until next time."

They rose and shook hands.

"Good afternoon, Master Rose." Marcel glanced through the office window. "And button that overcoat, young man. It would appear winter has arrived."

***

It had indeed.

The wind gusted hard and cold on his way home, and what had begun as a light dusting developed into a few inches of accumulation by the time David tucked Rachel into bed that evening.

When he asked what story she would like, she replied, "A frosty poem."

David smiled and retrieved the book of Robert Frost poems from Rachel's bookshelf. Their mother had loved the poems and read them to David when he was young, and to Rachel too.

"It's late," he said, sitting at her bedside and opening the book. "Just a short one tonight. Do you want to read it?"

A grin danced across his sister's face, and she sat up and wriggled closer. "Nature's first green is gold," she read, flawlessly. "Her hardest hoo to hold." She looked up at her brother. "What's a hoo?"

"Hue." He smiled. "It means its color."

"Then why didn't he say that?"

"I don't know, Rach. Sometimes people like to use different words once in a while."

> *"Her early leaf's a flower;*
> *But only so an hour.*
> *Then leaf sub... sub-sides to leaf.*
> *So Eden sank to grief,*
> *So dawn goes down to day.*
> *Nothing gold can stay."*

She looked up at David.

"Great job. Momma would be proud."

"Where does it go?" she asked.

"What?"

"The gold. Why can't the gold stay?"

David sighed. Poetry had never been his best subject. "It doesn't mean real gold, but things that are like it—bright, shining, hopeful." He paused. The last line, he realized, probably sounded anything but. "But the sun goes down at the end of each day. Seasons change. I think part of his message is to appreciate things while you can."

"That's a good message."

They looked up at their dad in the doorway.

"Bedtime, little lady." He looked past them and through Rachel's bedroom window. "Might not be school tomorrow."

"Yay!" Rachel squealed.

David smiled. His sister enjoyed school, but nothing could match the appeal of a snow day.

"I still need to work though," their dad said. "Maybe I can bring you with me for a bit, sweetie."

"Okay, but then I wanna go sledding. And have hot chocolate. And build an igloo."

"We'll see what we can do." Their dad chuckled. "But can't do any of that if you don't get some sleep. Goodnight, princess."

"Goodnight, Daddy."

"Speaking of my work," their dad said to David as they exited Rachel's room, "they're having kind of a cool contest, actually. Whoever is top salesperson for the quarter wins a spring vacation: England. One of the partners knows someone, I think, with connections to one of those authentic medieval castles. Kane Manor, I think it's called. The winner gets to take their family for a week. Pretty cool, huh?"

"Yeah, pretty cool."

They descended the stairs and walked into the kitchen. His dad poured himself a cup of coffee, while David got a glass of milk.

"Do you have a chance to win?"

His dad took a sip and looked up. "I don't want to jinx it, but yeah, I do. Been a good couple months, even in this market. If I sell the house on Randoli—" He crossed his fingers and knocked on the kitchen table. "—that's a million-dollar house. That would probably cinch it. Hmm. Actually, I need to look into getting each of us passports, just in case."

David nodded and sipped his milk. A vacation sounded pretty good.

"Now get to bed." His dad's coffee mug clinked as he deposited it into the sink. "You'll either have school in the morning, or a little sister who's going to be begging you to take her out in the snow. Either way, you need some rest." He turned back to his son. "Goodnight."

"Goodnight."

CHAPTER 15
Assembly

TO THE GREAT DISAPPOINTMENT OF MOST children, school was not canceled. Worse yet, for the students of The Crossing, an assembly had been called. These were, with rare exception, tedious affairs.

David shuffled in with a throng of listless-looking classmates and made his way to the back of the auditorium. Ever since he could remember, he'd preferred to sit in the back of rooms. He couldn't say why exactly, but he'd never felt comfortable being unable to see behind him — an apprehension which had become more pronounced of late.

He sank into a chair and watched as Principal Lardman made his way to the podium, appearing to David a bit uneasy, like an amateur comic anticipating hecklers.

"Good morning," he blurted. His words drowned in a reverberating static wail, and the students groaned and covered their ears. Dr. Lardman held the mic a bit farther from his mouth and proceeded with a litany of trivial announcements.

David, still not sleeping well at night, felt his eyelids becoming heavy.

He was uncertain if or for how long he'd drifted off, but next thing he knew, the siren song of a familiar voice coaxed him back to full alertness.

"David."

"Hey." He opened his eyes and smiled.

Amanda sat down beside him, leaned in, and gave him a quick hug.

He'd never been so glad for assemblies.

"As many of you know," Dr. Lardman said from the stage, "Harold Cheswick has taught here for many, many years. It is with mixed emotions I relay to you that he has taken an indefinite leave of absence to attend to personal matters."

A loud murmur spread through the auditorium, and David and Amanda exchanged glances.

"Mr. Rendicott has been serving ably in Mr. Cheswick's absence," Dr. Lardman continued. "We are grateful he has agreed to stay on for the remainder of the term. I know you'll give him your full cooperation and support, and join me in wishing Mr. Cheswick well, while respecting his privacy to the utmost."

The rest of the assembly consisted of remarks from the Student Council and a mini pep rally by the Spirit Squad, but David's curiosity kept him focused on Mr. Cheswick.

"I hope he's okay," Amanda said as they eased into the throng of chattering students exiting the auditorium.

They squeezed through the bottleneck emptying from the auditorium into the foyer, and veered left into the corridor, which led to hallways and classrooms.

Amanda gave him a quick hug. "Gotta get to class."

David watched her disappear into the sea of students, forgetting momentarily about getting to class himself. He stood as though rooted, intoxicated by the lingering memory of their interaction, until the bell, loud and shrill, jarred him back to reality and called him away to class.

Something always seemed to call to him.

He turned and scampered down the hallway, late again.

***

Their dad took them to services that Sunday, the first time ever without their mother. He said it had been too long, and that it was important not to lose their faith. They attended a non-denominational church, as their mom had always stressed the importance of being open and accepting of people's various beliefs.

Rachel's eyes grew wide as they entered the sanctuary. Dozens of long pews sat atop soft blue carpeting, and the walls, lined with intricate stained-glass panes, arched up to an elegant domed ceiling. She craned her neck upward, taking in the view.

"Okay, sweetie," their dad said, "time to sit down now. We have to be quiet, like we talked about, okay?"

Rachel nodded and clasped his hand as he led her down an aisle.

"Good morning," the minister said from the pulpit.

"Good morning," his congregants murmured back.

Minister Morgan was a tall African American man with slightly graying hair, which to David made him seem even wiser. He possessed a deep voice and kind eyes, and had officiated at his mother's funeral.

"A few months ago," Minister Morgan began, "we discussed the holy days of Rosh Hashanah and Yom Kippur, and as with all of our sermons, we have had many wonderful questions and good discussion on this topic." He looked out at his congregation. "It is believed that these are solemn days for reflection, atonement, and renewal, and that God determines who is to be written into the Book of Life and who is not. The ancient view embraces this quite literally, believing that such tablets exist. God opens these books each year and marks folks for the Book of Life or Book of Death." He paused and gestured to the congregation. "I have been asked on many occasions — usually after the passing of a loved one — how it is, exactly, that such a wonderful, good person could be *marked* for death, if we are to believe in the ancient teachings."

David leaned forward in his pew.

"A fair question," Minister Morgan continued. "I suggest we dig a bit deeper into the meaning of these days. Clearly, it cannot merely be the good or righteous are marked for life and the evil for death. We know all too well that many good people die each year, while many others, less good, continue to live. How can this be?"

He paused as a few congregants were still shuffling in, wearing sheepish expressions. The minister smiled at them and continued his sermon. "Everyone dies, of course. Many believe that these judgments of the Lord, these designations in these holy tablets, may not focus merely on our mortal lives, but instead speak to the matter of eternal life. It is believed that our deeds — good, bad, and otherwise — are recorded, and the truly righteous shall, upon their earthly passing, be granted eternal life. While we cannot profess to know the decisions of the Almighty, we keep faith that our loved ones have, through lives of righteousness and benevolence, achieved that eternal blessing. We also believe they are kept forever alive in our hearts, minds, and memories, that theirs is a beautiful and enduring legacy."

Rachel fidgeted in the pew. "I'm *bored*."

David put a gentle hand on her back. "Shh."

She curled her lip down and was, for the moment, quiet.

"When a congregation, a family, comes together," Minister Morgan said, "we sometimes refer to it as a gathering, an assembly—a showing of love and support and faith. There is also Biblical reference to the assembly of the first born: special, holy souls who are enrolled in Heaven. We come together, we pray, we cry, we laugh, we remember. We support each other during these toughest of times."

Rachel leaned her head on her brother's shoulder. "I wanna go...."

David put a finger to his lips.

Minister Morgan stretched his hands out toward the congregation. "Let us take a moment to remember our departed loved ones. May their souls be eternally blessed, and may we all say Amen."

CHAPTER 16
Illusion

"I'LL GO WITH YOU," AMANDA SAID.

"Thanks." David smiled. She had sat with him at lunchtime and pressed him about his suspicions regarding Mr. Cheswick. He'd shared what he'd overheard Lardman saying on the phone a few months back, and told her he'd decided to pay their teacher a visit. He'd considered phoning first, but Amanda suggested otherwise.

"He may say no," she said. "Depending on what's really going on, he may say no, but I bet he won't turn you away if you show up there."

They headed out after school. Mr. Cheswick lived only a few miles away, but it wasn't an easy jaunt. Despite the gleaming sunlight, a cold and bitter wind lashed at them as they walked.

The notion that Mr. Cheswick's situation somehow tied to everything else gnawed at David. It frightened him to consider just what that connection might be, but that fear was obscured by another consideration: Amanda. They moved briskly on account of the cold, but even so, time seemed to freeze as she walked beside him.

"How is Rachel?" she asked, her voice weighted with concern. "I'm sure all this has been so hard for her." She smiled and touched his arm. "For each of you."

David's throat caught, and he looked away a moment so she wouldn't detect the glistening in his eyes—he was so taken by her kindness. "She's hanging in there. She's pretty amazing."

"She has a pretty amazing brother."

He smiled and felt himself blushing. Then he stopped, and she stopped too. He wasn't certain if there was ever a perfect time for something like this, but this time felt about as right as any.

There, in the frozen light of the waning afternoon, he told her—everything. From the terrible night their mom disappeared, to the day at the creek, to the day at the cemetery, to the nightmares and everything Marcel had told him. She listened and watched him, and he watched her—looking for the dreaded signs of disbelief, or worse—but he saw only compassion and concern. When at last he'd finished, she stepped across the small space between them and shared an embrace he wished could last forever.

Alas, the day was ebbing fast, and they needed to resume walking if they were to reach their destination at a reasonable hour.

"Do you believe me?" David nervously glanced at Amanda from the corner of his eye.

"Until today, I didn't believe in those things." She stopped and looked in his eyes. "But I believe in you, and so yes, I do believe."

His heart soared as they continued walking.

"So you think Mr. Cheswick's situation has something to do with all of this?" Amanda asked.

"I don't know. Maybe. It kinda feels that way."

They quickened their pace. David's arm swung back with his stride, and when it swung forward again, Amanda caught it in hers in perfect rhythm.

Considerations of immortality, mystical creatures, and suspicious events were for the moment suppressed beneath the sheer giddiness of walking alongside the girl who'd captured his heart. They held hands and talked nearly the entire way—a long walk that seemed to him anything but.

When they finally reached Mr. Cheswick's house, he stopped and turned to Amanda. "Thanks for coming."

"Thanks for letting me."

He surveyed the property and frowned: no cars in the driveway. "May not be home."

Amanda's forehead crinkled as she stared at the house. "Let's find out. Something feels weird."

They went to the door and David knocked. Nothing. He rang the bell. Still no answer.

He looked at Amanda and shrugged. "Sorry." He started to turn around but paused when Amanda didn't follow suit.

With an almost imperceptible nod of her head, she motioned toward the front bay window.

David thought he detected a faint fluttering of drapes. A few moments later, a frantic clattering sounded from inside, and the front door swung open. The house was dark, and the figure in the doorway peered out at them like a hibernating animal seeing sunlight for the first time in a long while.

It was Mr. Cheswick, and yet it wasn't. He had profoundly changed—and not for the better. He looked haggard and pale. The front door, based on the sounds they'd heard on opening and the keys jangling softly in Mr. Cheswick's unsteady hand, must have been loaded with various locks and deadbolts. "What are you doing here?" he rasped, his eyes darting behind them, searching the area.

David cleared his throat. "We just wanted to see how you were doing. Sorry if it's a bad time."

Mr. Cheswick nodded and seemed to relax slightly, though his eyes kept shifting about. He quickly motioned them inside with his non-key-holding hand. "Come on, then. Inside, inside."

They scampered in past him. After sticking his neck outside and craning in all directions, Mr. Cheswick retreated back into the darkness and set about rebolting his fortress of a door, each lock responding with a resounding pop.

Amanda and David exchanged glances.

"Sit, sit," Mr. Cheswick said, his voice still hoarse, but when they stepped toward the couch, he gesticulated at them frantically. "No. Not *there*. They can see you there, even with the blinds drawn." He motioned them over to chairs at the opposite end of the living room. After they sat, he stood before them with a nervous and expectant look. "Well?"

"We just wanted to see how you were doing," David repeated, but he was still pondering what Mr. Cheswick had just said. *They?*

"We miss you," Amanda added.

Mr. Cheswick's features softened for the first time since their arrival, if only slightly. His shoulders sagged, and his lips trembled, as if he were struggling to conjure some semblance of a smile. "I miss you too," he said, barely audible. He looked at them, then down at the ground, shuffling his feet before darting once more toward his front window. He leaned forward, one knee on the couch, and nudged the blinds apart with his pinkie. After staring out a few moments, he returned to his visitors.

"Who are you looking for?" Amanda asked.

Mr. Cheswick regarded her. "Maybe who's looking for me," he said, but then seemed to immediately regret it.

"What—" David got no further before Mr. Cheswick waved his hand frantically again.

"Nothing, nothing. Forget it, I beg you. I've said far too much as it is."

David leaned forward, conflicted. Mr. Cheswick obviously didn't want to talk, but David needed answers, and it seemed apparent their former teacher possessed at least a few. He started to ask another question, but Amanda put a gentle hand on his.

She smiled and shook her head almost imperceptibly. "We're sorry. We'll go now." She nudged David, and they both rose.

"All right. That is best, I think." Mr. Cheswick escorted them to the door. When they paused there, he shook his head, fumbled for his keys, and muttered, "Forgive me." He unbolted the locks with trembling hands.

When he pulled the door open and David and Amanda stepped back outside, Mr. Cheswick again craned his neck and peered about. "Go straight home. Speak to no one."

David scanned the streets leading away from the house: not a soul in sight. "All right."

"Good." Mr. Cheswick receded back into the shadows like a squid into ink. "Thank you for visiting. Please do not do so again. And Godspeed to you both."

The door slammed shut, followed by the jangling of keys and snapping of bolts. Then the house fell silent, the only thing still audible the rising howl of the winter wind.

***

The news that Mr. Rendicott would replace Mr. Cheswick for the remainder of the year had been unsurprising, but that morning's class offered at least small consolation: the replacement teacher announced they would finally enjoy a brief reprieve from the study of conflicts and feuds.

"Current events." He jotted the words onto the chalkboard. "Imperative to keep up with them—newspapers, TV, and of course, everything is also online now. Keeping up with current events is to be alive with present history, the events that will become the history of tomorrow. Einstein said, 'The distinction between the past, present, and future is only a stubbornly persistent illusion.'"

David's mind wandered as he gazed outside, his thoughts drifting away like the wispy flakes that fluttered down from the gray dome of sky above. Here he sat at a desk when he had mysteries to solve, danger to thwart, and truth to discover. He glanced at the clock, which seemed to mock him with its tortuously slow advance.

Rendicott continued his lecture, explaining that their only assignment that week was to watch the evening news and be prepared to discuss it in class. At one point, his eyes seemed to lock with David's.

David looked down; Rendicott made him uneasy, but then again, many things did of late.

Time crawled for the remainder of the day—through the rest of history class and all the way up until the end of school, when it was at last time to see Marcel.

CHAPTER 17
Dangerous Ground

MARCEL'S DOOR WAS CLOSED WHEN DAVID arrived, and Mrs. Gittlebaum asked him to sit down and please wait. He took a deep breath, but as he exhaled, he realized he could faintly hear Marcel's voice through the wall.

Mrs. Gittlebaum stared intently at her screen, typing away. If she could hear too, she didn't show it.

"I am doing as you asked," David thought he heard. "Yes, yes, I understand. All is proceeding as planned. It should happen soon. No, we do not require Cerratus."

David heard the click of the phone being returned to its cradle, and he straightened in his chair as the door swung open.

Marcel motioned him over. "Good afternoon," he said, without his usual smile.

"Hi." David quietly slipped his backpack off his shoulder and took a seat.

Marcel sat down behind his desk and closed his eyes. He inhaled deeply, and when after a moment he opened his eyes, he'd seemed to return to the Marcel to whom David had grown accustomed. "Well, much to discuss, yes?"

David nodded.

"Where would you like to begin?"

"We went to see Mr. Cheswick," David said. "Amanda and I."

Marcel raised an eyebrow. "You saw Harold? How is he?"

"Not good, at least from how it looked."

Marcel frowned. "I am unsurprised, though I am sorry indeed to hear it."

"Are you upset with me for going?"

"Heavens no, my boy." Marcel appeared pained that David might have presumed otherwise. "Your compassion—and that of Amanda—is most commendable. I shall ever and always trust in your instincts, but it is upon dangerous ground we tread, as you are realizing more each day. Each action evokes a reaction. The gears of a great and ancient machine are turning, Master Rose."

"What do we do now?"

"I really don't know—a day at a time for now. At the doorstep of eternity, that is usually somehow best."

***

"He loves the snow," Robert said.

"Who?"

Robert looked at his best friend. "Santa Claus. Bear... duh! Hello?"

David grinned sheepishly. "I must have zoned out for a bit." Frosty puffs of breath punctuated his words as they walked Bear through the snow-crusted streets of Robert's subdivision.

"Ya think?" Robert chuckled.

The precipitation had descended throughout the previous day, blanketing streets and coating roofs like icing atop gingerbread homes. It glittered like a motherlode of spilled diamonds in the moonlight, lighting their way so that they didn't require flashlights. Bear pranced happily through it, pausing occasionally to sniff things no longer there, undeterred by the occasional deeper pockets into which he'd sink down to his haunches.

Approaching headlights cast an arc of illumination about them, and things went wobbly for a moment, as though they were teetering through a giant snow globe. Robert gave Bear a tug, and they moved from the road as the vehicle passed.

Bear suddenly pulled hard, sniffing the air and peering intently ahead.

"Someone's coming," Robert said.

They headed into the wind, wet flakes slapping against their squinting eyes as they attempted to distinguish the approaching figure. They could hear the crunching of footsteps.

Bear strained against his leash.

"Bear!" Robert put a second hand on the leash and braced himself.

"Hey guys!"

Donovan.

"Hey," David replied, curious at seeing him here.

Robert restrained his still-agitated pet.

"We stopped by your house to say hi," Donovan explained. "Your dad said you were over here. I decided to walk. What are you guys up to?"

"Just hangin'."

"Hey Robert," Donovan said.

"Hey."

"Cool dog." Donovan extended a hand toward Bear before pausing. "Is he friendly?"

"Usually."

Donovan started to pat the dog on the head, but Bear growled deeply and snipped at his hand. "Hey!" He yanked his hand back.

"Bear!" Robert struggled to pull the still-growling animal backward. His boots skidded in the snow. "I'm sorry. He's never done that before."

Donovan slipped his hand out of his glove and squinted through the unrelenting snowfall.

David could see a small indentation from one of Bear's teeth, but no blood. "Good thing you had gloves on."

"Still hurts." Donovan looked at Robert. "You shouldn't have a dog that bites."

Robert looked up with an expression David couldn't recall seeing in his best friend.

"I said I'm sorry!" Robert snapped. "David, let's go."

"Your dad wants you to come home," Donovan informed David.

Robert and Bear had continued walking, but now they stopped and Robert looked back.

David kicked some of the caked snow off his boots and shrugged. "Sorry," he called back to Robert. "I better go."

Robert shrugged too. "Gotta do what you gotta do."

CHAPTER 18
The Problem of Evil

THEIR ENGLISH TEACHER, THOUGH A SMALL woman, had posed a big question.

"If fate exists," Mrs. Brophy queried, "is it still our responsibility to make good choices?" She regarded her pupils with an expectant look. "Is it necessary to be a good person if everything may already be decided for us?"

David surveyed the faces of his classmates, spotting many vacant expressions — whether owing to the topic, or to this Monday morning the last week before winter break, he didn't know — but he welcomed any topic that deviated from the incessant study of conflict.

"Yes, Amanda?"

David abandoned the scan of his classmates and trained his gaze upon his favorite of all.

"It's not either/or," she said. "Socrates and Plato believed in freedom, even if fate played a role in things."

Harley Altman snickered from the desk in front of David. "Someone did her reading."

David kicked the back of his foot.

Harley whirled around. "Hey!"

"Knock it off, boys," Mrs. Brophy said. "Very good, Amanda. Can you elaborate?"

Amanda furrowed her brow in thought. "Well, they wanted people to take responsibility for their actions. They believed that even if destiny controlled things, there was still room for free will."

Their diminutive instructor smiled approvingly. "Nicely done, Ms. Keppinger. Even the Pythagoreans, who based many of their theories on a belief in patterns, numbers, and an order to all things, believed in some element of choice. Fate and destiny are recurring themes throughout countless classics—Oedipus, Macbeth, even Oliver Twist. The list goes on."

Something stirred inside David. He hesitated, then put up his hand.

"Yes, David?"

"What about religion?"

Mrs. Brophy raised an eyebrow. "Religion?"

"It's all about God's will. You always hear people say, 'God has a plan,' but then all these bad things happen to people—to really good people sometimes."

"Ah, yes," Mrs. Brophy said. "You've touched upon one of the most confounding dilemmas confronting religions throughout history." She arose from her desk and turned to the blackboard.

David could hear the rasping chalk, and when a moment later Mrs. Brophy stepped away, he stared, transfixed, at the four words she'd scrawled.

The Problem of Evil.

As though owing to reflex, David looked at Donovan, who was looking at him too.

"It's not a horror film," Mrs. Brophy said. "But it was—and is—a moral and philosophical consideration with which the world has struggled for centuries. People turned to religion to explain the world around them, but in time—as Ms. Keppinger noted—there grew some support for free will. Early Christians faced a dilemma. They wanted people to take responsibility for their actions and make good decisions, but they also believed in an all-knowing, all-powerful God. Furthermore, they believed evil existed in the world, and therein resided the problem. How could evil exist if God controlled everything, and God, of course, was good? The problem of evil."

She paused. "Any thoughts? David? You asked the question."

David felt eyes upon him as he responded. "Free will. God may be all-powerful, but people must still make their own choices."

Mrs. Brophy looked pleased. "Excellent. Yes, free will. This is true human freedom."

David glanced once more at Donovan, who flashed a strange smile.

"No matter the role of fate or faith," Mrs. Brophy said, "that does not relieve us of our responsibility." She regarded her students solemnly. "There is always a choice."

***

"Is it okay for Rachel to be in here?" David sat in front of the TV, watching the evening news per Mr. Rendicott's instructions. One story after the next seemed to be a tragic, violent one. They reported now about yet another fatal car accident in which an entire family had perished.

Their dad looked up from his book and glanced over at the TV. "You're right. Rach, can you go play in your room until dinner?"

Rachel began to protest, but her dad cast a stern glance, and she snatched up her toys and trudged upstairs.

"There's been a car accident... like... every day." David jotted notes in his journal.

"Yeah." His dad shook his head. "A shame." He pulled back the window curtain. Snow was falling again, and the wind sounded like wolves. "Well, the weather has been pretty bad."

The news veered into international updates, but the theme remained consistent: war, genocide, terrorism. Even the weather focused on the many accidents induced by the treacherous conditions.

When the news ended, David took notice of his dad's book: *Castle Vacations*.

"Fascinating stuff in here," his dad said. "Some amazing structures and history." He gestured at the castle depicted on the cover. "This one is a shell-keep. They had tower houses, motte and bailey, concentric castles — though I don't believe there are any concentric ones in England." He smiled. "See, I've been studying."

David raised an eyebrow. "Why?"

"Ah, well, I was going to tell you guys tonight at dinner, but... I made the Randoli sale."

"Cool. That's great!"

"Why, thank you, sir." His dad smiled. "It is great. First, because it puts some money in our pockets, but also because it means I've won the office contest. We're going to England — Tintagel Village, near Cornwall. Heard of it?"

David shook his head.

"Around five hours from London, I think, with a lot of history, a lot of legend. Cool stuff. Oh, and we all get to go — Donovan and Kathy too. She finished second, and our boss decided both our families could go. Pretty awesome, huh?"

"Yeah." David hoped the doubt in his voice wasn't as obvious to his dad as it was to himself. Anxiety welled up within him like a gathering storm, like the wolf winds outside their window, and he wondered a moment whether his dad could hear that too.

CHAPTER 19
A Note on the Door

WITH JUST A LITTLE HELP FROM David's dad, but mainly owing to their own efforts, the boys finished the treehouse before the harshest part of winter set in.

Rachel loved it, though she was, of course, too young to climb up unattended. She remained unfazed by that, as now that the snow fell, it was — to the delight of children throughout town — sledding season.

Kathy and Donovan came over for dinner that evening — something that had occurred on more than just a few occasions of late — and the boys spoke excitedly of their sledding plans.

"I'm going too!" Rachel said. She seemed quite pleased to have already reached this agreement with the boys.

Her dad nudged David. "You need to keep a good eye on her. People get hurt sledding sometimes. And you need to make sure she's not getting too cold. Okay?"

David nodded. "I will."

"Deer Creek, right?"

"Yeah." Deer Creek Elementary sat two blocks down the street and, owing to its modest hills by the back fields, was a popular destination when the snows came.

David helped clear the dishes after dinner. When he brought the leftovers into the kitchen, he glimpsed a note on the refrigerator door and plucked it out from under the magnet.

Cookies cooling on the counter.

He hadn't noticed it before, when he and Donovan had spotted the cookies a few hours earlier, after school, and happily consumed them. That had been very nice of Kathy. They'd shared some with Rachel, and it was then that they'd made their sledding arrangements.

David wadded up the note and prepared to toss it into the garbage, but then froze, the crumpled paper in one hand, a plate of leftover meatloaf in the other.

"Everything okay?"

He turned around to face Kathy, who looked at him with an expression he could not with certainty decipher. He slipped the note into his jeans pocket as inconspicuously as possible and conjured a smile. "Yeah. Thanks for the cookies."

"You're very welcome," she said after what seemed an unsettling extra second or two.

David opened the fridge and found a place for the meatloaf, then shuffled out of the kitchen, hands jammed in his pockets.

Donovan was helping Rachel with her coat.

David headed upstairs. "I'll just be a minute," he called behind him.

"Isn't your coat down here?"

He paused and glanced back to see Kathy looking at him expectantly. "Just finding a sweater."

Her smile appeared stuck to her face, as the note had been to the fridge.

He locked his bedroom door quietly, then removed the note from his pocket and unfolded it with care. He stared at those simple five words:

Cookies cooling on the counter.

His heart raced, his eyes glued upon the note. Something began to suggest itself inside him.

"David?" Donovan said. "Hey, dude, why's it locked?"

David opened the door. "Sorry," he said sheepishly. "Didn't realize I did that."

Donovan regarded him. "You ready?"

"Ready."

They left David's room and thumped down the stairs two at a time.

"Sounds like a herd of elephants," joked David's dad.

Rachel, bundled from head to toe, teetered near the front door, and it seemed a minor miracle that she could even stand. "I'm ready," came a muffled voice from somewhere within her ensemble.

As David headed to the hallway closet for his winter gear, Kathy followed him. "Didn't you go to get a sweater?" She leaned against the wall.

David faced her, and their eyes locked.

"Couldn't find it."

"Oh, that's a shame. Well, I hope you're warm enough out there."

"Thanks, I'll be fine."

She looked at him a moment longer before returning to the living room, where his dad had settled into his chair, feet propped on the ottoman.

David put an arm around his well-bundled sister. "Here we go."

She waddled alongside him as they headed to the door.

Donovan opened it, and a chilling gust swept in, but they stepped out, undeterred.

"Bye," David called behind him. He grabbed Rachel's hand, so very small in her mitten, and the three of them headed out into the frigid night.

CHAPTER 20
Perdidit Antiquum Litera Prima Sonum

IT WAS TIME TO VISIT CHESTER McVEE.

When Chester's mother opened the door on that cold Saturday morning, David felt an immediate pang of guilt. Mrs. McVee, a small and severe-looking woman with silver hair and silver-rimmed glasses, was in fact a very sweet person. David recalled the countless times she'd baked Chester and his friends cookies, given them rides to the movies, even made dinner for all of them. He felt bad that it had been such a long time since he'd visited Chester, but her face lit up upon seeing his.

"David Rose!" She beamed. "How very nice to see you. It has been too long. Come in, come in. How are you?" She cupped a hand over her mouth. "Oh my, I'm so sorry. It's been so long. I guess I haven't seen you since—well, since...."

"It's okay. I know it's been a long time. I'm sorry I haven't been over."

"Well," she said, regaining her composure. "I'm very glad you've dropped by. Chester will be delighted. He's in his room. You can go on in. Please let me hang up your coat. Would you like some cookies?"

"No thanks." David wriggled out of his coat and handed it to her, then headed through the living room and down the hallway to Chester's room. The door sat slightly ajar and eased open as he knocked.

Chester sat at his desk reading, his back to David. "David Rose," he said, not yet turning around.

"Hey, Chester. What, you know me by my knock?"

"I'm not that good." Chester slowly swiveled around to face his friend. "My legs don't work, but my ears still do. I heard you talking to my mom. Come on in."

David did so, closing the door behind him. He sat down on the edge of Chester's bed and took a breath. A ceiling fan whooshed in steady rotation above him, lightly tousling his hair. "How's it going?"

"Okay. To what do I owe the pleasure?"

"I want you to look at something for me."

Chester observed him curiously as David reached into his pocket and carefully extracted three folded slips of paper from a plastic snack bag. He handed his friend the notes.

Chester accepted each gingerly, and gently unfolded them one at a time. He turned back toward his desk and placed the papers adjacent to one another, under the light of his reading lamp.

Cookies cooling on the counter, read one. *Running out for milk*, read the next. The third was one his mother had given him years earlier, expressing her appreciation of the great brother he was to Rachel, asking him to always look out for her. He had kept it alongside the milk note in the back of his sock drawer.

"Any thoughts?" David asked.

Chester looked over at him and then back at the notes. He bent over each of them intently, looking from one to the other to the next. After about a minute, he glanced up at David. "There is the matter of both content and handwriting. Am I correct?"

David regarded his friend. "Yes." He sat down on the side of Chester's bed.

"*Cookies cooling on the counter*. Hmm. Who wrote this note?"

"Donovan's mom, Kathy."

"Ah," Chester said, still staring at the notes. "As for the other two, obviously they're supposed to have been written by your mother."

David raised an eyebrow. "Supposed to have been?"

Chester turned around. "I'm sorry if this is painful, but I doubt very much you came here just to show me notes that you believe are all from the person they're supposed to be from. Although it is okay if you have."

David's heart began to pound with an uncertain blend of exhilaration and fear. "Dad won't hear of it, but it has just never seemed right, that note: *Running out for milk*. And the fact they didn't find.. didn't find her...."

"Yes," said Chester quietly. "I see what you're saying."

David thrust his arms out to his sides. "But the writing... it's the same writing."

"Is it?"

David stood and walked over to the desk and stared at the notes alongside his friend. "It sure looks like it. I've looked at these a million times."

"Ah, but as Holmes said, 'It is far easier to find a needle in a haystack than another piece of hay.' Or something like that."

"Thought you preferred Poe."

"I do, but the quote seemed appropriate here. As it were, unless both of us have missed it, there is no needle that stands out here and grabs our attention.

The cookies note is Donovan's mom. The other two *appear* to be from your mother, but you suspect that may not be the case."

David shrugged. "So now what?"

"Graphology."

"English, please." David patted his friend on the back.

"*Graphology*: the study of handwriting, or at least the practice of studying handwriting. There is considerable debate surrounding its authenticity as a legitimate discipline, but it's frequently employed and has been found to be helpful in some matters."

David shrugged. "I'll try anything. Is this something you've studied?"

"Studied? I wouldn't say that. I've dabbled."

David smiled, knowing that dabbling was to Chester what exhaustive research was to most kids, maybe to most anyone. His smile broadened as he watched his friend open a desk drawer and retrieve a magnifying lens.

"Not trying to be a detective. I just need to see a little better." Chester bent back over the notes and peered at them intently. He remained in this posture for a considerable time.

Not wishing to distract him, David walked quietly back over to the bed and sat once more.

After maybe five minutes, Chester slowly swiveled around and regarded David with a serious expression. "Have you gone to the police about any of this?"

David swallowed. "My dad wouldn't go. I wanted us to, when it happened."

Chester considered this momentarily. "I understand. I can't imagine the effect all this had on him."

David nodded.

"But what about now? Have you wanted to take these notes to the police, tell them your story?"

David stood up again and walked over to Chester's window. "I went today."

"Good. Of course, that was the right thing to do. They're professionals and can provide the help you need."

"But they can't. Or at least, they won't."

Chester's expression remained solemn and more than a bit curious.

"One of their guys actually sat down with me at first," David explained. "A detective, I think — dressed in regular clothes, but he had a badge and gun and stuff. Pretty nice guy. We sat in one of those interrogation rooms, like on TV, with the two-way mirrors. Those are pretty cool. Anyway, the guy took notes, asked questions, seemed to be taking me seriously, but then...."

Chester looked at him expectantly. "Then?"

"Then a knock came on the window. It startled me, actually, a real urgent-sounding knock. The guy went out of the room for a minute, and when he came back, everything was different."

"Different how?"

"Well, he just kind of wrapped things up real quick after that — seemed disinterested, kind of blew me off. He asked me one or two more stupid questions, and then basically said if they hear anything, they'll let me know."

Chester nodded slowly. "Did you believe him?"

"Not anymore. Something had changed. I don't know who he talked to. Maybe his boss. Maybe someone told him they couldn't waste their time on the conspiracy theories of a stupid kid."

Chester leaned back in his chair, clasped his hands together on his chest, and gazed up toward the ceiling. The fan whizzed around and around. At length, he said, "They're not perfect circles, you know."

David looked at him quizzically. "What's not?"

"The rotation of the fan," Chester replied, still looking upward. "At first they appear to be. 'Round and 'round and 'round. It can transfix you, lull you. 'Round and 'round."

David watched his friend watching the fan.

Chester continued. "Life can be that way—the daily grind, routine—and we can be desensitized to details, to subtleties. But if you watch the fan more closely, if you truly concentrate, you can see through the routine a little, and you start to notice some things. It'll spin slightly higher or lower. It'll shake or quiver a bit. If it's extra cold or hot in here, it tends to run differently. Sometime there's an electrical surge, and it has a little hiccup. Sometimes it seems that even just the way the blades cut through the air affects the air, and that in turn affects the next rotation."

David listened and waited, knowing his friend wasn't just talking about fans.

Chester lowered his head and rubbed his neck. "Ouch. I've got to stop doing that."

David smiled.

Chester rotated his neck around slowly, first clockwise, then counterclockwise. "That's better. And now back to the matter at hand. They're not perfect circles."

David raised an eyebrow. "The fan?"

"The o's," Chester said.

"What o's?"

"The writing. Graphology. Come back over and take another look. Here." Chester handed David the magnifying lens as he approached the desk. "Use this."

David bent back over the three notes, peering through the lens, immediately struck by some of the nuances and details he could indeed distinguish. "Pretty cool."

"Yes, it's cool, but it's more than that. Are you comparing the three notes?"

David stood back up for a moment and stretched his back. "You mean two? We're trying to decide if the two notes from my mom are both hers?"

"Are we?"

David looked at his friend. "Okay, please just tell me. Please. You are amazing, Chester. Seriously, I'm blown away, but I've been waiting so long for this moment. I need to know what you're thinking."

"I appreciate that, David. I truly do. I know how much this means to you, but it is *because* of that, not in spite of it, that I'm trying to help you see this for yourself."

David took another deep breath. His pulse pounded. "Okay, I'm sorry. Which notes should I be looking at?"

"All of them. But your instinct was right. Let's begin with the two from your mother." He paused while David bent back down over the notes. "They look awfully similar, as you noted a few minutes ago, perhaps even identical, as the writing from the same person naturally should. But as you are now looking more closely, does it still appear as perfect of a match?"

David didn't answer immediately. He peered through the magnifying lens, looking from one note to the other and back again. "No. Close—real close—but not perfect."

Chester nodded approvingly. "Not perfect. I would concur. The o's. Focus on them. That's what caught my attention. The other letters seem spot on, a perfect match, but the o's.... What do you see?"

"They're close, but... but the o's in the milk letter...." He paused, his throat suddenly very dry.

"Take your time."

"I'm okay. Those o's are perfect. Perfectly round. Impressive, actually."

"They are indeed. And what about the o's in the letter to you about Rachel?"

David peered through the lens. "Not quite perfect. A little more oval, I guess. Just slightly."

"That's what I saw too. It's hard to make a perfect circle, even for someone with nice penmanship, which the author of all three of these notes clearly possessed."

David put the magnifying lens down and stood up. "So, what does all that mean?"

"I would only be guessing, but the perfect o's in the one note suggest that extreme effort was taken in writing it. One must wonder why, given that running out for milk is a rather quick and trivial act. It's curious that the writing would be so very neat and the o's so very perfect... if she wrote it."

"And if she didn't?"

Chester folded his hands again. "Well, that's another matter entirely. If she didn't, then we of course now come to the key question, the puzzle which brought you to the police station and then here today. If she didn't write it, who did?"

They sat silently for a while.

"And that begs a follow-up question," Chester finally said. "Who wrote it, and why did they take such care with their penmanship?"

David picked up the magnifying lens once more.

"Three notes," Chester said.

"What do you mean?"

"You brought me three notes... I assume for a reason. We've just discussed whether the two from your mother are both from your mother, but I assume you didn't bring me a note about cookies just for kicks."

David looked down at the cookies note and shook his head.

Chester continued. "Why did you bring it?"

"Something hit me. The note... when I saw it, something jumped out at me. I wasn't sure what, but something seemed familiar. And so...." David picked up the cookies note and the milk note as Chester waited patiently. "And so I compared these two. At first, it seems obvious they're very different, that two different people wrote them, but then...."

"But then you took a closer look."

"Yes, I took a closer look. And now, looking through *this*—" He gestured with the magnifying lens. " —I see it. It's there. Did you see?"

"*Perdidit Antiquum Litera Prima Sonum.*"

"Okay, I know *that* is not English.

"Forgive me. You are correct. It's Latin. *Perdidit Antiquum Litera Prima Sonum*. My chance to return to Poe. Inspector Dupin said it in 'Murders in the Rue Morgue.'"

"Okay... and it means...?"

"*He has ruined the old sound with the first letter.* Something hit me too." Chester grinned. "And it's always a bonus when I can slip in a Poe reference."

David furrowed his brow. "But I still—"

"Well, I didn't say it fit perfectly, but let's consider all this. We've detected subtle but distinct differences between the two letters supposedly penned by your mother, particularly the o's. We've also detected some similarities between two of the notes, also subtle, but as we examine things, also rather distinct."

David looked back and forth between the cookie and farewell notes.

"Again," said Chester, "the o's. They're our thread, our subtle clue, which upon closer examination becomes distinct. The o's we see in the milk note and in the note to you, we have discovered, are somewhat different. The o's in the milk note and the cookie note, however, are remarkably similar."

David put the notes back down on Chester's desk and began pacing the room. The enormity of what was beginning to suggest itself pressed in upon him.

"*He has ruined the old sound with the first letter,*" Chester repeated. "As that pertains to our discussion, the first letter is o — not literally, but the letter of interest to us. The o is the culprit, and if someone else authored the milk note, that person may have given themselves away with the o's. Ruined the old sound, if you will. Blown their cover."

"Are you saying...?"

"I am not saying anything, but permit me, for a moment, a Holmes reference. 'Once you eliminate the impossible, whatever remains, however improbable, must be the truth.'"

David spoke quietly. "Kathy."

"We must now accept that as possible — perhaps improbable, but it may be the truth."

David resumed pacing, his heart pounding once more, thoughts careening off one another at a dizzying pace. "But that means.... But what if...."

Chester held up a hand. "David, stop. We don't know anything for sure. I told you, it's only possible. Graphology is not an exact science. There may not be much to it."

David stopped his zigzagging of Chester's floor and looked at his friend, somewhat exasperated. "Wait a minute. You mean all this may not mean anything?"

Chester drew himself up in his chair. "I can't prove any of this, and I can't tell you what to think or do. All I've done is given you something to consider, and I dare say it was something you were considering anyway."

David returned to Chester's desk, scooped up each note, carefully folded them and returned them to the plastic snack bag, then tucked the bag into his jeans pocket. "You're right. I was. Thank you, Chester. Seriously, you rock."

Chester grinned sheepishly. "I have my moments. Or should I say, elementary?" He and David exchanged fist bumps. "What are you going to do?"

David stopped, his hand on the door handle. "I have no idea. There's just so much.... I don't know what it all means, or how it all fits together. All I know is that I have to find out."

"That's one heck of a door you're opening."

David drew a deep breath. "I know."

CHAPTER 21
Preparations

"I WISH THAT YOUR MOTHER WAS here," his dad said.

The late-afternoon sunlight poured in through David's window, warming him.

His dad smiled as he helped his son adjust his tie. "She would have loved to see you dressed up like this, and she would have been a lot better at helping you than I am."

"It's okay, Dad."

"We really need to get you a few of your own." His dad chuckled as David fidgeted with the end of the patterned, navy tie, which dangled near his waistline.

"It's fine. I'll have the jacket on." He grabbed the sport coat from his bed and slipped it on, tugging at either sleeve until it somewhat resembled a proper fit. He regarded himself in the mirror, grinning sheepishly at the kid looking back at him.

"You sure you don't want to ride with Donovan? Kathy hoped you would."

"Dad, he's taking someone. I don't want to tag along. Besides, I told Robert I'd ride with him. We're meeting friends there."

His dad sighed. "Okay, okay, I understand." He studied his son, who was fretting again with his tie. "Didn't mean to upset you."

"I'm not upset. Why are you staring at me?"

"Hey, give me a little credit. I think I can tell when there's something on your mind. Was there someone you wanted to ask?"

David groaned.

"Ah," his dad murmured. "I figured as much. Who was it? What happened?"

"I really don't want to talk about it."

His dad nodded. "Okay, but if you ever change your mind, I'm happy to listen. I know how it is."

David checked his watch. "Robert will be here soon." He started for the door.

"David."

He stopped, hand on the doorknob.

"I need you to try... with Donovan."

This was the last conversation David wanted to have. "I *have* been."

A horn sounded outside and David exhaled, grateful for the reprieve. He turned and scampered across the hallway and down the stairs.

"David!" Rachel had twisted around from her spot in front of the TV and now stood up and regarded him.

"Yeah, Rachel? I gotta go."

"Let me *see* you," she insisted.

He turned toward her, and she inspected him from head to toe with a serious expression before nodding in approval. "You look like a *movie* guy. I hope you get to dance with the best girl. Don't forget to tell her she looks pretty. Oh! And that you like her shoes."

David furrowed his brow. "Her shoes?"

Rachel sighed. "Yes, her shoes. Girls like that."

"Okay," David said, but his sister had already turned back around. He opened the door and headed out into the night, his heart beginning to thrum with a great many considerations.

CHAPTER 22
The Dance

EVERYTHING MOVED VERY FAST, AS STROBE lights pierced the otherwise darkened gym in sporadic flashes. A DJ spun records, and the students who'd packed into the gym all shouted to be heard.

"Come on," Robert said, raising his voice. "Let's go find Jelly."

David waded with his friend into the sea of bodies.

Jelly, as they affectionately called him one of their friends since elementary school, was in actuality a person, not a condiment. His real name, though his friends used it so rarely they sometimes required a moment to remember, was Anthony Carwell, and he loved jellybeans. Loved them. He was a bit round and generally jovial, though if provoked, he had a short fuse. He'd been known to steamroll classmates at gym if pushed too far, yet inevitably he'd feel guilty and apologize profusely.

He was apologizing now as they approached the far end of the gym. He evidently had bumped into a classmate, spilling the boy's plastic cup of punch. Thankfully, the student seemed in a forgiving spirit, and David and Robert quickly ushered Jelly away.

"How long have you been here?" Robert inquired.

"What?"

"When did you get here?" he shouted.

"Oh! Right at the start. They had a ton of cookies when we first came in." Jelly glanced around. "Hopefully, they'll be putting more out soon."

The song ended, offering a brief reprieve.

Robert smiled. "Thanks for the update. Who else is here? Flanagan? Half Caff?"

Jelly nodded. "Yeah, they're here. Flanny brought Esther Rimple. Esther Rimple!"

The boys understood Jelly's exuberance. *Flanny* referred to Rory Flanagan, one of their good friends, and one of the quirkiest yet shyest kids they knew. Although fun-loving and goofy with his friends, when it came to girls, he blushed crimson-red at the mere mention. The one person in all of ninth grade who might have been even shyer was Esther Rimple. A studious, reserved, quiet-as-a-mouse girl with thick glasses and seemingly endless rings of red hair, Esther was at first glance a bit plain-looking, but David always thought she had a nice smile—problem was, very few people had ever seen it. Perhaps Flanny had. Maybe he'd overcome his nerves and told her a joke. He always had a joke. In any event, the two of them getting together would have fetched long odds had anyone been wagering.

"Hey!" Jelly exclaimed as the next song began to blare. "It's Half Caff."

David smiled. Their gang did not lack nicknames. Chester, as an example, who had just pulled up alongside them in his motorized wheelchair, sometimes answered to Sherlock. They occasionally serenaded Robert with Bob, Rob, or even Robs, none of which seemed to faze him one way or the other. Half Caff, on the other hand, was a funny story. His name was Craig Firestone, a skinny kid with unkempt brown hair who had shown up in math class one morning with a cappuccino. The teacher immediately confiscated it, and Craig's friends couldn't wait for class to let out.

"Why the hell did you bring coffee?" Robert had demanded.

"I drink it sometimes," Craig had insisted. "Every now and then."

"Decaf or regular?"

"It depends," Craig explained. "If it's early morning... well, regular, of course, but later in the day, I sometimes have half-caff. You know, they make that. Half-caff. Half regular, half decaffeinated. So I don't get too wired."

"Coffee, or punch?" David asked him presently, gesturing at the cup in his friend's hand.

"Ha, ha. Punch." Half Caff looked behind him. "And I think they just put some cookies out."

"Where?" Jelly peered intently through the crowd.

"On the tables, by the punch."

After Jelly set off on his quest, Robert looked at David and shrugged. "Guess we're headed over there."

They navigated through the maze of students, some of whom were dancing, others just milling around. David exhaled upon arriving at the far side of the gym without having run into certain people. He wanted to see *her*, just... not with *him*.

"*Look* at these." Jelly marveled at the mountain of cookies adjacent the punch bowls. He started grabbing fistfuls and stuffing them into napkins.

"Jelly," Robert said. "We're civilized people, you know. Use this." He handed him a plate.

Jelly grinned sheepishly.

After they'd gotten their refreshments, they turned back and eyed the dance floor. David scanned the crowd, prepared to look away quickly, but the first person he recognized was Flanny. At first, he couldn't make out his dance partner, but after a moment, his eyes widened.

Esther Rimple. Esther didn't have her glasses on, and her fiery red hair flowed long and straight past her shoulders. She wore an emerald gown, and she was beautiful — beautiful and dancing. *Really* dancing. David watched in amazement as Flanny attempted to keep up with his date's frenzied movements.

He shook his head. *You can never really know a person.*

"David."

He started at the touch of a hand on his shoulder, but then a smile lit his face. Her hand seemed to linger an extra, glorious moment, and David blushed and fidgeted with his tie.

Amanda placed a gentle hand on his. "It's fine." Her eyes sparkled with kindness. "You look very nice."

"So do you." Remembering Rachel, he glanced at Amanda's feet. "I like your shoes."

She grinned broadly, lifting one foot off the ground as though posing. "Yeah? Someone told you to say that, right?"

David froze, but Amanda leaned over and gave him a quick hug. "It's okay. That was cute."

"Hey."

Robert nudged him and gestured to an approaching group of boys, led by Donovan. He was flanked on one side by Stefan Milano, a tall, good-looking kid with thick black hair, and on the other by Charlie Dougall, a burly sophomore with an infamous temper. Beady eyes peered out from Charlie's square head, atop which sprouted a crop of spiky dark hair. He was already a standout on the varsity football and wrestling teams. Even the Owen Gillespies of the school knew not to mess with him.

"There you are." Donovan glanced at David before returning his attention to Amanda. "I need to keep a better eye on you, huh?"

He laughed, but Amanda shot him a look. "Excuse me?"

Dougall smirked.

Robert stepped forward from the snack table and stood shoulder to shoulder with David.

"Is there a problem?" Donovan asked.

"That depends on you," Robert said.

David tensed as Dougall took a step toward him and Robert.

"If there is," said Dougall, "I can solve it."

Amanda stepped between them. "We're all here to have a good time. No need for any of this." She looked at David apologetically.

"You're right," Donovan said. "Let's go."

Donovan, Dougall, and Stefan had started to head off into the crowd when Donovan suddenly stopped, extending a hand in Amanda's direction. "Come on."

She looked at Donovan, then quickly back at David, her expression pained. "I'm sorry, but I came here with him. I better go." She managed a faint smile.

David did his best to reciprocate. "It's okay."

She slipped away into the throng of students, and David turned back to his friends and exhaled deeply.

Jelly gulped down punch, wiping sweat from his brow every few seconds. "Whoa. *That* was close." He nudged Robert with his elbow. "He had *Dougall* with him."

Robert shrugged.

Flanny and Esther had made their way over, breathing hard, their brows gleaming with sweat.

"Hey guys," Flanny gasped.

"Hey," David replied. "Hi, Esther."

"Hi!" Esther wiped her brow. "Whew. Hard to keep up with this guy."

Robert chuckled. "That's our Flanny."

"Hey, guys," Jelly said. "You missed all the action! Oh... also, they have cookies. See?"

Everyone laughed, and Jelly filled them in on the encounter with Donovan and his friends.

Finally, they moved on to other topics and set about trying to enjoy the evening. Every so often, David would glance across the gym and spot Amanda. He thought once or twice their eyes met briefly, but the distance made it difficult to tell.

Over the next hour, the music blared, the lights pulsed, and David and his friends meandered back and forth through the hordes of people on their side of the gym, laughing and shouting to one another above the noise. At one point, Mr. Delson shared a dance with Mrs. Delgado, one of the math teachers, much to the amusement of all present.

"Hello again."

Amanda. David smiled, but then quickly looked over her shoulder.

"Don't worry. They know to stay put back there. I told him I was getting more punch."

"Nice," David said. "Umm, won't he wonder why you didn't just get punch at the tables over by them?"

"Let him wonder."

David smiled and wiped a hand across his brow, feeling suddenly lightheaded.

"Wanna go outside and get some air? " Amanda asked.

He wanted nothing more.

She grasped his right elbow with her left hand and guided him toward the front of the gymnasium. The air in the foyer felt immediately cooler, but when they headed for the exit doors, Coach Anderson, one of the chaperones for the evening, blocked their path.

"Where you headed, guys?"

"Just outside for a minute for some fresh air," Amanda said.

"Sorry, not allowed. We're responsible for supervising you on school grounds. Gotta stay inside where we can see you."

"It's okay," Amanda said. As they headed back into the gym, she leaned over and whispered in David's ear. "Let's head for the back of the gym. I have an idea."

When they reached the far doors, she glanced around quickly, then started to push the doors open.

"Young lady," said a kind but emphatic voice. "Where might you be headed?"

David hadn't noticed Marcel there until now, and he couldn't help but smile upon seeing him. His counselor looked sharp in a brown vest suit and maroon bow tie.

"Hi, Mr. Fontaine," said Amanda. "It's getting so hot in here, and loud. We just wanted a few minutes to walk, get to chat a little. They wouldn't let us go outside."

Marcel smiled. "Well, I certainly appreciate what you're saying." He wiped his brow with a handkerchief, which he then folded neatly and returned to his vest pocket. "It *is* warm, and loud—

though I thought this might be the decibel level of choice for young men and women of your age...."

David and Amanda laughed and looked at him expectantly.

"...but I am afraid I must disappoint you with the same news as did my colleagues. For your own safety, I must prohibit you from leaving the gymnasium, I regret to say." He smiled again, but his voice was resolute.

David knew better than to persist. "No problem. We can just walk around in here."

They'd begun to move away from the doors when David felt a strong hand on his shoulder.

Marcel looked down at him.

"It's good to see you, David." He wore a conflicted expression, as though he wanted to say more.

David smiled. "You too."

As they left Marcel, David scanned the gym for Donovan and his gang. Surely they would be looking for Amanda by now.

Before he could fret any further, Amanda tugged at his elbow and ushered him to a back corner of the gym. She gestured back over to where they had been conversing with Marcel just moments before. "Look."

The spot was vacated, and they could see Marcel walking off toward one side of the gym, near the snack tables. He scooped himself a cup of punch, wiped his brow again, and began chatting with colleagues.

"It's our chance." Amanda nudged David again toward the back doors. No sooner had her hands pressed onto the door's release bar when another voice stopped them in their tracks.

"And where do you two think you are going?"

Rendicott. David's shoulders slumped. This would be bad.

Amanda sighed, seemingly resigned to the fate of being constrained in the gymnasium for the rest of the dance. "Just wanted to take a walk."

David watched curiously as Mr. Rendicott glanced around the gymnasium. When he looked back at them, his expression had turned sympathetic, paternal, like Marcel's moments before. It made him uneasy.

"Well, I suppose it's okay, but don't be too long."

Amanda looked up, surprised. "Really?"

Mr. Rendicott held up an index finger. "Not too long."

"Thanks!" they said in unison, and slipped quickly through the door Mr. Rendicott propped open for them.

David watched him step in front of the door, his back to them, obscuring them from sight as they moved quickly down the hallway.

The halls were dark, save for the faint auxiliary lightning, and as they got farther from the gym, it became eerily quiet.

"Here," Amanda said when they neared the end of the hallway. She took his hand, and they went into the stairwell.

They sat down side-by-side three stairs up, Amanda to David's left, the faint echoes of the dance seeming worlds away. It seemed to David vitally important that he not restrain Amanda's hand if she seemed to want to let go, nor relinquish it if she seemed to want him to hold on. He drew a deep breath and squeezed her hand so lightly that he wasn't entirely sure he had done so, or that she'd felt it. His heart raced in this brief moment of uncertainty, but when he felt her squeezing back, a current of happiness pulsed through him. Somewhere within him, by turns disturbing and exhilarating, notions of immortality and secret worlds swirled uncertainly, along with feverish questions about what had really happened to his mom. But even these, for the moment, were quarantined in deeper recesses of his mind, so that the world consisted only of him and Amanda, in this stairwell at the end of the hall.

She said, "I'm surprised Mr. Rendicott let us go."

"Me too." It seemed odd that Marcel had been the sterner of the two.

She looked at him, then down at her feet. "You guys are lucky."

David regarded her curiously. "Who's lucky?"

"You are." She slid off her shoes, leaned forward, and caressed the bottom of her feet. "*Boys.* Be glad you don't have to wear shoes like these. Dang, they hurt."

"I'm glad."

Amanda grinned. "Though that would be a sight."

They both sat silently a while, still holding hands, still smiling.

At length, her smile faded and her head slumped. "I'm sorry."

"What for?"

"Donovan." She shook her head.

"It's okay. You're not responsible for him."

She looked into his eyes. "You're too sweet, but I should know better. There just seemed to be something about him...."

David felt a pang of jealousy but empathized immediately. "I know. There is. There are times he seems so nice, such a cool guy, such a good friend, almost like...."

"Like what?"

"Like a brother." David shook his head. "And so many times, I've felt like the jerk in all this. So often now, I just don't know what to think or how to feel. "

Amanda turned toward him. "Hey, you're not a jerk. You're a good guy."

"Thanks."

"No, I'm serious. I can see it. You've just been through a lot—a whole lot."

Before he could reply, the last sound he wanted to hear reverberated down the darkened hallway.

"Amanda?" Donovan's voice called out, unmistakably.

They could hear other voices too, and footsteps, and David knew Donovan had his entourage in tow.

"Amanda!"

She gestured behind them, up the stairwell, but David shook his head, resigned. "I'm tired of running."

They stood up together, hands still clasped. Though he knew a potentially ugly confrontation awaited, he was far more upset that his time with Amanda had been interrupted so soon.

She leaned toward him and brushed her lips against his cheeks, as lightly as a butterfly's wings, then stepped back and smiled. "Ready?"

They stepped out from the stairwell into the dimly lit hallway at the precise moment Donovan and his friends arrived.

"Well, well," said Charlie Dougall. He looked like a hungry animal that knew it was about to eat.

Stefan Milano stood to his left.

Donovan addressed Amanda. "You shouldn't have said yes if you wanted to go with David."

"We're just talking," she said. "Is there anything wrong with that?"

Donovan had turned his attention to David. "Thought we were tight, dude."

"You knew I liked her," David said quietly.

"You should have asked her then."

"Hey!" Amanda stepped between them. "I am not anybody's prize. I made my own decision, and yes—" She looked at Donovan. "—I chose to come with you. I don't need your permission to talk to David or anybody, but I should have told you instead of sneaking off. I'm sorry."

Even through the darkness, David could see Donovan's eyes soften.

Stefan eyed the developments uncertainly, but it was Dougall who spoke next, pointing a finger at Amanda.

"You don't get off that easy. You don't do a dude like that—come with them to the dance, then ditch 'em for another guy. Especially a dweeb like this one." He jabbed a stubby finger into David's chest and sneered.

Before he realized he was doing it, David wrenched Dougall's hand from his chest and shoved him back toward Donovan.

Dougall's eyes registered a moment of shock before boiling over with rage. He pointed his finger again. "You're dead."

Amanda's eyes widened, and she scrambled out of the way as Dougall barreled past.

David knew well that Dougall had never lost a fight and had hurt many kids, but the notion of retreating never entered into his considerations. Instead, he shifted his posture slightly to one side—his left leg leading—and assumed an easy combat stance. He somehow had time in the fraction of a moment before Dougall set upon him to think: *I have a combat stance?*

Before David could test its effectiveness, Donovan's voice rang out, resolute. "No!" He had stepped forward and corralled Dougall's arm before it could rocket forward.

Dougall whirled around. "What the hell, man?"

Donovan stood his ground. "No. We can work it out." He looked past Dougall at David. "We're brothers, right?"

David glanced at Stefan, who looked to be affixed to the wall, staring wide-eyed, and then met Amanda's gaze. She smiled hopefully, and he looked past Dougall's still cocked fist at Donovan. "Right."

Donovan smiled, but Dougall finally wrenched free of his grip and whirled toward David once more.

"Hey!" Mr. Rendicott's unmistakable voice thundered down the hallway.

Everyone froze; even Dougall knew not to push the issue. He glared at David, as though marking him for a future date.

As Rendicott neared, David's eyes again locked with Donovan's. He could not read them in the slightest.

CHAPTER 23
The Eyes of March

THE ALTERCATION AT THE DANCE mandated more counseling sessions. David had long since come to savor his time with Marcel, but when he strolled into the office after school that afternoon, Mrs. Gittlebaum informed him in a melancholy voice that Mr. Fontaine no longer worked there, and he would be seeing a new counselor.

David's heart sank. Though he still couldn't fully believe the notions of immortality and magic that Marcel had, in these last several months, confided to him, they had nevertheless instilled in him an unmistakable air of excitement and hope. Now the air seemed to rush out of him, the excitement and, most importantly, the hope disappearing along with it.

"Would you like to talk with Dr. Lardman about it?" Mrs. Gittlebaum offered.

David nodded, but when Lardman welcomed him into his office and asked him to sit down, David quickly regretted his decision.

"Mr. Fontaine unfortunately is no longer with the school," Dr. Lardman said. "We have a new counselor, and you may begin seeing him immediately. Okay?"

David's mind churned with distressing questions, each of which begged additional ones, and none of which seemed to possess answers. Maybe Marcel had just been crazy all along, a well-intended old man out of touch with reality. Maybe David was crazy too.

Still, something wasn't right. Indeed, something was very, very wrong.

"David?" Principal Lardman regarded him expectantly. "Are you ready to see Mr. Cerratus?"

"Yeah," he lied.

When David came out, Mrs. Gittlebaum poked her head into the counselor's office. "David Rose is here."

"Thank you," a deep voice replied from within. "I'll be out in just a moment."

Mrs. Gittlebaum stepped back, closed the door, and smiled at David. "He'll be out in just a moment."

David shifted back and forth on his feet.

Mrs. Gittlebaum looked up at him. "It's been a tough time, hasn't it?"

"Yes." Her acknowledgement provided a small bit of comfort, a matchstick of light in a moment that had otherwise gone dark.

She nodded and lowered her voice to a whisper. "Strange times, too. What I try to do is just stay to myself and do my job. Hopefully, what I don't know won't hurt me."

David looked at her, unsure how to reply.

"I guess what I'm saying," she continued, "is maybe you should do the same. Try not to worry, and don't ask too many questions. Maybe whatever is going on will eventually pass."

David managed a faint smile, and as he did, the door to the counselor's office swung open.

A tall man with thick dark hair and a large, square jaw looked down at him. "David Rose." The man motioned toward the open office door. "Please come in."

Mrs. Gittlebaum looked at David hopefully, and he managed another faint smile before putting his head down and trudging into the office.

When the tall man closed the door behind them, the light from the reception area faded, and the already dim office grew darker still. Mr. Cerratus asked him to please sit, and as he did, he thought once more of Mrs. Gittlebaum's advice. His appreciation of her words did not, unfortunately, correspond with any optimism that they would prove true.

He glanced outside at yet another cold, gray afternoon. The clouds didn't float past, as they often did. They'd settled in.

It seemed to David to be the longest of winters.

***

By the first day of March, the clouds began to lift and sunlight warmed the air. They had PE outside, and when David came back in for English class, he was glad for his seat near the window, where he could still feel the sun on his face.

"*Julius Caesar*," Mrs. Brophy said. "You should be almost done now — it was one of the assigned readings. Let us start with Brutus and Cassius. Villains? Heroes? Yes, Jeffrey?"

"Villains," replied Jeffrey Colloway, a thin boy with a clump of blond hair that looked as though it spent considerable time compressed under hats. "They committed murder, and betrayed a friend."

"Good points. It *is* difficult to put an exonerating light on such acts, but does anyone have another view of the matter? Amanda?"

David looked up.

"They felt justification for their acts," Amanda said. "Cassius rejected the idea of Caesar's power. He believed in fighting it, believed in free will."

Mrs. Brophy smiled and retrieved a copy of the book from her desk. She flipped around for a moment until she found the desired page. "Very good, Amanda. Cassius says, '*Men at sometime were masters of their fate. The fault, dear Brutus, is not in our stars, but in ourselves.*'" Satisfied, she closed the book. "Cassius and Brutus assassinate Caesar but are themselves defeated in the end. Does this suggest one philosophy trumps the other? Was Caesar's death inevitable, a nod to fate? Or did his lingering impact on those who vanquished him and those he ruled constitute a defiant testament to free will, even in the face of death?" She smiled again, seeming to recognize that she'd given her pupils a sufficient amount to consider. "I think you get the point. If nothing else, perhaps one lesson is this: be certain who your friends are."

***

David was relieved to have the house to himself for a few minutes after school. He grabbed an apple from the kitchen, then went to the living room and sank into the easy chair to crunch into his snack. Still a few weeks to go before the trip, he wished somehow it could be canceled or, better yet, that they could go without Donovan and Kathy.

He heard the front door opening and the familiar patter of seven-year-old feet darting in.

"We're home, David!" Rachel giggled as she entered the living room and saw him. "Oh! You're right there!" She dropped her backpack onto the floor and ran over to her brother.

"Yeah, I'm right here. Hey, Dad."

"Hi, David. How was school?"

"Good."

"Good." His dad leafed through some mail he'd brought in. "I'm headed to the computer for a little work, okay?"

"Sure."

"Did you have a good day, David?" his sister inquired, in her very best big-person voice.

"Yeah. How about you?"

Rachel furrowed her brow in contemplation. "We had hard work today. We had to write a whole pear graph."

David smiled. "Paragraph?"

"Yeah. Pear graph. The teacher helped us a little."

"Well, that's okay."

"Did *you* have hard work?"

"Not too hard, but I do have to start my homework."

"What's it about?"

"Well, it's reading. A play about a man named Julius Caesar. We learned about it today, since it's March fifteenth."

"Why today?"

"Because he got killed on this day, a long time ago, and ever since then, people say, 'Beware the Ides of March.'"

"What's that?"

David got up from his chair. "Let me show you."

He went to the front hallway, retrieved his backpack, and pulled out his history book. He flipped through some pages and pointed to a picture. "That's Julius Caesar. He was a Roman leader around two thousand years ago."

Rachel's eyes widened. "That's a long time ago."

"Yes, it is. He was the leader of the Roman Empire, a very important guy. Anyway, Ides of March.... Caesar was a dictator, and some people didn't like him. They wanted a different kind of government, and on March fifteenth all those years ago, a group of senators assassinated him. That means they killed him. So, ever since then, there's been a phrase: Beware the Ides of March." He looked up from his book and experienced an instant pang of guilt, as his poor little sister looked mortified. "Don't worry." He patted her head. "It's just a figure of speech. Kinda means, just be careful."

Rachel exhaled, then eyed the piece of fruit in her brother's other hand. "I want an apple too." She headed for the kitchen but stopped at the edge of the living room and looked back at him. "Are they big?"

David raised an eyebrow. "The apples?"

"The *eyes*," she explained impatiently. "The eyes of March."

CHAPTER 24
For Every Action

AS MUCH AS HE'D GROWN TO look forward to his sessions with Marcel, David quickly began to dread his time with Mr. Cerratus, who volleyed questions at him like jabs he had to parry and deflect — such as right now, as the counselor looked up from some notes and regarded him from behind his desk.

"Why don't you explain your hostility toward Donovan?"

Why don't I explain my hostility toward you?

"Many incidents this year," Cerratus continued. "Fights, problems. Any explanation for all of this?"

David looked down. He trusted this man about as far as he could spit, and he couldn't spit far.

"In that case —" Cerratus leaned over his desk. " — I recommend we find out."

David crossed his arms.

"You have endured a lot of stress. Would you concur?"

David nodded slowly.

Mr. Cerratus looked at his notes for several mores seconds, then back up at David. "Fights, nightmares, even that incident at the creek."

David stiffened. The idea that this man had access to all he'd shared with Marcel was extremely unsettling. "A lot of kids go through stuff."

"Indeed they do."

They regarded each other a moment, David wishing he could be anywhere else.

"But the matter of your mother's passing must be the most difficult of all."

David felt his hands balling into fists. Maybe it was natural for a counselor to ask about such a thing, but hearing it slither from this man's lips felt as if he'd been struck by a venomous snake.

"That must have been a great trauma," Cerratus said. "For all of you. It must be a great trauma still."

David stared out the window at the clear blue sky, as if doing so long enough might somehow transport him away on the wings of his contemplations.

"PTSD," Mr. Cerratus said. "It's a modern term: Post-Traumatic Stress Disorder. When someone suffers great trauma, the stress can manifest in a variety of unhealthy ways. In your case, nightmares, conflict, all that you've been experiencing. David?"

He reluctantly returned his attention from the window.

"But there is hope—treatment, coping. The first step is digging down and getting at the root of the issue. Once that occurs, the road to recovery may begin. Awakening to the origins of things can be quite powerful."

He smiled—the first time David could recall him doing so—but it was an unpleasant, misplaced-looking expression, more triumphant than sympathetic.

"The stronger it is, and older it is, the more spectacular the moment. Real epiphanies, bolt of lightning stuff." Cerratus got up and walked around his desk to the window. "A fine day." He closed the blinds, and the room quickly darkened. He then returned to his desk and sat. "I don't believe Mr.

Fontaine ever tried this technique with you. Have you ever heard of regression hypnosis?"

David regarded him warily. "No."

"It can be an effective technique. Basically, it involves hypnotizing the patient and recovering old, often suppressed memories."

"I'm a kid."

"You're the required age!"

David drew back in his chair as though struck, but Cerratus's face softened.

"I'm sorry. What I mean to say is, you're a young man now, a fine man. At any rate, this technique can prove effective in getting to the root of current problems. In this case, your hostility toward Donovan, and that demonstrated in the other incidents you've had this year. If we can deduce some underlying issues, then perhaps we may chart a better course of action to help you. After all—" He paused and looked at David. "—I *am* here to help you."

David glanced toward the door.

"What say you, David Rose?" Cerratus leaned forward in his chair, grinning again. "Have you ever been hypnotized?"

"No. Are you supposed to do that with students?"

Cerratus's grin thawed. "You have been mandated to attend these sessions. You are expected to cooperate with whatever course of action we deem best."

"We?"

"The school, of course. We want what's best for you. Shall we begin?"

David didn't respond, but Cerratus stood up and walked over to the door, paused a moment, then quietly locked it. David swallowed and tensed in his chair as the counselor turned and approached him.

"Try to relax." Cerratus rotated a chair until it faced David. He sat down and retrieved a small bag from his desk, placed it on the floor, and removed a CD. "Soothing sounds." He grabbed a CD player from his desk and popped in the disc.

It sounded to David like Irish music, similar to what they played at O'Tierney's Pub and Grill, or on those River Dance shows his mother used to watch.

"Celtic."

David exhaled but tensed back up as Cerratus again reached into his bag. He didn't know what to expect—a swinging pendulum, or perhaps one of those dizzying spirally things? He raised an eyebrow upon glimpsing the large photograph Cerratus had withdrawn.

"Kind of fits our theme," Cerratus said. "Goes well with the music, usually helps a person relax."

David studied the picture: a countryside with rolling hills, sprawling canopies, a farmhouse, a river, and grazing animals.

Cerratus propped it up against a lamp adjacent to where they sat, leaned toward David, and held his hands up near his own chest. "Now, try this."

The counselor brought his hands closer together, then slowly touched the tip of each index finger together. He moved them apart, then slowly repeated the action.

He looked at David. "Can you try that? Slowly touch your index fingers together."

Well, this is easy. David did as asked.

"Good. Again, please."

David touched his fingers together, separated them, and repeated.

"Excellent." Cerratus motioned with his head toward the picture by the lamp. "Please keep doing it, and look at the beautiful picture. Focus on it."

He did, and a wave of peacefulness began to wash over him. Although voices within him called out urging caution, they sounded far away, and he couldn't help but let himself be carried off. He was so very tired.

"You're doing great," Cerratus said. "Breathe deeply. In...." He modeled the gesture for David. "Out. In... out. Good. Keep touching your fingers together... and apart... and together. Breathe in... out. Take in the picture. It's beautiful, isn't it? The hills, the fresh air... feel it on your face, refreshing and relaxing you. Can you feel it? Are you there?"

He was. It felt like the time he'd gotten his wisdom teeth removed and they'd given him nitrous oxide. He'd faded into a pleasant numbness, knowingly, yet powerless to resist.

"Savor it." Cerratus sounded increasingly distant. "Feel the breeze caressing your face. Now look around. Can you see it? It's wonderful — the hills, the cottages with swirls of smoke spiraling up from little chimneys, the animals, the sea in the distance, the cliffs. Turn around now, slowly, and behold the splendor of the great structure. Do you see it? Do you remember?"

David Rose on the hillside was unaware that David Rose in the counselor's office was slowly nodding. He trained his attention on the immense castle that stood before him, and a great consciousness swirled within him, like the smoke from the cottage chimneys.

A faraway voice said, "Tell me what you see."

David didn't answer. He just stared at the castle, transfixed.

"David Rose." Impatience simmered in the counselor's voice.

David felt vulnerable, like the time with his wisdom teeth. Who *was* this man, and what was this strange world into which he had steered him?

Precisely at this moment, and for no apparent reason, he thought of physics. Not that he knew anything about the subject, but Chester—enrolled in the class typically reserved for upperclassmen—had recently mentioned how they'd been studying Newton's Third Law of Motion. *For every action, there is an equal and opposite reaction.* David had not given the notion a second thought, but now it occurred to him that so many things had happened to him in the last year and a half—happened *to* him, acted *upon* him, and he'd reacted. Always he'd reacted. Perhaps it was within his power to change gears, or at least throw a wrench in them.

No time like the present.

Willing every ounce of concentration he could muster, the David Rose in the counselor's office and the David Rose on the hillside joined with spectacular fusion. His soul was ablaze with power and possibility, and he restrained a smile, for Mr. Cerratus must not see. Fully and simultaneously in two places, David's mind and focus were one.

On the hillside, a man David didn't recognize approached, wearing what appeared to be medieval armor and wielding a long, tapering sword. Although David possessed no weapons, he understood he was about to engage battle on two fronts.

Back in the office, Cerratus continued his own assault. "You are remembering, aren't you?" More a statement than a question.

Go along, David told himself. *For now.* "Yes."

"Good. Remember. See it all. Feel it. There is someone else there with you now, correct?"

"Yes."

On the hillside, that someone now stood perhaps twenty feet away. David had hoped to catch a glimpse of his eyes through the slits in the gleaming helmet, but he could no longer wait, couldn't take a chance that the knight and his sword might be harmless figments of his hypnosis-induced hallucination.

He called upon a reservoir of concentration, and the scene before him swirled and shifted. When he emerged from the strange vortex, he found himself back in his own head, just him in the counselor's office. He kept his eyes closed.

Mr. Cerratus addressed him again. "Can you describe him?"

Every ounce of concentration. "It looks like a knight."

"Excellent. Who is he?"

David was silent. Something in him wanted to go along with Cerratus, to let himself be led to wherever and whatever might await him, because as dangerous as it might be, he might also find there some of the answers he so desperately sought. This was not the path Marcel thought best, however, and despite the fact he'd never fully believed everything Marcel had told him, he harbored no doubt about which counselor he trusted and which he didn't.

"I can't see," he finally replied. "He's in full armor."

"Look at him. Look again. Surely you must know."

David inhaled deeply. *Time to throw a wrench.* His heart pounded. "I think you know."

Silence. Then, "You know what you must do."

"Tell me."

"You know," Cerratus said, an edge quickly returning to his tone. "You must know!"

David held on. "Tell me."

"You do not require my direction. You know who you are, who he is, and what must occur."

"You must tell me. I must be sure."

"Surely you know! It is.... It...."

Cerratus fell silent.

After a few moments, David slowly opened his eyes.

Cerratus was scribbling furiously in his notebook. A few moments later, he looked up, as though having felt David's eyes on him. "Okay, that will be enough for today." He returned to his notes.

David took a deep breath, exhaled slowly, and stood. He retrieved his backpack and slung it over his shoulder. He wondered if Mrs. Gittlebaum would still be at her desk. It seemed he'd been in there a very long time.

He walked to the door but paused and turned around. "Are we finished?"

Mr. Cerratus stopped writing and looked up at him, his eyes cold and hard as a winter sky. "For now."

CHAPTER 25
Burning

IT SEEMED TO DAVID AS THOUGH an hourglass had been upended. It was now just a few weeks before their vacation, and he wished it would be scrapped, or that Kathy and Donovan would bow out. His apprehension ran far deeper than anything he could articulate—it churned in secret places within himself, places at once close yet always out of reach. It found voice in the innocent, knowing eyes of his little sister, who, since he could remember, had demonstrated a perception well beyond her years.

From the first, Rachel had been leery of Donovan and Kathy—a natural reaction, perhaps, but David knew better, because he knew her. Something else hid just beneath the surface, like how you could sometimes tell a storm was coming, not because of what you saw but because of the feel of things.

None of this would be enough for their dad, however. They needed proof. If David pressed the matter without evidence, he would only alienate him further. He couldn't take that chance.

When push came to shove—literally—hadn't Donovan stood up for him at the dance? Once again, David felt at odds with himself. Once again, the feeling seemed unsupported—if not contradicted—by fact. Marcel had always praised David's instincts and told him to heed them, but Marcel was gone, and though David missed him terribly, with each passing day their time together became an increasingly distant memory.

Kathy and Donovan came over for dinner that night. It seemed they were never far away, always close, as though circling, waiting.

But for what?

Kathy brought flowers, and his dad found a vase for them and put it on the table as a centerpiece. Dinner went off uneventfully, and afterward they went to the living room. His dad left the light off and instead lit the candles atop the stands on either end of the couch—something he did on occasion to wind down and relax.

They laughed and spoke of the upcoming trip and played board games—though not strictly by the rules, out of consideration for Rachel. David left the chess set aside. It required an excruciating patience that he didn't know if he possessed, and there was risk: if you drew your opponent in, only to make a false move yourself, you would pay a steep price.

His dad and Kathy sat alongside one another on the couch, while the kids sat on the other side of the coffee table, on the floor.

"Rachel," David said, "tell everyone what you said before bed last night, about the trip."

A knowing smile spread over his sister's face. "You mean about Momma?"

Out of the corner of his eye, David thought he saw Kathy tense, and he could feel his dad's eyes on them.

"Yes, about Momma."

Rachel nodded solemnly and looked at the others. "David told me I could take a picture of her with me on the trip. That way she gets to go too."

The room fell silent. The candles flickered, and skittish shadows danced on the walls. "That's right," David said. "Why don't you go get the one you chose and show us?"

Rachel jumped to her feet and sprinted for the stairs. A soft but determined clip-clop indicated her ascent.

David suppressed the grin tugging desperately at the corners of his mouth. He bowed his head a moment to gather himself, then looked back up with what he hoped was a casual expression. He glanced at Donovan, whose own demeanor appeared more curious than anything else. Looking to the couch, David caught his dad's gaze first; he appeared unsure, even pained.

What registered in Kathy's eyes left little doubt. They burned hotter than the candle flame on either side of her.

Her eyes locked with David's—searing into him, searching and angry—but then she conjured a smile and said with a troubling sweetness, "Well, that is just lovely."

His dad turned toward her and smiled nervously.

The clip-clopping sounded again, and moments later Rachel bounded back into the living room and wedged herself between the adults on the coach.

David's smile required no coaxing.

"Look, Daddy." Rachel pointed at the picture she'd retrieved. "It's from when I was still in Mommy's *tummy!*" She beamed, and David knew that in the picture their mother beamed too, radiant in a white dress, her hands caressing her rounded belly. Joy shone in her eyes. "Isn't she pretty, Daddy?"

Kathy had accommodated Rachel by scooting over to her left, near the end of the couch. Now she jumped to her feet. "Oh! Oh my!" She'd knocked the candle off the stand and onto the ground, where a small flame had begun to singe through the carpet. "It's burning."

David's dad scooped Rachel up in his arms and took her from the living room. "Water, David."

David scrambled to his feet and rushed to the dining room table. He snatched the vase with the flowers, ran back into the living room, and poured the water from the vase onto the flame. The flowers fell to the ground too. Thankfully, the fire had only progressed a few inches and was immediately extinguished. It hissed as it fizzled out. An acrid smell filled the air as a small plume of black smoke wafted upward, flattening and fanning out in narrow charcoal waves as it hit the ceiling. When it reached the smoke detector, the red light flashed and the alarm rang out, shrill and unnerving.

Rachel covered her ears with her hands and buried her head in her dad's chest.

"Well," he said, smiling weakly. "At least we know it works."

After the boys helped clean up the mess, David's dad suggested that, in light of everything, it was probably best to call it a night.

David could not argue. The alarm, after all, had sounded.

CHAPTER 26
A Promise Renewed

THAT NIGHT, AS DAVID SETTLED INTO bed, a small, muffled sound issued faintly through the vents and walls that separated his room from Rachel's. He had to hold his breath a moment to be sure, but he soon heard it again—barely audible but, now that his mind registered the source, jarring. It was a sound he braced for every evening after putting his sister to bed. He hurried down the hallway to her room.

His own eyes began welling before he eased open Rachel's door. She lay in her bed, a piece of paper clutched between trembling fingers. Moonlight filled her room with a soft glow.

David rushed to her side. "Rachel."

She looked up—as though just noticing he'd come in—and threw her arms around him. She buried her face in his chest, and soon he could feel her hot tears, which spread in blotches across his shirt like a spilled drink. The paper—a note their mother had written her—remained clutched in her hand.

He delicately took it and slipped it under the pillow. "It's getting wet. It'll be safe there."

She looked up into his eyes, blinking fiercely. "You promised."

And he had, that afternoon of his birthday months ago, when he'd made a vow to find out what had happened to their mother, to look for her. Guilt washed over him, not because he'd forgotten or hadn't been trying, but because he'd allowed himself to become distracted.

In fairness, the distractions had been considerable. It had been all he could manage to cope with the life-rattling news of immortality—as well as his lingering doubt about all of it. He'd grown determined—if it were indeed somehow true—not to succumb to the sinister plans of his enemies, whoever they might be.

Yet now, as Rachel squeezed him even more urgently, he understood the most important way to achieve that was by not allowing them—and the dark and mysterious world in which they operated—to forestall or prevent his pursuit of the truth, of the promise he'd made. Maybe all of this related to their mother, and maybe not, but in his heart of hearts, he believed her to be alive, and all that mattered was finding her.

He patted Rachel's back, plucked some tissues from the box atop her nightstand, and dabbed her still-welling eyes. "I'm sorry. I haven't forgotten. It's not easy, is all." He put his hands on her shoulders and looked her squarely in the eyes. "It may take a long time, and I know that's hard to hear, but I need you to be patient and to trust me."

She nodded and plucked some tissues of her own. David couldn't help but smile as she reached up and gingerly blotted his eyes.

"If she is out there," he said, "I *will* find her. No matter how long it takes."

Rachel managed a smile and embraced her brother one more time.

Consoled that his sister appeared at least slightly more at peace, he gazed out her window. The moon—

not full, but nearly — seemed to smile back at him, comfortably cradled in unending blankets of black space.

When Rachel at last fell asleep, David crept back to his own bed. Resolve coursed through his veins, but he shut his eyes, knowing he needed to rest, to somehow quiet the fitful notions ricocheting through his mind. Tomorrow would be a new day, but where to begin? He still had so very little to go on.

The sands of the hourglass, meanwhile, continued to empty.

CHAPTER 27
The Light of Day

DAVID ASKED ROBERT, AMANDA, AND Chester to meet him that afternoon—a Saturday—at Moreland Farms. He'd told them everything, and they had remained, especially Chester, skeptical about the whole notion of immortality. Who could blame them? Still, they remained unconditionally supportive of *him*. They didn't question that the things David said had been happening, indeed, had, and none of them begrudged him in the least his unshakable doubt over what had truly happened to his mother on that fateful night.

He didn't tell his dad where he was going.

Chester's mother dropped him off—he'd told her they were doing some research on the history of the farm, an entirely believable explanation, coming from Chester.

The rest of them rode their bikes.

Though located just a few miles from his home, and though he'd spent countless hours there with friends in the past, for the past year and a half, David had steered clear of the place whenever possible.

Not because of Old Man Moreland, though that would probably have been forgivable. Ever since David could recall, neighborhood kids had whispered about the mean old man and his haunted property. Urban legends aside, David avoided the location because it marked the spot where his mother's accident had occurred, her vehicle skidding on the ice before crashing headlong into a set of propane tanks at the edge of the farmer's property. David's conviction remained strong that things did not happen as they'd been told, and the time had come to test the courage of that conviction.

It was past six o' clock by the time they all managed to get there. David had hoped to have a look around in the light of day, but their families had all insisted they eat dinner first, so now their window of opportunity had shrunk considerably.

They met at the western outskirts of the farm, where a small section of public land connected Moreland's property to the road. Neighborhood kids hung out there sometimes, throwing footballs or watching the animals graze. Some years ago, when David was very young, the farmer had run a few hundred head of cattle on his land. He'd sold them off a few years' back, but David remembered staring wide-eyed as the old man's sheepdog chased and herded the gigantic, stamping beasts. Their stampede had churned up great plumes of dust and rung in his ears like thunder.

As soon as Mrs. McVee's vehicle turned out of sight, they began walking—Chester on foot with the aid of his cane, the rest of them alongside their bikes. Their true destination lay about a quarter mile down the road, where it happened. David didn't know what, if anything, he expected to see or accomplish; he only knew it was something he must do. Obviously, he couldn't expect any physical evidence so long after the incident, but he thought it might be less about clues or evidence than about *feeling* his way through.

The sun had begun to fade, but sufficient daylight remained to reveal that Old Man Moreland had replaced the propane tanks. They spread horizontally across the ground like herded missiles. David headed for them, surprised that a wide swath of land encircling the tanks remained charred. One of the primary sources of his lingering doubt remained the horrifying explanation that his mother's body had been entirely consumed by flames—not burned beyond recognition, but *entirely consumed*. Not a stitch of clothing, not a bone fragment—nothing had been found. He was no forensic expert, but he'd found this difficult to accept. Now, eyeing the browned arch of grass extending from the tanks, he considered that perhaps the fire had indeed been that hot.

"Propane burns extremely hot," Chester said, giving voice to David's thoughts. "Upward of four thousand degrees, I believe."

David didn't break stride. "Is that hot enough to... to...."

"Forgive me for this—" Chester breathed hard as he walked. "—but I recall once reading that most cremation ovens operate between 1,500–1,900 degrees." He cast a quick glance at David. "So... yes."

"Dude." Robert came up alongside them. "What exactly do you read?"

"Ah, don't ask."

When they reached the tanks, David put two hands on one and steadied himself. Though his skepticism—along with a promise—had led him here, he now seized with the realization that he very possibly stood on the spot where his mother had died.

Robert and Chester stood silently by their friend.

In the distance sat the Moreland homestead, bathed in irregular shafts of sunlight that filtered through the outstretched arms of the towering oaks encircling the yard.

Amanda had not spoken as they'd made their way to the tanks, but now she was staring back at the road, her back to them. "Is this the same spot where the tanks were before — when it happened?"

"It is," Chester said. "I remember reading that, and if you examine where the burnt grass begins to — "

"It's okay." Amanda pointed back out toward the road. "I believe you, but doesn't anyone else find that strange? It has to be a hundred yards from here to there."

Chester's eyes narrowed, as they so often did when he was deep in thought.

"What's the speed limit there?" Amanda asked.

Everyone looked at Chester.

"Thirty-five," he said.

Amanda regarded David and spoke quietly. "Did your mother speed?"

David's heart quickened. "No. She never got a ticket in her life, and she always went ridiculously slow at night, especially if the roads were bad."

"Which they were." She looked in his eyes. "I came here with an open mind, to support you, more than anything else, but I had my doubts. Now...." She turned once more toward the road, shielding her eyes against the setting sun. "Now I wonder. This far away, the speed she would have had to be going.... Didn't they say her car struck the tanks straight on?"

David nodded.

"Well, no road intersects this one, so she would have had to have been speeding, really speeding, and somehow veered sideways and raced through the snow all the way to this spot. Is that even possible?"

David swallowed hard and shook his head. "No."

No one, not even Chester, suggested otherwise.

CHAPTER 28
Threads

"WHO?"

David—lost in his thoughts—hadn't even been fully aware he'd spoken. His friends looked at him expectantly.

"The man in the long dark coat," he repeated.

"What man?" Robert asked.

"After my fight with Gillespie, back in the fall, I got sent to Lardman. While I waited, some strange, big guy in a dark coat kind of barged in, and I heard him arguing with Lardman about Mr. Cheswick."

"I remember that." Robert gestured at David and Amanda. "And didn't you two visit him? Cheswick, that is."

David nodded. "We did, and he was real nervous."

"Scared," said Amanda.

Chester placed a hand on one of the tanks and furrowed his brow. "The matter of Mr. Cheswick remains a curious one, to say the least, but are you suggesting it's in some way related to all that's been occurring?"

David shrugged and looked skyward. Wild streaks of purple and orange lit the sky beneath the gathering darkness. "I don't know, but think about it: what happened with my mom, what happened with Mr. Cheswick, the notes I brought you, that strange man in the coat. Not to mention everything that's been happening with me, and everything Marcel told me. All of these things are crazy, but they happened. So what's crazier—believing crazy things that have happened, or believing they're all a coincidence?"

They all looked at Chester, whose eyes once again narrowed in contemplation, as though he were filtering all David had said through the formidable labyrinth of his mind, attempting to sift useful information from useless sediment. Trying to convince him of something was like trying to argue a geometric proof, but this was new territory—for each of them. The old rules, it became more apparent with each passing day, no longer applied.

Chester finally nodded solemnly. "I think you make a very good point."

David smiled.

"I know how much this means to you," Chester continued, "and how much is at stake, so I won't pretend to have any idea how these things are connected—only that, yes, they may be."

David looked back at the road, and slowly turned in a circle. "I wish somebody had seen something."

"Maybe somebody did." Robert gestured beyond the tanks to where the Moreland house stood. Even from that distance, such an explosion would have commanded the old man's attention.

David nodded. "He had to have heard it, maybe seen something." He took a step past the tanks, but paused. Through the haze, he could make out a hand-written sign some twenty yards ahead:

Trespassers will be shot.

He looked back at his friends. "You guys can wait here, if you want."

Amanda stepped over to him and stood by his side.

"What the hell." Robert joined them. "We've come this far."

David frowned and looked at Chester. "You shouldn't come. No offense, but I mean, if we have to run all of sudden...."

Chester ambled over to them. "Your consideration is duly noted. I can't imagine he's likely to open fire, but if he did, I'm not so sure I would be safer taking cover behind those." He nodded back at the tanks.

Amanda smiled. "He has a point."

The parcel of land separating them from the Moreland house seemed to make up the farmer's front yard, with most of his crop-lined fields sprawled out behind and to either side of the residence. Negotiating their way through one of those would have been far more difficult, and more likely to arouse the old man's ire. They had a clear path to the house, but it wasn't lost upon David that this also meant Moreland had a clear path to them.

Despite the fear stoked by this consideration, he welled with an unusual calm as he and his friends moved forward. The angle of the sinking sun pointed a finger of light ahead of them, casting their path in a glittering radiance, which, against the canvas of lush grass and encroaching shadows, seemed to David somehow magical. It wasn't that he expected magical answers from the old man, or even any answers at all. Perhaps, more than anything, he was just happy to finally be moving *toward* something and not away.

When they reached the creaky front porch, they paused and stood shoulder to shoulder. David swallowed, stepped forward, and rapped on the front door.

It swung open almost immediately, startling each of them. The old man's face was weathered, as though shaped through the years by the same elements that had shaped his land. He was also, of course, old — older than the four individuals on his porch combined.

His eyes raked over each of them, and he said in a thick, gravelly voice, "Saw you comin'. See pretty much anyone and anything that's comin'."

David extended his hand. He could see it trembling but did not withdraw it. "My name is David Rose, and that's why we've come — to ask you about things you've seen."

The farmer nodded and, after an uncomfortable moment, thrust out his own hand.

David gripped it and shook; it felt like grasping a gnarled stump of wood. "This is Amanda, Robert, and Chester."

Moreland nodded again, and David's friends nodded in return.

It appeared they would not be invited inside, and this suited David just fine.

"My mother —" He gritted his teeth as his insides knotted. " — was the one who hit the tanks that night."

"Rose. Yes, I know who you are." He looked in David's eyes. "I'm sorry for what happened." His voice had in no way softened, nor his expression, but in the consistency of his hard and unchanging demeanor resided an unmistakable sincerity.

"Thank you." David gestured behind him, toward the tanks and toward the road. "It never made sense to me, what happened: why she went out that night, in those conditions, why she'd be going that fast, how there could be... could be nothing left, no witnesses. I just wanted to ask you, since you live here, if you were home when it happened, if you saw anything?"

Moreland's gaze traveled out toward where David had gestured, as though traveling back to that terrible evening. He stared for several moments, shrouded in waning daylight, before looking back to David. "I was home. I heard, and then saw... a horrible explosion. I've also wondered how—and why—a person would be traveling so fast on such a night."

A hopeful ember flickered within David. "Right. Right. So, what did you do?"

"I went out there fast as I could. Got my boots on and threw on my coat and ran out there. A terrible sight. I knew whoever it was would be—well, I'm sorry son, but what I'm saying is that I knew they'd be gone. No one could survive that. The responders got there fast. It was a hell of a thing. A frozen night, but it was an inferno out there."

David swallowed.

Robert put a hand on his shoulder.

"I'm okay." David looked back up at the old farmer. "I guess what I'm asking is, did you see anything else?"

"Yes."

The immediacy of the old man's reply cut into David's consciousness like a blade. His voice scraped against his throat like sandpaper. "What?"

Moreland's expression became severe. "Now, don't go lettin' your mind wander off to crazy notions when you hear what I tell you." He paused and regarded David, as though awaiting his assurance. "I almost missed it, owing to the smoke and flame and snow, but I don't miss much here. What I saw, young man, when I finally headed back inside that terrible evening, were footprints."

David's eyes widened, but the farmer raised a cautionary hand. "Mind what I told you. Sure as I'm standing here, they were not the tracks of a woman. They were large, too large for your mom—a man's boots. I've seen pretty much every track that man, woman, child, or animal can make. I can tell by the shape, by the depth, and by the space between prints what I'm lookin' at, and I'm telling you these prints belonged to a man, and a pretty strappin' one at that."

David inhaled deeply. His heart thundered like the stampeding cattle. "Did you follow them? The tracks, I mean? Where did they go? I—"

"Son." Moreland again held up a hand. "Folks cut through my land all the time. At the time, I didn't think much of it. No other vehicles on the scene, so I didn't figure it had anything to do with what happened. My guess is it didn't. Figured whoever it was had passed through just before it happened."

"So," Chester said, undeterred as the old man's eyes fell sternly upon him. "Where did the tracks go?"

They followed Moreland's gaze over to the edge of the woods lining the southern acreage of the farm.

"Like I said, folks cut on through here all the time, like it's their own damn property."

"I don't blame you for being bothered by that." Amanda managed a smile against the hardened stare that now fell on her. "We would never do it without permission, but would it be okay if we cut across in the same direction and looked around the woods a bit?"

Moreland furrowed his brow, but then shrugged. "Knock yourself out." He dismissed them with a wave of his hand.

"Thank you, sir," David said.

The first hint of warmth flickered across the old man's features. "I'm sorry for what happened, son. I'm not sure what you hope to find in those woods, but if poking around there a bit is something you need to do, then you just go right ahead."

"Thank you."

When the front door thumped shut, the four of them turned and stepped off the groaning porch. A receding column of light illuminated the rectangle of land separating them from the woods, gradually succumbing to a dome of shadows cast by the tree line and setting sun.

Chester consulted his watch before glancing westward. "Around seventeen minutes of daylight left, give or take."

Robert grinned and shook his head.

Amanda stretched her shoulders. "Then we better get moving."

"I'm not entirely certain what we're looking for," Chester said.

"Me neither." David had already paced several strides ahead. "But I think I'll know if I find it."

***

Since time had become very much a factor, and since he would be unable to navigate through the woods, Chester stayed behind with Robert while David and Amanda raced ahead. Once through the tree line, they slithered their way past jutting branches and fallen limbs. The advance of night accelerated quickly under the thick canopy, and they squinted through the haze in an attempt to distinguish their surroundings.

The old farmer had not exaggerated his complaint about passers-through—cans, bottles, wrappers, and various other trash cluttered the forest floor, alongside branches and leaf litter. David and Amanda rummaged their way through bits of it, picking up a bottle here and a wrapper there, but ultimately released each item, as none suggested anything resembling a clue.

As the world around them darkened, they wound their way back, guided by the faint and fragmented shafts of light that managed to breach the woods. David peered directly ahead toward the tree line, shielding his face from the slash of head-high branches, so he hadn't seen the cluster of thorny bushes jutting waist-high as he passed. He now grunted as his shirt snagged on a jagged knot of brambles, halting his progress. He wrested himself free, but forfeited a small patch of cloth from his shirt.

Amanda, seeing that he had stopped, made her way over to him. "Oh." She frowned upon noticing the torn shirt. "Bummer. You okay?"

A curious expression crept over her face as he stayed silent, fixating on the bush. Visibility had become even more strained, but as she followed his eyes, he was certain she saw that it was not his shredded square of clothing that had stolen his attention. He was indeed staring at a torn cut of cloth, but a different one. This one appeared to have been impaled there for quite some time, having deteriorated to the point where it wasn't much more than a frayed patch of threads.

The cloth was black, perhaps from a shirt, or trousers, or even a coat.

CHAPTER 29
Covenant

HIS WINDOW FACED EAST AND, ON most days, filtered the morning light, but when he awoke that Saturday morning at dawn—one week to the day before they would be departing—there appeared only the pale glow of fragile daybreak and, beyond it, impending darkness. The thunderclouds moved in like a procession of charcoal aircraft carriers, and David knew that upon their thunderous arrival, Rachel would seek refuge in his room, as always.

He slipped out of bed and crept the length of the hallway to the bathroom. By the time he returned to his room, the storm had settled vocally overhead, and soon the frantic patter of his sister's pajama-clad feet approached down the hall.

Eventually the fireworks quieted, but when the downpour that accompanied them showed no sign of relenting, David managed to convince Rachel that they must go about their day. Their dad and Kathy had an office party that night, and David and Donovan were to stay with Rachel.

He hadn't told anyone about the visit to Moreland's property or the piece of cloth, and his friends had cautioned against drawing conclusions. The bit of fabric could belong to anyone, and even if it did belong to the mysterious man in the dark coat, they still had no idea of his identity or what—

if any—connection he had to all that had been happening.

After putting dinner out, his dad and Kathy departed, scurrying out to the car beneath the daggers of pelting rain.

After dinner, Donovan helped David clear the dishes, and they put a movie on for Rachel, who plopped down cross-legged in front of the television.

"Not too close," David told her, and she rolled her eyes and scooted back.

The boys sat a few feet apart on the couch, each busying themselves with their phones. After a few minutes, David felt eyes on him and looked up.

"I'm sorry." Donovan looked him squarely in the eyes.

It had become increasingly apparent to David that things were not always as they seemed, but something in Donovan's expression and tone felt sincere. "Thanks. Me too."

And he was. Not that he believed himself the instigator in any of this—whatever *this* was—but he couldn't deny having permitted so much to unnerve him. He'd hardly been at his best in many of his reactions.

"Sometimes things just come over me." Donovan dropped his voice to a whisper upon receiving an admonishing glance from Rachel. "Like at the dance."

David tended to believe him, as he could wholly relate. This did not, however, provide a great deal of comfort—allowing it to do so felt like lowering his guard. Something seemed always to be hanging over them—over *him*—just out of sight and out of reach, and he'd no interest in becoming an easier target.

When it came time to put Rachel to bed, she protested mildly, but the storm had awakened her early and her eyes looked heavy. David read her a bedtime story, and when he finished, he noticed Donovan leaning in her doorway.

"Goodnight, Rach," Donovan said.

There was, for a moment, only the steady thrum of rain, until David gently nudged his sister.

"Goodnight," she mumbled.

"Only one week to the trip. You excited?"

"No!"

David startled as his sister sprang from her bed like a cornered animal. She darted past Donovan, who sidestepped her like a matador eluding a baby bull.

"Rachel!" David stood up as her footfalls pattered down the stairs.

"Sorry," Donovan said. "Didn't know she felt that way. Should we go get her?"

"I'll go." David sighed, then froze as a different noise sounded from downstairs, a quiet but unmistakable *click*, followed by a *whoosh* and the suddenly much louder chant of rain upon pavement. He and Donovan locked eyes, then raced downstairs and into the foyer, where the front door stood open, swaying slightly from the gusting wind. Rainwater had already begun pooling near the door.

David stepped outside, shielding his eyes with his hand, and peered out into the night.

"Rachel!" Receiving no answer, he groaned and walked farther into the yard. "Rachel! You're gonna get soaked!"

As was he. In just those few seconds, his clothes had become saturated and his hair lay slicked over his forehead. A low rumbling sounded somewhere in the not-too-distant darkness, and every few seconds the black sky became awash in chalky illumination. He'd long known his sister's distrust of Donovan and Kathy—a sentiment that in some ways seemed to run deeper than his own—but he hadn't realized it could induce her to do something like this.

He shuddered, pulled his collar up around his neck, and turned back to Donovan, who had just stepped outside. "I have to go find her!"

"I'll go with you!"

David shook his head, beads of water snapping off his forehead. "No! What if she comes back and no one is here? Wait for her!" He peered once more into the deluge before turning back to Donovan. "She can't have gotten far."

Once he saw Donovan step back into the house, he broke into a trot down their lane, splashing through rippling puddles and little streams, which wound their way toward the sewers. At every lawn, he paused and shouted for his sister.

This did not bode well for their trip. He'd resigned himself to its inevitability, and hoped things would at least be tolerable, but with Rachel this upset, things wouldn't be easy. In most moments, his sister was sweet as an angel, demonstrating a concern for others remarkably beyond her years, but every so often a fire sparked within her, and she could be unsparing in her words. David worried what this could lead to, odd as such a consideration might be, given her age.

The first pangs of protectiveness had reverberated through him the moment he'd laid eyes on her in the hospital—this tiny, swaddled thing resting in their mother's arms in the narrow prism of light intersecting the otherwise shadowed room. David would forever remember the words his mother had written and spoken to him about looking out for Rachel, but really, they'd never been necessary. It pulsed as a covenant in his blood, his DNA, in the very fabric of who and what he was. Unbreakable. He did not regard himself in any way heroic, for this conviction existed beyond any measure of conscious choice.

This scared him the most: not that he didn't know what he might do should she ever be threatened, but rather the unquestionable certainty that he knew exactly what he would do.

It was also why, with every step he took without locating her, his soul welled with overwhelming dread and guilt. He was to look after her—tonight and always—and as of this moment, he was failing miserably.

***

It had only recently occurred to Rachel that she sometimes saw things a little differently than other people did—saw and sometimes heard. This would help explain a good many things. Sometimes they were good and wonderful things, and sometimes not, like what she saw when Kathy looked at her, or Donovan, just moments ago in her bedroom. She would get so frustrated with others—especially David and Daddy—for not noticing, but now she realized they probably weren't seeing the same thing. Surely, David would have said something if he had seen what she did—if he had seen that standing in her doorway was not a handsome, smiling teenage boy, but a snarling, bearded man with hatred in his eyes.

Sure, he'd changed back to Donovan a moment later, but she'd learned that the bad ones could be sneaky like that. It frightened her, and even though she trusted her brother, the look in Donovan's eyes—the look in whomever or whatever had been standing there—had upset her so badly that her only thought was to run away and hide so he wouldn't find her.

She'd known immediately where she would go. Though she'd slipped on the way up, she'd caught herself and made it inside, where she now cowered in a corner of the small structure, shivering and wet, hoping more than anything that her brother would discover her first.

**

At the end of the lane, drenched and with no sign of his sister, David stopped. Marcel had cautioned him that the world would only become more uncertain and chaotic and that, in the toughest moments, he must retain his composure and think things through. Even though she'd burst from her room in a fit of emotion, Rachel was not likely to have run aimlessly and endlessly through their neighborhood, especially in this downpour and in the blackness of night. She'd probably circled out back of their house before deciding to return in short order.

David's stomach seized. He'd left her alone with Donovan.

He began to sprint.

**

When she heard the ladder creak under someone's weight, she didn't know whether to be terrified or relieved. Donovan and her brother were around the same size, after all. There were actually many things similar about them, a thought that upset her whenever it surfaced in her mind.

The creaking grew louder, as the person had reached the top of the ladder and was now — she could feel — staring into the treehouse at her.

She began to cry.

***

The door flew open and thunked against the wall as David burst into the house.

"Rachel?"

Nothing.

"Donovan?"

Only the sharp drumming of rain responded. Donovan hadn't closed the door, and larger puddles pooled in the entranceway. David moved toward the unlit dining room, which looked out into the backyard through bay windows. Queasy with fear, he didn't worry about the muddy tracks he stamped onto the floor with each step.

A tremendous flare of lightning erupted, framing the backyard in brief but perfect resolution.

He froze where he stood.

***

Donovan reached for her. The lightning flashed every few seconds, bathing the treehouse in an amber glow and casting Donovan's reaching arm in grotesquely long shadow. Rachel scampered backward until her body pressed flush against the far wall of the treehouse.

"Rachel!" Donovan called. "You've got to come with me!"

She tucked her chin into her chest and turned her body so that her back was to him.

What's taking David so long?

"Okay, I'm coming in to get you!"

"Stop!"

Donovan froze at the new voice, and Rachel lifted her head.

"David!" cried Donovan. "I've got to get her out of there!"

As if to punctuate his point, the sky lit up again, followed by an ear-splitting *snap*. A flare caught the corner of David's eye, and he turned in time to watch a sizable limb splinter and fall from an oak in their neighbor's yard. He looked back at Donovan, perched near the top of the aluminum ladder. Donovan was right—there was no time to lose.

"Okay!" David rushed to the base of the tree. "But push the ladder down—can't take a chance with this lightning!"

Donovan nodded, hoisted himself fully into the treehouse, and then swiveled back around.

"Look out!"

David moved aside as Donovan kicked the ladder away. It teetered momentarily before clattering to the ground with a *bang*. David used his foot to push it a few feet farther away before returning to the tree.

"Rachel!" he called, cupping his hands to his mouth. "Let Donovan help you. I'm right here. I'll catch you, I promise!"

He shielded his eyes against the downpour and rapid-fire flashes of lightning. He could just make out Donovan disappearing into the treehouse.

The ensuing moments felt an eternity. David's gut was a reservoir of uncertainty: had he, in trying to do what he thought safest under the circumstances, placed Rachel in even greater danger? *No*, he told himself, gritting his teeth. *No!* Even if all Marcel had shared was true—if this dark and magical world of immortality were real—Donovan was still a kid, like David, and in his heart of hearts, David didn't believe Donovan would hurt his sister. He *couldn't* believe it.

When Donovan and Rachel appeared at the edge of the treehouse a moment later, David exhaled gratefully nonetheless.

"I'll lower her down!" Donovan yelled over the downpour.

David extended his arms as high as he could and braced himself. "All right!"

He squinted against the liquid darts and watched as Rachel—her hands clenched in Donovan's—swung her legs out from the edge of the treehouse. On his toes, David could just graze her muddy, bare feet with his fingers.

Donovan lay prone on the floor of the treehouse—it would be impossible for him to pull Rachel back up.

Suspended helplessly as lightning flashed and rain slashed her body, she called to her brother. "David...."

"You're going to have to let go! I've got you." David peered past her to Donovan, whose face tensed with the strain of his burden. "Let her go, Donovan. I'll catch her!"

And David did, though the impact propelled him backward and he stumbled and fell, his back thudding against the squishy yet unforgiving earth.

He'd clenched his eyes shut, and when he opened them, his sister's were mere inches away.

"Hi, David."

"Hi." He eased her off, and together they got to their feet. He gently nudged her in the direction of the house. "Get inside. I've got to help Donovan."

"I want to stay with you."

"Rachel, it's dangerous out here. Get inside. I'll be right there."

Once she reluctantly trudged toward the house, David returned to the base of the tree.

Donovan sat at the edge of the treehouse, his legs dangling out. The lightning had become so insistent that the entire yard was bathed in an eerie, near-constant glow.

"Gotta hurry!" Donovan twisted his body, propping himself up and pirouetting like a gymnast on a vault until his back was to David. Maintaining a tenuous grip on the rain-slicked floor of the treehouse, he lowered himself until he was dangling helplessly in the night.

"Ready!" David harbored little hope of catching Donovan, but planned on breaking his fall as much as possible.

He braced himself, and when the impact came, both boys crumbled to the ground, the air whistling out of David. For a moment, he gasped like a fish out of water, but his breath quickly returned, and Donovan pulled him to his feet.

"David!"

Both boys looked toward the house. Rachel had only made it as far as the back door, where she stood dripping and shivering under the canopy. They hurried over to her, and David grasped her hand.

As he turned to lead her back to the front of the house, the night flared brighter yet, and each of them flinched as a deafening crack detonated nearby. David's eyes widened as the treehouse burst into flames. He immediately worried the entire tree would become engulfed and set the house ablaze, yet somehow the conflagration seemed limited to the treehouse itself. The fire burned through it methodically, as though consuming it in reverse order of how it had been constructed, plank by plank. Each of them stared — mesmerized — as the entire structure disintegrated in alarmingly short order and crumbled to the ground in a shower of sparks. The rain quickly doused the last crackling embers, and plumes of acrid smoke spiraled up from the charred remains.

David didn't know how long they stood, entranced by the smoldering spectacle, but at length he nudged Rachel and led her back to the front of the house. She'd had quite enough for one evening.

CHAPTER 30
Another World

BY THIS POINT, DAVID WAS USED to unanswered wishes. Even after what happened the night of the fire, their dad did not cancel their trip, claiming that now they all needed a vacation more than ever.

They flew into New York and, after a brief layover, boarded another plane for the nearly seven-hour trip to Heathrow Airport in London. Rachel had asked to sit next to David, and tensed as the plane taxied around the runway. When it finally accelerated for takeoff, she grabbed her brother's arm and maintained her grip until well after the plane had eased into the morning sky. Only after they reached cruising altitude—thirty-three thousand feet, so said their captain—and the flight attendants delivered snacks did she relax.

A small screen descended from the overhead console, and David pressed some buttons and found a show for Rachel. He removed some headphones from a plastic sleeve the attendants had provided and handed them to his sister. "Put these on."

She did so, and after she seemed settled, David put on his own earphones and listened to music. Occasionally, Donovan would turn around from the seat in front of him and make small talk, but after a while David reclined his seat and closed his eyes, which soon grew heavy. The drone of the engines quickly lulled him, and the chatter of the passengers faded as he drifted off, strange voices speaking to him in his dreams, beckoning him onward.

***

He awakened as the plane began its descent. Rachel appeared visibly exhausted. They'd lost an hour upon arrival in New York, and London was an additional four hours ahead. Now would come the long 5- to 6-hour drive to Cornwall, where they would likely not arrive at the castle until close to midnight.

After they'd landed at Heathrow and retrieved their luggage, a sleek black limousine pulled up to receive them. Rachel was too tired to be impressed; she stretched out on one of the long leather seats, placed her head on her dad's lap, and fell fast asleep.

David was tired too, but the bright lights and grandeur of downtown London drew his attention. He peered out his window as their driver shared tidbits about the more notable landmarks.

Donovan seemed equally intrigued.

As for their destination, their driver referred to it in prideful tones. "Cornwall is a ceremonial county of England, a beautiful place. The peninsula is bordered to the north and west by the Celtic Sea, and to the south by the English Channel. To the east resides the county of Devon, across the River Tamar."

Fatigue ultimately triumphed over curiosity, and David drifted off.

The next thing he knew, his dad was gently pressing his shoulder. He sat up and rubbed his eyes, and they widened as a spectacular, looming structure came into focus.

They had arrived at the castle, in the main village on Tintagel Island. David had been impressed by the pictures he'd seen, but even those hadn't done proper justice to the majesty of the place.

Rachel saw it too. She'd been a bit tougher to awaken, and crabby at first, but she raised her head from her dad's shoulder as he lifted her out of the limousine. "Are we staying *here*, Daddy?"

"Yes, baby, we are."

"It's like another world."

David's body was stiff from the day's travel, and upon extricating himself from the limousine, he bent forward and backward and slowly stretched his back. When he straightened up, he froze. The castle was enormous, surreal, something from a storybook, and... it felt for a moment like yet another of his vivid dreams. An elongated drawbridge extended from it, stretching over a large, dark moat, which snaked around the grounds. A series of chains reached down and across from the castle wall, attaching to segments of the bridge. Overhead sounded the fluttering of wings and honking of geese. A light breeze blew, and it smelled like the sea.

Kathy came up alongside David's father and touched his shoulder. "It's beautiful."

Rachel buried her head in her dad's shoulder.

David inhaled deeply and glanced at Donovan, who stood a few feet away, staring at the castle. David didn't begrudge his awe. The structure, even merely the portions they could see, was breathtaking. It towered over the land like a great watchman, rising from legs of spiraling towers until, at its summit, it rounded to a magnificent crown lined with door-sized windows, which gazed out like dark eyes upon the land. The towers varied in height, the tallest of which appeared to be at least forty feet. A procession of large flags jutted from each, and every few moments, the sea winds broke over the land like a wave, setting the flags rippling and flapping louder than the soaring formations of geese overhead.

They each stood and beheld the castle—save for Rachel, who rested in her dad's arms, and their limousine driver, who dutifully retrieved their luggage from the rear of the vehicle.

At length they heard approaching footsteps and a jangling of keys, and the large steel gates of the drawbridge swung open with a deep and prolonged rumble. Two impeccably dressed servants, men of perhaps fifty years with neatly combed hair, strode quickly toward them. One continued past them and joined the limousine driver in the retrieval of their luggage, while the other stopped before them.

"Good evening, honored guests." He bowed. "Welcome to Kane Manor." He greeted each of them with what looked to be his best attempt at a smile, and it seemed to David he gazed at him an extra moment or two. Then he circled past to assist with the luggage.

"We can help," said David's dad. "David and Donovan and I. It's a lot of bags."

"Thank you, sir, but we wouldn't think of it. You are our guests. You have traveled long and far. Please—" He gestured toward the drawbridge. " —follow us."

They began walking, except Donovan, who remained rooted to his spot, still gawking at the castle.

"Donovan!" David called.

Donovan finally broke out of his trance and jogged over to them. He sidled up alongside David and nudged him in the ribs. "Here we go."

A sprawling tarp roof and interspersed metal slats on either side of the drawbridge bestowed the sense of a great tunnel leading them onward toward some grand adventure. Every few feet, candlelit lanterns crowned the intersection of the slats and roof, bathing the corridor in an eerie, churning brew of shadow and light.

"Note the wooden floor," said the servant leading their way. "This is, after all, a drawbridge, designed to be raised and lowered, and a concrete or steel floor would simply be too heavy." David and Donovan nodded, and the servant, who'd paused momentarily, seemed pleased by the boys' interest. "As it is, there are already heavier elements." He gestured toward the slats to either side of them and to the tarp above. "All of this adds weight, but in medieval times, the drawbridge had to be raised quickly at times, and so they were constructed as light as possible. These lighter bridges connected to a gatehouse, and when raised, would stand flush against the gate, offering an additional barrier against attackers. They used ropes or chains, connected to a windlass in a gatehouse chamber, to raise or lower the bridge. Only these lighter bridges could function without some sort of counterweight." He stomped his foot on the deck beneath him and smiled. "Ours is a little sturdier, I dare say, the whole structure quite a bit heavier, so counterweight beams extend into slots in the gatehouse floor." He winked at the boys. "Of course, we rarely need to raise the bridge. Haven't been attacked in quite some time. I hope you gentlemen don't have anything planned."

The boys grinned, and the servant did likewise before turning and continuing toward the far end of the drawbridge. They passed through a gatehouse and arrived at the foyer at the front of the castle—a large, steel-wrought archway that encased a massive mahogany door. The emblem of a shield and sword gleamed from the top of the door; *Kane Manor*, read the inscription emblazoned upon the blade.

One of the servants set down his bags and pushed open the heavy door, and David peered into the darkness that greeted them. The servant retrieved the bags, stepped inside, and beckoned each of them onward.

Once inside, David's eyes gradually adjusted. A few lanterns and torches offered faint illumination, and the great chamber in which they stood slowly came alive. David couldn't help but be impressed—like another world, as his sister had observed. Their entire house could comfortably fit inside.

Lavish, unlit chandeliers descended from the high ceiling like stalactites. The movie screen-sized walls were scarcely visible, due to the number of paintings and sculptures and other medieval effects that decorated them.

"Amazing," Donovan murmured.

"I am assuredly glad you think so." The possessor of this deep and confident voice stepped from the shadows.

David furrowed his brow, as the voice seemed strangely familiar, but as he looked at the man more closely, this notion faded. He couldn't recall seeing him before.

He was handsome, perhaps mid-forties, sporting a light-blue shirt and navy dinner jacket. His dark hair was neatly combed, and he boasted a muscular physique.

David wondered how they'd failed to hear his approach.

The servant cleared his throat. "His Lordship, Sir Edmund Kane."

The man approached David and Rachel's dad, bowed, and extended his hand. "Welcome, friends, to my home. I am thrilled beyond measure that you have come."

Their dad gently placed Rachel down and returned the handshake with vigor. "Thank you for sharing your beautiful home with us."

"It is my pleasure." He bent toward Rachel, who threw her arms around her dad's leg as though hanging on to a tree in a storm. "It is an honor to host such a beautiful princess."

Rachel smiled but did not move from her dad's side.

The man straightened up and gently took Kathy's hand. "My lady."

Kathy smiled and gave a slight curtsey. "My lord."

The man moved to the two boys, extending a hand first to Donovan. "I couldn't help but notice your interest." He motioned toward the armor and artifacts surrounding them.

Donovan grinned. "Yes sir."

"Excellent. I dare say you shall have opportunity in your time here to get a much closer look. Would you like that?"

Donovan's smile expanded ear to ear.

"I rather thought so." The man chuckled before turning his attention to David. "And, of course, the same goes for you." He offered his hand. "I hope for you the adventure of a lifetime. Many of our guests describe their time here as a home away from home.

We shall do all in our power to assure you each feel the same."

He squeezed David's hand tightly, nearly to the point of discomfort, but David attributed this to their host's strength and enthusiasm.

"But now —" The man gestured with outstretched arms. " —I imagine you are all exhausted from your journey and would like to be taken to your quarters for the evening."

He snapped his fingers, and the servants, who'd been waiting dutifully, snatched up the luggage and stood at attention. Two more servants scurried from the shadows and awaited their master's instructions.

"Our guests are weary. Show them to their quarters. See if they would care for a refreshment before retiring. See to it that they have anything they require." He regarded his guests. "My staff will see to it you are well cared for. Do not hesitate to inquire after anything you may desire — anything at all. Get your rest." He looked at the two boys. "You shall need it. Much is planned for you, and it begins tomorrow. We shall dine in the Great Hall in the morning, and I shall apprise you of our itinerary. Until then —" He offered a sweeping bow. " —I bid you good evening." He began walking back toward the shadowed far end of the foyer.

"Thank you," David's dad called after him. "But if I may...."

The man stopped and turned back around. "Of course."

"I just wondered... this castle... It's incredible. Concentric, right?"

Their host eyed him for a moment, and a smile crept over his face. "Indeed, sir, it is."

"I thought so. Thank you."

The man began to turn around again, but froze as David's dad spoke up once more.

"One more thing."

This time, the man's smile took a bit longer to reappear. "Sir?"

"Concentric castles... I know the books aren't always right, but I thought I read there weren't many of these in England."

The man scrutinized him momentarily with an expression difficult to interpret. "You are correct. Your knowledge impresses me. This is, in fact, one of scant few."

David's dad nodded. "Thanks. I guess the authors forgot to mention it."

"They did not forget. I desire, as they say, a low profile, incongruous though that may sound from one possessing of a castle. I have had good fortune in achieving at least a modicum of privacy." He articulated this last word with a distinct *ive* as in *give*.

"Thanks," David's dad said again. "I certainly understand. We're thrilled to be here. Good evening."

Their host executed a final bow. "Good evening."

CHAPTER 31
The Great Hall

"PLEASE," THEIR HOST URGED WHEN THEY'D gathered the next morning for breakfast, "call me Edmund."

David was relieved. He'd been wondering how to address him: "Sir," "Mr. Kane," or even "Your Lordship," to which the manor staff seemed beholden. David was particularly uncomfortable with this latter option, but these considerations quickly evaporated as he eyed the feast now being laid before them.

Some other guests were lodging at the castle and had joined them around the banquet table. Edmund made the introductions: Mr. and Mrs. Delancey, who resided in Wales and visited the manor a few times a year; Mr. and Mrs. Fingerish, business associates of Edmund, with their ten-year-old daughter Sydney in tow; and two men of about forty years — rough-looking — whom Edmund introduced as the McAlister brothers. They each nodded without expression and returned to their breakfasts. "Hunting buddies," Edmund explained with a grin. A beautiful greyhound lay at the feet of one brother, who occasionally slipped it morsels from his amply filled plate.

David hadn't known other guests would be there, but overcrowding was not likely to be a problem — Kane Manor was enormous. The Great Hall was no exception. Much like the vast foyer, numerous paintings, sculptures, and medieval trappings populated the walls and protruded from the high ceiling. A crucible of interlocking swords gleamed directly overhead, coming to a diamond point at its tip, and a huge chandelier ten feet above the banquet table illuminated their feast. The hall appeared roughly the size of the school auditorium back home, and conjured notions of royal gatherings from centuries ago, but David's attention returned to the moment at hand as savory platters of food continued to be placed before them.

"A little sampling of medieval fare," Edmund said. He looked at Rachel, who seemed simultaneously impressed yet leery of the heaping mounds of unfamiliar food rising before them on the long marble table. "And a few contemporary offerings should your taste buds not be feeling quite so adventurous just yet."

Rachel spotted a cartoonishly large platter of pancakes, a crown of butter melting atop the towering stack, and smiled.

David yawned. "Sorry," he said sheepishly. It was ten o'clock, but they hadn't gotten to bed until well past midnight. He'd shared a room with Donovan, and their quarters were lavish — spacious, soft, warm beds with down comforters and an array of fluffy, colorful pillows.

"No worries at all. You had a long journey." Edmund gestured at the generous spread before them. "Please, indulge to your heart's content, and I will do my best to orient you to a bit of the history of this place."

A servant looked on dutifully over their shoulders, passing whatever food they desired, even dishing it onto their plates for them — for the children, juice, water, milk, and tea. In addition to these, the adults were offered wine, as well as a hot breakfast drink Edmund called caudle—a blend of egg yolks, honey, wine, and bread crumbs. If any of their beverages began to empty even slightly, a servant promptly refilled it to the brim.

"This is amazing." Kathy sipped some wine. "Everything, absolutely sumptuous."

"I am pleased you think so. I shall share your compliments with our esteemed chefs." Edmund lowered his voice slightly and smiled. "As well as I compensate them, they'd *better* be good."

Rachel was making quick work of her pancakes while eyeing a nearby platter of food uncertainly.

"Herbolace." Edmund pointed at the tray in question. "Quite tasty, in my opinion. Somewhat a mix between scrambled eggs and an omelet, filled with eggs and herbs and sprinkled with grated cheese." He took a bite from a serving on his plate. "Ah, exquisite."

Rachel stuck with her pancakes, but many of the guests sampled most everything on the table, each item kindly explained by their host. There was pottage, a soupy stew with bits of dried bacon; fresh fish; and rastons, large rolls made of sweetened bread dough enriched with eggs.

"Kind of like a brioche paste," Edmund said.

For dessert, a delicious rich custard, and at the end of the meal, two manor staff wheeled out a beautiful sculpture of a wild stag.

"Incredible," said David's dad.

"Sotelte," Edmund noted, "and it is edible—carved of hard sugar."

A few *ooh*s issued from around the table, and a servant stepped forward and prepared to parcel off pieces for the guests.

"Daddy...." Rachel tugged at her dad's arm, her eyes wide.

He looked down at her. "What's the matter, sweetie?"

"It's an animal, Daddy. We shouldn't eat it."

Several of the guests smiled.

"Rachel," her dad said. "It's okay, honey. It's not real."

"I *know*."

"It'll taste like candy. I'll bet you'll like it."

They would not find out, as Rachel refused to sample the sweet creation. She cringed when the servant proceeded with lopping off sections of the sugary creature.

Sydney, moved by Rachel's distress, came over and gave her a hug. "It's okay, Rachel. I won't have any either."

Rachel smiled.

"Hey," Sydney offered, "want to go look around with me?"

Rachel nodded and started to push back in her chair, but paused and grabbed her dad's arm. "May I, Daddy?"

"Sure, baby, go ahead." He touched Sydney on the arm. "Thank you, young lady. You are very kind."

Rachel and her new friend scampered off toward some of the sculptures jutting from one of the walls.

The rest of the guests enjoyed samples of the sotelte. David found it tasty indeed, though he kept glancing at his sister, feeling somewhat guilty.

Edmund leaned forward and addressed his guests in a slightly lowered voice. "While it is just us adults...." He paused briefly, letting David and Donovan soak up the compliment. "Permit me to touch upon a related topic: The Hunt. I consider it my pleasure, privilege, and responsibility to provide experiences as authentic as possible in replicating traditional castle life, and The Hunt is a fundamental part of that. You are here at an opportune time, as Fence Month, the closed hunting season in England, commences in June. More details will be forthcoming, but The Hunt shall be in two days, weather permitting, and our prey—" Edmund lowered his voice further yet. "—will be none other than that sacred creature whose likeness we are indulging in presently."

David's dad raised an eyebrow. "The stag? Really? How is it hunted?"

"Naturally, rifles and other firearms have been popularized in the last many years, but that would not constitute an authentic homage to the medieval life you hope to experience, would it?" Edmund smiled. "Bow hunting, good sir. It is the noble way."

David's dad cleared his throat. "Thanks. Forgive me, please, but I think I read that bow hunting is illegal in the UK, some sort of act passed in the early eighties?"

Edmund gave him a curious look, much as he had the previous evening in the foyer, but it was not this that caught David's most rapt attention.

The McAlister brothers had stiffened in their chairs at the end of the table, and sat glaring at his dad.

Edmund made the faintest dismissive motion with his hand, and the brothers looked down.

"I continue to be impressed by your knowledge, Mr. Rose." Edmund smiled pleasantly.

"Benjamin, please."

"Of course. Benjamin. I admire a man of study."

"But am I right?"

Edmund paused a few moments before answering. "You are indeed, and it is now I must humbly prevail upon you to bestow upon me some modest benefit of the doubt. As with many rules, many laws, there is often a bit of gray, the occasional exception, a matter, perhaps, of interpretation. The authorities know I, in fact, revere any prey we hunt, that I do not abuse the privilege, and they have come to realize, I believe, that theirs is a tough enough job without having to occupy themselves with a triviality such as this." Edmund smiled and extended his hands outward, palms upturned. "I implore your understanding, and I dare say it just might prove an experience not one of you shall ever forget."

They returned to their dessert, and the guests chatted excitedly.

Rachel and Sydney ambled around the periphery of the hall, marveling at the seemingly infinite number of artifacts and gleaming objects. A servant brought them each an ice cream cone, at which they lapped happily as they circled the spacious hall.

Edmund took a final bite of sotelte, wiped his mouth with a silk napkin, and cleared his throat. "Permit me to apprise you of our itinerary for these next few days. Today shall be fairly casual. Some of you got in quite late last evening and deserve a day to relax and get settled, and perhaps explore the castle a bit. There is much history here, and some wonderful quarters to explore. Of course, I am blessed to own a rather generous expanse of property. You may ride our prize-winning horses, try your hand at archery, or perhaps engage in a spirited game of cricket. How does that sound?"

A general murmuring of approval ensued.

"Excellent. As I mentioned, in two days comes The Hunt, an essential part of castle life, of the social order, and one ripping good time. Be sure to get your rest tomorrow evening, as those participating shall gather before sunrise. The following day, we'll explore the castle ruins, one of the highlights of any visit to Tintagel. As fate would have it, we are to be treated that day to an added phenomenon—the rare and stirring spectacle of a full solar eclipse. I have restored vast sections of the castle—such as that you dine in presently—but I wished to preserve parts of the ruins on the far end of my property, near the sea. They are alive with history and—" He regarded David and Donovan with a smile. "—a bit of ancient legend as well."

Rachel and Sydney arrived back at the banquet table, still clutching their ice cream cones, reciting a list of the many wondrous things they'd just seen.

"And now," concluded Edmund, "our fair princesses having rejoined us, I shall bid everyone a wonderful day. Enjoy the castle. Enjoy my home. I have been fortunate enough to be able to enjoy quite the collector's life." He gestured toward each wall and up toward the domed ceiling. "What you see here, and in the other sections of the castle, is but a tiny sampling of that which I have been privileged enough to amass: artwork; artifacts; literature; photographs; odds and ends that help connect us to peoples and cultures, sometimes from centuries gone by; sands from shores of faraway lands. They represent a lifetime traveling the world, searching for history, for those treasures that connect our past and present and perhaps future as well."

The guests were quiet, save for Rachel, who'd lost interest in their host's words and was crunching away at her ice cream cone, down to which she had now gnawed.

"You're hardly an old man," David's dad said to Edmund. "That is some lifetime you've been able to live."

Edmund's eyes sparkled. "You are again quite right."

"Have you found everything you've searched for?"

Edmund responded not by looking at David's dad, but by looking David squarely in the eyes. "Not yet."

CHAPTER 32
Archer's Paradox

Thwack!

Donovan's arrow whistled though the air and pierced its target true. Thankfully, the target was an inanimate, silhouetted man, its body superimposed in three segments on rectangular pads. Appreciative clapping sounded from the gallery.

On the overcast, gray morning, the thicker overlays of fog from the moors had largely dissipated, only a few wispy strands lingering overhead. Beyond the range on which they stood, David could see another, presently vacant. Adjacent to that sat the livery and stables.

"Nice job," he said. "You've shot before?"

Donovan shook his head, looking genuinely surprised. "No. Lucky shot, I guess."

Three successive bull's-eyes later, this theory seemed harder to believe.

"Bully!" exclaimed their shooting instructor, Mr. Samuels, a short, bald man around sixty years of age. He had wowed the gallery moments earlier with his own impressive marksmanship on shots of increasingly greater distance.

Donovan clearly had taken notice of his instruction.

"Magnificent shooting, lad." Mr. Samuels turned and handed a bow and arrow to David. "He shall be tough to best, young man, but simply worry about doing the best you can. Now, which is your dominant eye?"

David regarded him uncertainly. "Dominant *eye?*"

"Yes. The bow is to be held in the hand opposite your dominant eye."

"I'm not sure."

"Worry not." Mr. Samuels gestured at the bow. "Are you right-handed?"

David nodded.

"Good. Then let us guess that your right eye is dominant. Your left hand shall be your bow hand."

David lifted the bow in his left hand and tried to simulate the stance Mr. Samuels had demonstrated during training, his left foot nearest the target.

"We are using a compound bow." Mr. Samuels pulled an arrow from the quiver. "They are designed to reduce the force required to fold the string at full draw. This permits the archer more time to aim carefully. It is the most popular form of bow used in your home country."

He handed David the red and yellow arrow. The arrowhead and nock — terms explained by their instructor — were a coffee-brown color, imprinted with the elegant Kane Manor insignia.

"The arrow has, of course, evolved through the years as well," Mr. Samuels continued. "Wooden originally, but being prone to warping, those gave way in many instances to fiberglass, aluminum, carbon fiber. The most popular — used in Olympic archery and by us here today — are the durable composite arrows. Notice the fletching — painted, yes, but all composed of feathers from birds hunted on these very grounds."

David did his best to listen but struggled to place the arrow.

"I am pleased each of you has joined us today," Mr. Samuels said. "Archery enjoyed great popularity here in England at the end of the eighteenth century, particularly among the gentry, and particularly owing to a growing fascination with medieval lore. Later, the work of Sir Walter Scott increased its popularity further still. Archery societies sprang up like wildflowers."

He turned back to David, who was still struggling with his arrow. "Ah, that can indeed prove a pesky process. I shall assist you momentarily. I suggest you first practice your stance a moment or so, all right? In the manner I presented."

He turned back to the gallery. "For you lovely ladies here today, you should know archery became quite the rage with women as well. Many became highly accomplished." He returned his attention to David. "Your posture looks good. All right then, let's place the arrow."

David held the bow in his left hand and attempted to insert the arrow with his right. A pesky process indeed — the arrow would not lodge in while the string was limp, but attempting to draw it back required use of the hand in which the arrow was gripped. After a few failed attempts, Mr. Samuels stepped in.

"Permit me." He guided David's hands through the process. "Of course," he called back to the gallery, "for centuries, archery constituted far more than mere sport. These were valued weapons during countless wars and conflicts, until the advent of firearms, which rendered them essentially obsolete in warfare. Of course, firearms had their shortcomings, especially early on — poor rate of fire, susceptibility to moisture, and inaccuracy of many shooters. Alas, their sheer power and distance ultimately made them the weapon of choice, but there are still those—" He stepped back now, as David seemed at last to be ready. "—who favor the bow as a more elegant, chivalrous choice." He smiled. "I dare say I count myself among them. All right, young master, I believe the range is yours." He took another step back.

David inhaled deeply, drew the bowstring back as far and taut as he could, and eyed the target. Suddenly the painted eyes seemed to flutter to life, the featureless face contorting, transforming. David stared, unbelieving, as it became Donovan's face, sneering at him, daring. Then Mr. Cerratus. Then their host, Edmund Kane.

David's right hand came off the bowstring, the arrow dropping harmlessly to the ground. Murmuring came from the gallery behind him.

Mr. Samuels approached and placed an arm on his shoulder. "Are you all right?"

David nodded. His throat was dry and he was sweating, despite the moderate temperature and gentle breeze. "Sorry." He cleared his throat. "Just got a bit dizzy."

Mr. Samuels patted his shoulder. "No worries. No worries at all." He motioned toward some servants who stood dutifully some fifty yards away. "Some iced water for our young guest, please."

David inhaled again, already feeling better. "I'm fine." He saw Donovan looking at him. "Can I try again?"

"But of course, if you're sure you're all right?"

David nodded. He could feel many eyes on him.

A servant arrived with water, served in a chalice too fine, it seemed to David, to be used at an archery range, but everything seemed done to excess here. He gulped down the water and handed the vessel back to the servant, who received it impassively.

"Thanks."

He retrieved his bow and arrow from the ground and aligned his body so his left leg stood closest to the target. This time he placed the arrow into the bowstring without incident, elevated the bow, pulled the drawstring back as far as he could, eyed his target, and readied his shot. A bull's-eye, as Donovan had achieved, meant the "heart" of the inanimate man, and David steadied his grip and aimed accordingly.

He released his shot.

The arrow snapped forward and surged towards its destination with a great *whoosh*, and David knew instantly he had shot well. The arrow impaled the target—not a bull's-eye but a good shot nevertheless. The gallery applauded politely. David glanced at Donovan, who clapped also, but it bothered him that Donovan's shot had been better.

"Well done. Well done." Mr. Samuels stepped forward and gave David another arrow. "You get two more."

David's second shot achieved similar results to his first.

Mr. Samuels, applauding again, stepped forward with the final arrow and addressed him loudly enough for all to hear. "May I ask you, did you aim for the heart?"

"Yes."

Mr. Samuels smiled and nodded. "I thought as much. Forgive me, I should have advised each of you on that point."

David paused his final shot and gave his attention to their instructor.

"The Archer's Paradox. In order to hit his shot, to pierce his target true, the archer aims not for the center of that target, but just beside it."

David turned back to his target and trained his gaze upon the "heart." He allowed his focus to drift incrementally to just next to center. Breathing slowly, deeply, he cleared all thoughts from his mind, drew the bowstring taut, and let his arrow fly.

Whoosh. Thwack.

The advice had been sound, his aim true. Still not a bull's-eye, but close, perhaps six inches off. The gallery applauded again, and David smiled and handed the bow back to Mr. Samuels, who patted him on the back.

"Bravo!" Mr. Samuels faced the gallery. "One more round of applause for our two young champions."

Donovan came over and extended his hand to David. "Nice job."

"Thanks. Not quite as nice as yours."

Mr. Samuels put a hand on the shoulder of each. "An impressive performance, both of you. I possessed not a fraction of your skill at that age. I'd hate to choose between you. Good thing you're friends." He chuckled, then turned and headed to the gallery to retrieve the next shooter.

Rachel and Sydney had made their way to the range, and his sister smiled and waved upon seeing him.

He waved back.

Something caught his attention on the far range, which until now had remained unoccupied. A tall figure had appeared and was lining up for a shot. David squinted, was and recognized one of the men with the hound from the morning's banquet—one of the McAlister brothers. Whichever one it was took aim, paused, then released his shot. The arrow cut through the air with tremendous force and pierced its target with a decisive *whap*. The shooter quickly loaded another arrow, took aim, and released again, piercing his target perfectly once more.

The man repeated this action again and again, and even from his fairly distant vantage point, David could observe the precise clustering of arrows.

Not one had missed.

CHAPTER 33
Battle

A BATTLE WAS SCHEDULED FOR AFTER dinner that evening. This was, after all, a castle, so reenacted duels seemed par for the course.

Speaking of which, his dad, along with their host and several other guests, had enjoyed an afternoon of golf, something David couldn't recall him having done in years.

"Incredible," his dad replied when David inquired as to how it had gone. "I guess nothing here should surprise me. The course was amazing."

"How did you do?"

His dad sighed. "I played okay—ninety, bogey golf. Not bad for my first time on this course, but Edmund won, shot even par. He's damn good."

If the morning banquet was extravagant, the feast presented them at dinner was downright regal. Roast pheasant and a whole suckling pig were the featured entrees, served with countless side dishes. More guests had arrived and indulged in the seemingly limitless buffet. A quartet of musicians sat in a near corner of the hall, serenading the guests with classical overtures.

Rachel and Sydney sat adjacent one another, chattering away, eating and playing. David was happy for this. Rachel didn't even seem fazed by the pig with the apple lodged in its mouth, even as servants carved savory chunks from its roasted hide.

They dined for nearly an hour, gorging themselves, several of the adults enjoying more than an ample share of alcoholic beverages. While dessert arrived, the evening's entertainment began to assemble about twenty feet from the banquet table. Even Rachel glanced up occasionally from her chocolate mousse to marvel at the unfolding scene.

Manor staff had erected a rectangular series of stanchions, enclosing a space of roughly thirty by twenty feet. Small chains threaded between them, and a network of interlocking mats formed a floor within the enclosure. Garnering the most attention was the pile of medieval armament gleaming in the center of the "battlefield."

Rachel tapped her dad on the shoulder. "Are they going to fight in there, Daddy?"

"Not for real. It's called a reenactment. They try to make it look real so we can see what it was like back then, but they are trained and won't really hurt each other."

"Good."

Edmund leaned toward her. "Your father explained that well. Now I need to go explain it for the rest of the guests." He smiled, stood, made his way over to the enclosure, and turned to face the banquet table, dismissing with a wave of his hand a servant who had approached with a microphone. The chatter and revelry gradually subsided around the table until all eyes fixed on their host.

He gestured toward his guests. "Please, continue to enjoy your desserts, beverages, anything you desire while we commence with the evening's entertainment."

Behind him, a small group of muscular men gathered, attired in intricate layers of interwoven garments. A pretty, fair-haired woman joined them within the enclosure, wearing an elegant white dress.

"As a few of us were discussing at the table—" Edmund caught Rachel's eye and winked at her, and she smiled. "—we are presenting for your enjoyment a reenactment of medieval battles from centuries gone by." He gestured toward the enclosure. "Though we enjoy quite an ample space, it is, of course, inadequate to allow for replication of a full-scale military engagement. Such replications have occurred for centuries, originally in the form of tournaments, which, while just short of genuine hostilities, were certainly of more gravity than mere sport. In fact, for some time they were free-for-alls, largely unregulated, the only distinction between them and actual battles being the acknowledgement of participants and guests that they were, in fact, not such. But yes, people were injured, and yes, people died. King Henry II of France, in fact, was killed by one of his constables. What our space does permit is recreation of one of the time-honored practices of medieval lore—the duel."

Edmund stepped aside a few paces to allow a clearer view for his guests, as the men put on the heavy coats of armor. "You have surely taken notice of the impressive physiques of our combatants, as well, perhaps, of that of our fair lady."

Twittering arose from some of the guests, and the woman in the white dress looked down demurely.

"The men had to be strong," Edmund continued. "A typical outfit of plate armor and chain mail suit weighed, on average, fifty pounds. To maintain the agility and precision required in battle, one had to boast exceptional strength—and, of course, skill."

One of the female guests whistled in appreciation, prompting a chuckle from their host and a bow from the nearest combatant.

Edmund resumed. "Quality armament was critical. Even the horses wore it. But the knights were layered head to toe. Note the arming cap beneath their helmets, and the hood beneath that, called a coif. Each of these added additional weight to the already burdensome mail and armor, but it didn't stop there. Observe the additional gear, those smaller plates that link the solid metal plates. Although they provided additional protection, they weighted down a warrior further still."

The men finished putting on their gear, and muscular or not, David wondered how they were even able to stand. Donovan's eyes widened, and upon glancing back at the enclosure, David realized why. A team of servants were presenting the weapons. Everyone watched and listened as Edmund described even more components of the gear, but David's attention, like Donovan's, was now riveted upon the weapons.

Their host smiled at their interest. "Okay, now the good stuff. Jonathan, if you please."

The combatant who had bowed playfully a few moments earlier scooped up a shield and a large blunted axe, and approached the edge of the enclosure.

Edmund gestured at him. "Let us start with the shield. Effective weaponry was important, but most knights would have told you that a sturdy shield, and the proper ability to employ it, was paramount."

The shield was spectacular. Its golden hues glimmered in the brilliant lighting of the Great Hall, framing a crimson Kane Manor insignia superimposed on the same dragon emblem David had observed other places throughout the castle. He peered at it more closely. Another more subtle depiction—eerie, even—glinted from the shield. When Jonathan shifted slightly, the lights captured the image in greater contrast: the beautiful, mournful face of a lady in white with flowing blonde hair, remarkably like the pretty woman presently seated within the enclosure.

"The shields were called targets," Edmund informed them, "and apropos this name could be, for if a warrior could degrade or destroy that of his enemy, the odds shifted heavily in his favor. Now, the battle-axe...."

Jonathan hoisted the weapon upward with his right hand, still clutching the shield in his left. With a great and furious cry, he swept the axe downward, as if unleashing his wrath upon some unseen enemy. Its blunted head slammed into the mat, the collision reverberating throughout the hall. Several approving murmurs followed.

"As you can see," Edmund said, "knights had to possess prodigious power, like Jonathan here, weighted down and wielding a heavy target and axe. Jonathan, thank you. Frederick, if you please."

Jonathan nodded, bowed, and retreated toward the back of the enclosure as another combatant stepped forward.

"Knights had a lethal arsenal at their disposal," Edmund explained. "Too many to detail here, but they could be classified into a few broader types: bladed hand weapons, which were your daggers, knives and swords—countless variations of each. Blunted hand weapons, including clubs, maces, hammers, picks, and morningstars. There were the pole arms, which included pikes, spears, lances, and dozens more. And of course the range weapons, such as javelins and crossbows." He looked toward David and Donovan. "I understand some of you made quite the impressive debut earlier with the latter."

David and Donovan shot each other prideful glances as their host pointed at Frederick. "No crossbows today, however. We will focus on two of the most common and lethal weapons in the arsenal of the medieval knight. Jonathan has demonstrated the power of the battle-axe, but now we come to the true icon of that golden age of chivalry and honorable combat — the sword."

On cue, Frederick reached for the long holster on his sword belt — or baldric, as Edmund had noted — and with a great flourish unsheathed the gleaming blade and sliced the air with a loud *swoosh*.

"Observe the majesty of this great weapon," Edmund gushed. "This is the broadsword, the earliest of medieval swords from the sixth century. Its two-edged blade measures nearly three inches at the base and tapers down to a finely cut point. This one weighs in at four and a half pounds and extends forty-two inches — one of the longer of its type."

David looked at Donovan, who leaned so far forward in his seat that David was surprised he hadn't fallen out.

"Sir Frederick," Edmund inquired. "Are you ready?"

Frederick carved the air with a few more lightning-quick sweeps of his blade before sheathing the weapon.

Behind him, another fully regaled knight arose with a clatter. He lunged toward the fair maiden and grabbed her roughly. She screamed and struggled as the knight dragged her toward one end of the enclosure.

David looked nervously at Rachel, who appeared quite concerned as their dad put a hand on hers.

"And now...." Edmund receded slowly into the shadows. "A knight must defend his honor and that of his true love. His enemy is formidable. The outcome shall hinge upon the ability and will of the combatants, and perhaps the hand of fate. May the battle begin."

With that, the combatants rushed each other ferociously, swords crashing together like cymbals, the lights from the great chandeliers refracting off the blades like lightning. The knights shoved one another and stepped back, but only momentarily. Seconds later, they rushed forward again with a great cry, relentlessly raining blows upon the other.

Most of the guests leaned forward in their seats, eyes wide. David looked at Donovan, who stared at the action with a glazed, faraway look. David returned his own focus to the duel, but suddenly the room was spinning. With each furious crash, he grew dizzier, until he swooned and lurched sideways from his chair. He was stayed by a strong grip.

"David," his dad said. "What's the matter?"

David sat up slowly. "Nothing." He offered his dad a faint smile. "Just zoned out a minute." He grabbed his water glass, which trembled in his grasp, and took a sip.

His dad appeared skeptical, but patted him on the back and returned his attention to the enclosure.

Across the table, Donovan was staring at him. Their eyes locked momentarily, but another clattering of swords drew their focus back to the battle.

When it concluded—the fair maiden saved, her honor defended, the villain vanquished—the knights stood and bowed, the maiden curtsied, and the guests in the Great Hall broke into thunderous applause.

Edmund, who had returned to his seat at the head of the banquet table, again approached the enclosure, likewise applauding. "Bravo!" He gestured admiringly toward the actors, who bowed once more before exiting the hall. He then turned and faced his guests as staff scurried forward to deconstruct the battlefield. "Never ceases to amaze me. I am glad you enjoyed it. These reenactments pay homage to the tournaments that were so popular and so very critical to English society for centuries. It was a crucial training ground for young knights, such as our valiant David and Donovan seated at our table tonight, to hone their skills—riding, shooting, fighting... a golden opportunity for knights to impress, to secure employment with great lords. Others found vocations through these tournaments, such as the job of a herald, which was critical, as he would carefully chronicle the names and arms and results of each combatant. Women were integral too, sometimes hosting the events, sometimes providing the prize. Sometimes... well... they *were* the prize. Nothing incited an impassioned battle like two warriors seeking the favor of a beautiful lady, much as you witnessed here tonight. I truly hope you have enjoyed this taste of medieval culture and history. Tomorrow, for those participating, you shall get another taste of a vitally important custom—The Hunt."

David turned to his dad. "Are we doing that?"

His dad looked uncertain, and when he didn't immediately answer, Donovan leaned toward David. "Dude, it'll be so cool. You've gotta do it!"

His dad looked at Kathy. "Are you letting Donovan go?"

She nodded. "I spoke to Edmund about it, and he assured me it's safe. He says they've taken kids even younger. I think it'll be fine. I think they'll enjoy it." She smiled at David.

His dad inhaled deeply, then shrugged. "Do you *want* to go, David?"

David looked at Donovan, who regarded him expectantly, and then back at his dad. "Sure."

Near the enclosure, their host was concluding his remarks. "The Hunt was indeed every bit as important a sport to the knight. In France, Northern Italy, and, of course, here in England, landowners prized their properties as game reserves, and protected them fiercely against poachers or other enemies. Land became more and more scarce, and such sprawling reserves could only be enjoyed by the wealthier nobles. Professional huntsmen were employed to protect the game and the hounds."

David looked over at the McAlister bothers, who were watching Edmund without expression, their loyal canine at their feet.

"Enjoy as much food and drink as you care for, but then rest up, dear guests. Those joining in The Hunt must rise early." Edmund's gaze settled on David and Donovan. "It promises to be a day to remember."

CHAPTER 34
The Hunt

"EVEN AS FOG CONTINUES TO LIE in the valleys, so does ancient sin cling to the low places, the depressions in the world's consciousness."

David was uncertain who had spoken. It was too early for speaking. The day had begun in darkness, save for the ghost-white quilt of fog that hovered over the vast expanse of Kane Manor—over the hills, woods, stables, ranges, and lakes—which enshrouded even the castle itself, as though to protect its secrets. *Early* had indeed meant *early*, as David's dad had roused him and Donovan at five, and after a light breakfast, they'd gathered as instructed near the equestrian range.

A tall, distinguished-looking gentleman inhaled deeply, seeming to savor the moment. Apparently, he had spoken. He looked to be maybe sixty, dressed in khakis, a red sweater-vest, and a brown, unzipped hunting jacket. Wisps of gray hair peeked out beneath a checkered gray deerstalker.

"Dewitt Bodeen, an American." He reached into an interior pocket of his jacket and withdrew a pipe. "Hope no one minds." He placed the stem in his mouth and struck a match. The embers flared orange in the darkness. "A little illumination to light our way." The man chuckled, tight plumes of smoke spiraling slowly upward before congealing into the canopy of fog. "And a tradition for me, for better or worse."

"Tradition is honored here."

By now, David recognized *that* voice. It seemed to rumble through the earth beneath them.

Edmund emerged from the shadows and shook the pipe-smoker's hand vigorously. "Good morning, Charles. I trust you slept well?"

"As always." Another spiral of rings ascended leisurely.

It seemed as if more guests had arrived every time David looked. He was too tired to count, but at least twenty had already gathered for the hunt, only about half of whom he recognized. Along with him and his dad and Donovan, there was Edmund, Mr. and Mrs. Delancey, Mr. Samuels from the archery range, and—somewhat to David's chagrin—the McAlister brothers, who approached through the mist.

Several greyhounds trotted alongside, tails arched, noses to the ground. Every few steps, a few would turn and dart back into the fog. David couldn't be sure, but he thought he heard something back there, a faint rustling, but then it vanished, as if swallowed up by the fog. One of the brothers would stay the dogs each time with a forceful call. The canines fell into line adjacent their masters as they came upon the group.

The rest of the guests, whom David didn't recognize, perhaps had just arrived that morning—or maybe earlier, and he simply hadn't encountered them yet.

"Dad." David grabbed his dad's arm and tugged him a few feet away from the group.

"What is it?"

"Rachel."

His dad looked at him. "She's back at the castle."

"What will she do while we're gone? Who will be with her?"

His dad placed an arm on his shoulder. "David, it's all right. Kathy is spending the day with her. She thought it would be a great opportunity for them to get to know each other. You know, bond a bit—a little girl time."

Before David could reply, Donovan stepped over and nudged him. "Look."

Two white vans emblazoned with the Kane Manor insignia pulled up, headlights piercing the darkness with tunnels of pale illumination. Each driver got out, walked briskly to the rear of his vehicle, and opened the doors. The guests lined up, roughly half behind either van, to receive their weapons. They emerged with bows and quivers in hand, as if moving through some sort of ammunitions buffet.

"You have all either hunted with us before, or received shooting instruction, or both," Mr. Samuels called to the group. "Some more recently than others. As always, veterans of Kane Manor hunts, kindly grant your patience for our newer brethren. As we always say, safety first."

He gestured at the McAlister brothers. "Most of you know Patrick and Mason, our esteemed huntsmen. They maintain our glorious hounds, as well as capture and care for our sacred prey. Gentlemen, have you readied the quarry?"

"We have, and the dogs are anxious."

The sleek canines fretted near the feet of their owners. Every few moments, they would sniff the ground and the air, and glance back in the direction from which they'd come.

"Excellent. Where our beautiful greyhounds are purebloods, our hunting techniques here are something of a hybrid. There are various methods of deer hunting, including stand hunting, which I fear would not offer the level of excitement or authenticity we wish to provide you. There is general hunting, which involves pursuing the prey by foot—most of us shall indeed engage this method today, though several will be on horseback. There is also a deer drive, wherein the prey is flushed toward a line of hunters—too simple, and too barbaric for our tastes here at Kane Manor. We honor our game, and believe any worthy prey requires the patience and dignity of a great pursuit."

A flicker of sunlight glinted behind them, and David regarded it in wonder. He'd never seen the sun rise—not that first golden break of light, anyway—but there it was, just a thin line of fire beneath a still vast crescent of darkness. It seemed to him an invaluable bit of comfort, like a match struck in a dark room.

"Our time draws near," said Mr. Samuels. "Our brave hounds shall assist in our hunt, which brings us to our final technique—stalking. Stalking involves stealth, pursuing the prey with patience, eventually moving in closely enough to take your shot. Now, are there any questions?"

"Yes." David's dad moved through the crowd and toward the front of the group.

"Yes sir?"

"I know you said everyone has hunted before, or had training."

"Indeed, sir."

David's dad looked pensive.

The hounds snorted and stomped. A small group of men on horseback had arrived while Mr. Samuels was speaking, and their horses snorted and stomped too.

"Ah, good morning, men," Mr. Samuels greeted them. "I see you're astride our illustrious Dartmoors." He approached one of the horses and patted its neck, and the animal whinnied its appreciation. "Kane Manor boasts one of the best stables in England — Dartmoors, Suffolk, Shire, the classic English Thoroughbred, and many more. Forgive me, sir... you were inquiring?"

"Well, these boys—" David's dad gestured at him and Donovan. "—have never hunted, and they just had a few hours of shooting yesterday. I've actually had none of the above, but they're kids. Are you certain it's safe, two kids running around the moors with people shooting arrows around them?" He looked at some of the guests. "Forgive me, I'm sure you're all terrific shots, but like I said, they're kids, it's dark...."

Edmund stepped forward from the shadows.

David had forgotten he was there.

"Permit me." He placed a hand on Mr. Samuel's shoulder. "You are, of course, quite right to inquire about the welfare of your young charges. As Mr. Samuels noted, safety is one of our unshakeable tenets. You are joined by experienced hunters this morning. My master huntsmen—" He nodded in the direction of the McAlister brothers. "—supervise every hunt and assure the safety of all guests. My horsemen do likewise, in addition to preventing the prey from escaping the property. Seems like forever that we've been holding these hunts, with nary a serious injury to any of our esteemed guests." He looked at David's dad and smiled.

The sun breached the horizon more urgently now, the darkness and fog beginning a hesitant retreat.

"And with that," said Edmund, "we must not tarry. Tradition holds that our hunt commences at sunrise. Patrick, Mason, will you do the honors?"

One of the brothers nodded and walked briskly away. The group began to fan out, and Edmund stepped away from the vans, his own weapons in hand.

"Tradition," he called out to the hunters. "As always, to win the hunt is a high honor. To the noble knight or fair maiden who makes the kill go the considerable spoils: a plaque, an engraved chalice, and permanent inscription in the annals of Kane Manor history. We have special guests today, my friends, and so it is a very special hunt."

David flinched as a gunshot rang out from somewhere just beyond the lingering recesses of fog.

Edmund smiled. "Worry not. We shall not be hunting by firearm. Patrick has merely signaled us that the prey has been released. Now it is time. Weapons at the ready, my friends. *May the hunt begin!*"

CHAPTER 35
Safe as Can Be

KATHY SMILED SWEETLY. "I'VE ALWAYS wanted a little girl of my own."

"I already have a mother."

Kathy's smile melted away.

Rachel didn't care for the expression that replaced it, so she looked at the pretty horses instead. She'd pleaded with her dad to take her with him when he awoke so very early that morning, as she didn't want to be left alone with Kathy. He'd assured her it would be fine, and told her she would get to go to the stables and see beautiful horses, just like the collection she kept in her room at home, only for real.

A chill lingered in the morning air. Kathy wore a leather jacket, which glistened like a wet seal in the sunlight. Rachel had on her favorite pink-and-blue hoodie. It was still early, and they seemed to be the only ones there, aside from the horses, of course. Rachel liked the gray ones. They were smaller than the others, but sturdy-looking, and so pretty. She smiled as one snorted and approached her at the edge of its pen.

"She's taken a shine to you, it seems."

Rachel turned around to see a kind-looking man with a gray moustache looking down at her. He looked dressed for riding. He smiled, and she smiled back, glad to no longer be alone with Kathy. He reminded Rachel of her granddad.

"What is your name, my lady?" When she told him, he smiled again and patted the horse's neck. "Mabel, please bid good morning to Miss Rachel." He turned around and bowed his head to Kathy. "Where are my manners? Forgive me. My name is Sanford Hollenbeck, stable master here at Kane Manor. Everyone calls me Sandy."

Kathy extended a hand, and Sandy grasped it gently.

"Kathy McCourt."

"A pleasure." Sandy returned his attention to Rachel, who had returned hers to Mabel. "Seems you've made a friend."

"She's a pretty horse," Rachel said.

"A pony, actually. A New Forest pony. Lord Kane adores them. He loves all equines, truly, but I'd venture to say the New Foresters are among his favorite. They are a native breed of the British Isles, and many still run free there."

Kathy pointed at two other ponies on either side of Mabel. "They have different colors. Are they the same breed?"

"They are indeed. The New Foresters sport a variety of coloration, though most are of variations you see here — gray, chestnut, and bay." He squatted alongside Rachel and pointed at the pony to Mabel's left. "That one is bay, Rachel, more of a reddish-brown."

Rachel nodded, but her attention remained on Mabel. "Can I ride her?"

"Rachel," Kathy said.

Sandy straightened up and looked at Kathy. "Well, if it's all right with you, Rachel can ride. New Foresters are renowned children's ponies. Mabel is even-tempered, and many youngsters have enjoyed a ride on her."

Rachel looked up at Kathy. She didn't like the feeling of hoping to gain her approval, but she really wanted to ride Mabel.

"I don't know, darling," Kathy said. "I'm not sure your father would approve."

"He *would*." Rachel curled her lower lip downward and looked up at the two adults with wide eyes.

"Well, shoot. Now how can we resist that?" Sandy looked at Kathy. "I'll be with her, of course. She will be safe as can be."

"Well," Kathy said, "I suppose it would be okay."

Rachel smiled.

"Excellent!" Sandy patted Rachel's back. "Excuse me for just a few minutes." He checked his watch. "My staff shall be arriving soon. We shall get the equipment and ready Mabel for your ride. Kindly wait here. I shall return straightaway." He strode quickly away and out of the stable.

Rachel looked down. It was just her and Kathy again.

"Rachel? Are you happy I'm letting you ride?"

"Yes."

Kathy regarded her expectantly.

"Thank you," Rachel said softly.

A low buzzing arose, and Kathy retrieved a cell phone from her jeans pocket. She looked at the screen, then quickly turned around and quietly answered the call. After a quick glance back at Rachel, she walked a few feet in the other direction, cupping a hand over her mouth.

Rachel welcomed the interruption. She looked back at Mabel, but something else suddenly caught her attention—something off to her right, at the opposite end of the barn, away from where Kathy still paced back and forth, preoccupied with her call. Rachel had heard something and *seen* something, out of the corner of her eye. She looked once more back at Kathy, who'd walked a bit farther away, and then ambled over to the windows at the far end of the stable.

The world outside looked like something from her storybooks, with rolling green hills, towering trees, and glimmering lakes. Farther off stood the tree line of a tall forest. She wondered what animals made their home within, but wasn't certain what she had seen or heard.

Then, there it was again.

It was *fast,* so fast that Rachel rubbed her eyes and looked again to be certain she had indeed seen it. She had. It had covered at least fifty yards in the brief time it had taken her to rub her eyes and reopen them, but there it was.

The deer was magnificent, with majestic antlers so large it reminded Rachel of a moose. It sprinted past quickly, powerfully. And no wonder, she realized with horror. It was running for its life. She knew this even before she noticed the group of hunters in pursuit. She frowned as she remembered her dad and brother were out there too.

How can they be a part of this? There must be some misunderstanding.

She turned around and glanced at Kathy, still at the far end of the stable, busy with her call.

She needed to find her dad and David. They would make everything okay. She thought of Sandy, who would be back momentarily to take her on a ride with Mabel, but there was no time to lose. She would explain everything to Sandy later.

She reached for the knob of the door adjacent to where she stood, pulled it slowly open, and paused as the door squeaked, casting a final glance back at Kathy.

She slipped quietly out the door, pulled it softly shut behind her, and headed out into the morning, in the direction she had seen the deer run.

***

Donovan seemed dissatisfied with the pace. After a few minutes of moving forward as one large group, several smaller cohorts had splintered off and headed in their own directions. It would likely be a long hunt, they had been cautioned—Kane Manor unfolded over hundreds of acres of varying terrain, and the stag would prove elusive quarry.

"This is the part that worries me," David's dad said as the group fragmented. "Everyone going this way and that, arrows flying everywhere. You read about hunting accidents all the time."

Donovan seemed more concerned with their progress—or lack thereof. "I would love to be the one to make the kill."

David doubted they would even find the animal, so vast was the property. Frankly, that would suit him just fine, but every few minutes or so, Donovan, moving increasingly ahead of them, would glance back with an agitated expression.

"Want me to just go on up ahead with him?" David offered. "At least get him to stop bugging us?"

"I'll go with you," said his dad. "Sorry, I'm just a bit preoccupied, thinking about Rachel and Kathy. I hope it's going okay."

"Why don't you call?"

His dad looked at him, then nodded. "Okay, one quick call." He withdrew his phone from his pocket and switched it on—they'd been asked to keep all electronic devices off during the hunt.

Up ahead on the next rise, Donovan stopped and looked back at them, hands on his hips.

The phone powered on, and his dad dialed. "Hi, it's me. I—" He paused and listened.

David grew cold as he watched his dad's face turn ashen.

"I'm on my way." His dad returned the phone to his pocket and looked at his son. "Rachel's missing."

The words registered in David's mind like a piece of a puzzle he didn't wish to assemble. "But Kathy was with her."

"They were at the stables. Kathy took a quick call, and the next thing she knew, Rachel was gone."

"Dad—"

"I'm going." His dad turned around and eyed the route they'd taken. "I'll find her."

At that moment, a great commotion arose from just over the next hill.

"There he is!"

"I have a shot!"

Father and son locked eyes.

"I'm coming with you," David said.

"No."

"Dad!"

"I'll head for the stables, but you better look for that stag."

"Dad, I want to help you find her!"

His dad stepped over to him and gripped his shoulders firmly. "I have to look near the stables, because that's where she disappeared." More cries echoed over the hills. "But you know how she feels about animals.... She could be out here somewhere."

A wave of nausea swept over David. In the echoes of his mind, he heard the loud *thwack* of arrows penetrating targets on the range.

"Look out for her." His dad set his bow and quiver on the ground.

David regarded the weapons. "Don't you think you might need those?" He knew that probably sounded crazy, but he'd felt compelled to ask.

His dad gave him a strange look. "David, even if I see the stag, I don't have time to try to shoot it. This stuff will slow me down."

David shook his head. "That's not what I me —"

His dad didn't let him finish. "David, you have to get these ideas out of your head. Everything will be fine." His dad gazed out at the landscape a moment before settling on his direction, and broke into a trot.

David turned around to see that Donovan had stopped again, far ahead this time, looking back impatiently once more. Beyond him, the hills seemed to sprawl endlessly.

Rachel could be anywhere.

David looked at his bow, gripped firmly in his left hand. His dad was right — it would slow his pace — but he wasn't about to leave it behind.

"He's in the woods!"

David glanced one last time at his dad's weapons, which sat on the hillside as though left behind by a vanquished warrior, then turned back, hoisted his quiver up higher on his shoulder, and ran as fast as he could toward Donovan.

CHAPTER 36
Isaiah 11:6

"I'LL HELP YOU FIND HER," **DONOVAN** said.

"Thanks. We'll have a better chance if we split up. We can cover twice the ground." David looked about at the hills, which rolled out in every direction, and gestured toward the woods about a half mile beyond Donovan. "I'll head there."

Donovan pointed eastward, where, in the distance, the spiraling turrets of the castle crested over the hills like a tilted crown. "I'll go that way."

David nodded and hoisted his weapons once more on his shoulders. "We have to find her."

"We will."

They locked eyes momentarily before turning to go their separate ways.

***

Back home, when she was very young and her mother still with them, Rachel discovered that she had a way with animals. Well, some animals, anyway. Bunnies in particular seemed to like her, and would let her get close and even touch them gently. Momma would take her to the park and she would pet them, or sometimes it would happen in their own yard at home. Rachel couldn't understand why the bunnies seemed to be so shy and ran away from most other people, even David, but she felt lucky that they let her get so close.

So far, the deer was not acting like the bunnies. It was being a bit shy, and it was fast. It would whoosh by, a blur, then stop in the distance and look back at her, giving her just enough chance to keep following. She smiled.

Maybe it's playing a game with me.

Her smile disappeared when the quiet was disrupted by a clatter of hooves and the echo of hunters calling out to one another. She could also hear barking—angry, hungry barking—not a friendly bark, like Robert's dog, Bear. The deer apparently heard it all too, because it turned and raced off in a blink. Rachel sighed. If she saw the hunters and the dogs and the horses with their clattering hooves, she would be sure to tell them to be quieter.

She yawned. This was a tiring game, but she didn't want to keep her new friend waiting. She ambled off in the direction he had sped, just as fast as she could.

***

The sun had finally and fully breached the thin horizon, but when David at last reached the tree line and crept into the forest of towering conifers, it was as though dawn had not yet broken. It was eerily quiet. He'd heard of tragic hunting accidents in which people had been mistaken for game, and in this thicket, a small child might be all too easy to confuse for prey. As he advanced, the trees thinned out and a bit of a pathway opened before him. Sections of rumpled, indented grass gave clear indication both man and horse had preceded him. He followed the trail as it penetrated deeper into the woods.

He walked for several minutes, the only sound his breathing and the occasional crackle of twigs snapping underfoot, but suddenly he paused. Branches snapped in the not-too-great distance. It sounded like something large, too loud and forceful for a squirrel or rabbit, or even a stag. As whatever or whoever it was moved closer, David instinctively knelt to the forest floor, trying to obscure himself behind a thick bush.

At length, the source of the commotion moved into view: the McAlister brothers, on horseback, with several hounds keeping pace.

The dogs trotted hunched over, noses to the ground, looking as though onto a scent. This was good, David reasoned, indicating that maybe the stag was near. If so, Rachel might be nearby too.

He decided to let them all pass before resuming his search, but as he knelt, his quiver of arrows growing heavy and his knees beginning to throb, he realized they were not moving on. The hounds—David had counted three—had darted off in different directions, and David watched as the McAlisters slowly guided their horses away from one another.

The brothers hadn't uttered a word, but one had nodded toward the other, who guided his steed farther away and disappeared from view, probably following the lead of one of the dogs.

David watched the remaining brother vigilantly, desperately hoping not to be spotted. It struck him as a rather irrational thought, as Edmund employed the brothers to help oversee the hunt, so it would not be unusual to find them out here keeping an eye on things. He remained still nonetheless, until....

A strange noise, alarmingly close, startled him, and he twisted around, awkwardly and audibly.

No more than a yard away, one of the hounds stood staring at him. He couldn't believe he hadn't heard it approach, but there it stood, fangs bared. It repeated the noise—an angry, guttural snort—and David looked past the seething canine at the other McAlister brother, twenty feet away, staring at him with a smile that made something in David's stomach twist.

When David stood up, the hound growled deeply and bared its fangs, gnashing the air in the small space between them. The two other dogs came sprinting back from wherever they'd run off to, and joined the third, hackles on end. They growled and gnashed the air too.

The brother who'd ridden up behind the first hound barked a guttural command, and the dogs broke ranks and began encircling the periphery of the area in a frenzied sprint.

Hesitant as David was to take his eyes off the snarling beasts, he turned around to check on the other brother, who had, of course, spotted him too and moved a few feet closer, smiling the same unnerving smile. David realized that a direct line could be drawn from one brother through him and to the other. All the while, the hounds continued their frenetic circling.

This was truly bizarre—he was not the prey, and yet here he was, surrounded, trapped, and watching with incredulity as one brother turned in the saddle and retrieved his crossbow. David quickly turned back to face the other brother, who, still grinning, had done likewise.

As the hounds raced and foamed, David felt himself reaching for his own weapon as if someone else were controlling his actions. His mind scrambled desperately to recall Mr. Samuels's shooting instructions and the archer's paradox.

The McAlister brothers reached for their arrows.

With hands shaking and heart pounding, David reached for his arrows.

"There!"

David stared as everything disintegrated into chaos.

Something fast, faster even than the circling hounds, sped past. The stag.

The dogs gave chase, and the McAlister brothers, astride their horses and arrows primed, did likewise.

Was it just another crazy coincidence?

The McAlisters seemed strange and ill-natured to begin with, but maybe they'd pursued the stag into the woods and loaded their arrows to ready their shot. Maybe David had just been in the wrong place at the wrong time — again.

What other explanation could there be?

Somehow, even this strained credibility. After all, the brothers were there to guide and supervise the hunt, not to kill the animal themselves.

He had no time to make sense of it, as the stag was close, and Rachel could be as well. Coincidence or not, the McAlisters and other hunters followed in armed pursuit. David wanted to shout out — to call after the brothers and caution them to stop, tell them his sister could be somewhere out here — but his voice would not come, and maybe this was just as well. Inexplicable as it might be, something inside him told him that alerting them to Rachel's presence might be the *last* thing he wanted to do.

And so he ran, the stillness from just minutes ago replaced by pandemonium. He could hear the McAlisters and their entourage of beasts as they tromped through the thicket. He could hear his own desperate panting as he raced with every ounce of energy he could muster, the thickening layer of bramble and branches clutching at him, scratching him, snapping in angry protest in his wake. He could hear more voices now too, and more hooved footfalls. Clearly, additional hunters had joined the pursuit.

He ran, and the woods grew thicker and darker still. The noises grew louder, bursting forth from all around him in terrible disharmony: trampling horses, angry hounds, shouting huntsmen, and the one sound he'd feared most of all—the sickening *whoosh* of loosed arrows. He ran, but with every step grew less certain whether he was running *toward* something or from it. The forest seemed to be swallow him whole as the commotion intensified.

Then, it stopped. All of it.

The horses, the hounds, the voices, the snapping branches—all had gone quiet. The eerie silence returned, somehow different this time. David stopped too, and stared directly ahead. No more than fifty yards away, a break in the thicket sprawled at last, an open space awash in the most glorious light. He approached it slowly, and with each step the picture assembled into gradual coherence.

It was the strangest of sights.

The illuminated swath loomed conspicuously—a gleaming finger of light within the enveloping palm of darkness. David crept closer and spotted a gathering of hunters—most on horseback, some on foot—frozen, it seemed, in a semicircle. The horses shifted impatiently but seemed likewise subdued. The dogs appeared to be leashed, and crept gingerly along the outskirts of the gathering.

As David looked, each of the hunters looked too, but not at him—they stared, transfixed, at someone, or something, that David couldn't see. His mouth went dry and his heart seemed to pause, as though teetering on a great precipice between all it had ever known and all that was now to come.

Fear coursed through his blood, making it heavy, weighing him down, but something compelled him, and he cried out and broke into a sprint. A few of the hunters glanced his way, but only briefly. The rest remained mesmerized by whatever it was they had partially encircled.

When David reached them, he pushed his way through, past man and beast. As the cluster of bodies gave way, the funnel of light intensified, so much so that he was momentarily blinded by its radiance. He breached the arc of hunters and at last came upon that which each of them beheld.

Then he saw.

His mother hadn't been terribly religious, but she loved a particular Biblical passage, and though he'd never given it much thought, he'd drawn comfort from how much it seemed to comfort her. It came to him now in the sweet timbre of his mother's voice. Isaiah 11:6. "The wolf shall dwell with the lamb, and the leopard shall lie down with the kid; they shall not hurt nor destroy in all my holy mountain; for the Earth shall be full of the knowledge of the Lord, as the waters cover the sea."

As his mind registered that which still transfixed all others present, a whisper escaped his lips in unison with the memory of his mother's words.

"And a child shall lead them."

Beyond the crescent of hunters, as though oblivious to their presence, knelt his sister. She was not alone. The weight of the world seemed to fall from David's shoulders as it appeared she was unharmed, but now a new anxiety swept over him: she had found the stag. At first, he thought it was dead, because it was splayed motionless on the ground, its head — crowned with long, corrugated antlers and surely weighing more than all of Rachel — rested at her feet. Its eyes were open, and its massive torso, coated with thick, bay fur, slowly expanded and retracted. Rachel soothed it, leaning over it in the grass and gently stroking its tufted mane.

David gasped. The animal was enormous, far larger than he ever realized a stag could grow. It looked to be at least eight feet long, and easily weighed a half ton. With one contortion of its massive body, it could easily crush his sister or impale her with its jagged crest, and yet it seemed inclined toward neither. It lay peacefully by her, calmed by the touch of her tiny hand, unmoving save for its slow, deep breaths and the intermittent blinking of its saucer-sized, chestnut eyes. Rachel gazed at the creature tenderly, both child and beast bathed in morning light.

David stepped slowly forward, but the animal began to stir, so he paused.

"Rachel," he whispered.

His sister looked up and smiled upon seeing him. "David!"

The stag stirred again, but Rachel patted it, and it became still once more.

"Rachel," David said again. "You have to come with me."

She appeared confused. "But he's scared. I don't want to leave him alone."

David glanced at the hunters, some of whom started to shift around a little, craning their necks to see, murmuring to one another.

He looked back at Rachel, whose attention had returned to the great beast. "Is he hurt?"

"No." Rachel's eyes narrowed as she looked past her brother to the group of hunters. "But *they* were going to hurt it."

David slowly extended his hand. Though the creature seemed totally, if inexplicably, under his sister's spell, he knew this could change in a heartbeat—with horrific results. "It's okay now. You need to come with me." She shook her head, but he kept his hand extended and smiled at her. "Rachel, please."

She looked up at her brother and held his gaze a moment. Then she bent down on her hands and knees and placed a kiss on the animal's mane. She sighed, then got to her feet. The stag saw this and began to do likewise, slowly at first, but then it rolled from its prone position and scrambled quickly upright.

David swooped in and pulled Rachel away as the antlers of the great beast swept perilously close.

The hunters continued to emerge from their trance, growing more animated, some even fumbling for their bows.

"Easy!"

The cry rang out from the rear of the group, a deep and familiar voice. Its owner worked his way through the cluster of hunters, which parted to let him pass.

David scooped Rachel up into his arms, and the stag snorted and stamped anxiously behind him as

Edmund Kane reached the front of the assembled group.

More voices called urgently, and the group gave way once more.

David smiled as his dad appeared alongside Edmund. He paused momentarily, staring wide-eyed at his children, then rushed to usher them away from the agitated animal.

The stag now stood alone before them, appearing greatly distressed.

Rachel tried to go to it, but her dad held her back. "Daddy...."

The blood of the other animals seemed to be roiling too now. The horses whinnied and bucked, and the hounds snarled and strained at their leads.

The stag stamped and pitched and pirouetted, and David watched in amazement as it seemed to lock eyes once more with Rachel before darting for the tree line.

Several hunters, including the McAlisters, drew their weapons. One raised his bow and took aim.

Rachel screamed in protest, and her dad restrained her as she struggled to break free.

The brother released his shot, and David flinched as the arrow buzzed past, the slap of air upon his cheek confirming its proximity. He whirled around and, after a moment, spotted the arrow lodged in a bush at the tree line.

Rachel smiled.

The brother seethed.

A great commotion and shouting arose from all around, and David smiled upon seeing that his dad was seething too, trying to get to the brother who'd taken the shot. The horses and hounds paced and snorted, and the hunters seemed to do likewise.

Edmund spoke again, loudly, raising his hands into the air, and gradually the clamor eased, the hunters fell quiet, and even the animals slowly calmed.

"Easy," Edmund called. "Lower your weapons, if you please."

The hunters did as requested, even the McAlister brothers, though they could not have looked less pleased, particularly the one who'd loosed the errant shot.

"Why the hell was he shooting?" David's dad demanded. "That could have hit my children!"

"I understand your displeasure," Edmund said. "But a cornered animal that size poses a significant threat. Patrick, I assure you, was simply firing a warning shot to scare the animal off."

David's dad narrowed his eyes and shook his head.

"I am sorry our hunt shall not on this occasion end in the traditional manner, but the safety of our guests is paramount, and we have a child in our midst." Edmund looked at Rachel and smiled. "Besides, there are other important facets to our tradition at Kane Manor, and to the ancient tradition we honor—among them, valor." He gestured at Rachel. "Our brave young lady did not wish to see our prey harmed, and she acted to protect it." He knelt down before Rachel, grabbed her shoulders gently, and looked her in the eyes. "And you, my dear lady, seem to possess the rarest of gifts, a great kinship with all living things." He smiled again, stood back up, and looked at David. "That is something I deeply admire. We would all do well to protect the things we hold dear."

Donovan, quiet since arriving on the scene, looked at Edmund and cleared his throat. His quiver of arrows remained slung over his shoulder. "Will we be able to finish the hunt?"

The McAlister brothers circled back together on their horses and eyed their master anxiously. David could swear he saw one of them licking his lips.

Edmund looked at Donovan warmly but then twitched, as though startled, and looked down.

Rachel tugged at his hand. She stared into his eyes and slowly shook her head. Edmund seemed to shift uncomfortably—the first time David had glimpsed even the slightest hint of unease in their host's demeanor—but Rachel tugged at his hand again.

Edmund managed a smile, and his voice refilled with its familiar resolve. "I am sorry to disappoint you, good sir, but it would seem our fair maiden here was, in fact, the first to bring the noble beast to heel, albeit in her own way. Let us consider the hunt to be over, and to our young victor is granted her wish, to see the animal run free."

Donovan's expression showed his obvious disappointment.

Edmund placed a hand on his shoulder. "Buck up, young man, and do not fret, for even grander things await. I urge you to rest well tonight, for tomorrow promises to be extraordinary. " He looked at Donovan squarely. "You've come a long way, and shall not be disappointed."

Edmund faced the hunters. "Those on horseback are free to begin your sojourn back. I shall dispatch jeeps for all those on foot who would prefer a conveyance back to the castle. You need only traverse back to the edge of the forest from which you entered. I suggest walking as a group. It is indeed all too easy to lose your way in here. All of our recreational activities shall remain open for your enjoyment, our kitchens as well. And, of course, another sumptuous banquet awaits this evening."

The walkers began to disperse toward the path that wound its way out of the woods.

Rachel scrambled up onto her dad's back, her arms wrapped around his, her cheek pressed to the back of his neck. "I wanna go home."

CHAPTER 37
The Boy with the Book

THE FOG CLUNG LOW AND HEAVY to the land as they drove. Some commented on its beauty, but David had grown weary of things unseen. He'd wanted to return home after the previous day's drama during The Hunt, but short of that, he'd hoped at least to sleep in. No such luck. Today's excursion would take them to the ruins overlooking Tintagel Island, and Edmund was adamant about getting an early start. David rubbed his eyes, his head propped against the window of the shuttle escorting them to their destination, the glass cold against his cheek.

It was, thankfully, a short ride. When they arrived, he slid out and stood up stiffly.

Rachel shimmied across the seat and swung her legs out of the van. Her feet pedaled the air in an effort to reach the running board, and David grabbed her before she could fall.

"Careful there." Edmund, having taken his own transport, stepped forth from the mist.

"It's okay," Rachel said. "David always catches me."

"Most fortunate." Edmund patted her atop the head.

A handful of other guests arrived in a second shuttle and made their way over: Sydney and her parents; Mr. Samuels from the archery range; and a young boy of eight or nine years, clutching a book with colorful medieval depictions on the cover. He tugged excitedly at his parents' hands, while his mother smiled down at him with tired-looking eyes, and his dad yawned.

"Good morning, everyone," Edmund said. "I am sorry I missed you at breakfast. I wished to arrive a touch early, to assure all was in order for your visit."

David shielded his eyes against the breaking dawn.

"That reminds me. We must not tarry if we wish to be in prime viewing position for the eclipse." Edmund motioned beyond them. "We walk from here."

The sun advanced gradually, parting the mist like a veil. Rachel scrambled up into her dad's arms, and he gestured toward a small isthmus that pointed out to the sea. "Look at the view."

The castle remnants were remarkably intact in some sections, crumbling in others. Rugged cliffs sprawled out above them, dotted yellow with wildflowers. Far below, the Celtic Sea — part of the Atlantic — stirred beneath the beckoning sun. Slow, undulating waves appeared, shaking off the blanket of fog that had sheathed its waters only minutes before.

David saw that the isthmus pointed toward something more. Beyond the slice of land that stretched before them lay an island, glimmering in the sunrise like a fallen jewel. From the center of the island jutted majestic ruins of a once great castle. It looked to be a healthy climb to the structure, once they made it to the island. He squinted at what appeared to be a narrow wooden bridge swaying in the awakening inlet winds, and the lone artery between the mainland and the island.

They walked silently for a while, as though Edmund understood doing so would help his guests absorb the majesty of this place more than anything he might tell them in this moment.

Ten minutes later, they reached a steep stairwell that spiraled down to the bridge.

"Steady on the bridge," Edmund called out. "Keep a hold of the little ones — the gusts will surprise you."

Sydney's father appeared apprehensive. "You sure it's strong enough for all of us?"

"Heavens, yes, though I can understand your concern. It is, in fact, built to sway, like buildings in an earthquake, and is far sturdier than it appears. It is trusty, my friend, but do hang on."

David began to descend. The surroundings had imparted to him a strange sense of tranquility, but as he reached the bridge, a loud hiss sounded, and a great plume of mist erupted up from the sea, so high that it licked at the underside of the bridge. A cluster of dark clouds had intruded on the otherwise gleaming horizon.

"Pretty cool," Donovan said. He nudged David and pointed across the bridge at the island.

Where the bridge connected lay an abbreviated beachfront, but the rest of the island's periphery ascended up sheer, towering cliffs. Those who once occupied the castle had certainly been well-protected from an enemy's approach.

A low rumbling rose in the distance as the spate of dark clouds mushroomed and edged closer. David and Donovan followed their host onto the bridge.

Halfway across, Edmund stopped. "A good spot to immortalize the experience," he called.

Several guests held up cameras and phones and began snapping pictures.

The boy with the book scrambled to the front of the group, tugged at Edmund's arm, and pointed out toward the caves lining the shore below. "Tell us about those."

Edmund smiled. "We get many questions about the caves." He eyed them wistfully. "Over the course of hundreds of thousands of years, the rocks at the shoreline were eroded by the sea, and several irregular caves were formed—quite spectacular, and rather unique in their relatively adjacent formation. Two of them afford easy access from the footpath. They are high enough to walk through and will take you through all the way to the other side of the island head." He wore a satisfied, faraway look.

The boy with the book looked out toward the caves, then back at his book again. He tugged at Edmund's arm once more. "Merlin."

Edmund's eyes glinted. "Ah, yes. Merlin. His cave resides beneath us, where you now gaze. It passes completely through Tintagel Island, emerging through West Cove. The great wizard made it his home in his duty as teacher and mentor to a young man who would be king."

The boy with the book stared out toward the caves with wide eyes, and cried, "Arthur!"

His mother had made her way up to him and placed a hand on his shoulder. "He just means in the legend, sweetheart." She smiled politely at their host. "The legend of Arthur."

Edmund smiled back.

"I *believe* it, Mom." The boy pointed once more toward the caves, dislodging his mother's hand from his shoulder.

"'Fairytales are more than true,'" Edmund said. "'Not because they tell us that dragons exist, but because they tell us that dragons can be beaten.' G.K. Chesterton, if you'll forgive a prideful reference to an English scribe."

The boy's mother smiled weakly.

"Well," Edmund said, "let us press on."

The climb to the castle looked to be an arduous one. One hundred concrete steps, Edmund had said, but as David began to climb, it looked more like a thousand. The winding path was narrow and steep, and Edmund told them that ascending to the summit was forbidden during bad weather. It was easy to see why, as one misstep might mean a long and perilous fall.

David looked back at the group to see that his dad had put Rachel down, and she trudged alongside him, her hand in his. The wind had increased with the elevation, and with each gust, his sister's hair tufted and streamed behind her, as though for a moment she'd taken wing. Glancing skyward, David could see the lattice of clouds still massing above them, a bruise-colored smudge on an otherwise sea-blue canvas. The quadrant housing the sun remained clear, though a shadow had begun to creep across it.

A hand fell on his shoulder.

"Eyes on the path, good sir," Edmund said. "Things can get a bit treacherous up here, if you are not careful."

David nodded and looked past Edmund at the winding, jagged crag, of which a considerable portion remained to be scaled. The thunderheads rumbled, and another geyser of mist vented from the churning sea below. He looked back in time to see the spent droplets disintegrating onto the bridge, over which the last members of their group had just crossed.

Five minutes later, they'd completed their climb.

Sydney's father lagged a bit behind, and she scampered back to him, tugging at his hand. "Come *on*, Dad."

Her dad wiped his brow with a handkerchief and gulped air upon reaching the group.

"A healthy trek." Edmund patted him on the back.

Beyond him, the summit plateaued out into a vast expanse of open meadow, punctuated in spots by eroded stone sections of the castle. Some fifty yards away, laborers scampered about, busily assembling some sort of exhibit. They each wore a crimson, hooded robe emblazoned with the Kane Manor insignia.

"My staff is preparing some of the crown jewels of my collection." Edmund explained that the site had once been home to the castle's great hall, which now lay largely in ruins. He stretched his arms out toward the ruins, as if he wished to somehow embrace them. "My castle," he said softly, as though to himself. Then, more audibly, he said, "And beyond us, the island of Tintagel. The parish of Tintagel boasts fewer than two thousand souls—yet roughly one hundred times that number visited in the past year. And no wonder. Its history is rich, its pull magnetic."

The boy with the book tugged at Edmund's arm now. "What about *Arthur*?"

Edmund looked down at him. "I like a man who gets right to the heart of things."

The boy with the book turned and peered out in the direction Edmund now pointed, northeast of the ruins.

Edmund turned back to his guests. "Camelot Castle Hotel, built in 1899 upon Barras Head. The magical call of Arthur, of Camelot, lures people here from across the globe, but the Knights of the Roundtable did not hold court at a hotel. Legend holds that one of the castles of Tintagel may have been the birthplace of Arthur himself. In 1998, excavators discovered a slate with a simple inscription: Artognou."

"Arthur," said Sydney's father, who seemed to have at last caught his breath. "I took Latin in college."

Edmund smiled. "Quite right."

The boy's eyes had managed to grow even wider, like small moons upon his face.

The skies rumbled again as several men carried a large marble slab into the enclosure.

David returned his attention to their host.

"Historians insist there is no compelling evidence to confirm any of this. Thus, as for the veracity of these legends, it is up to each of you to make up your own mind."

The boy with the book looked at Edmund with a solemnity unique to children. "I believe."

Edmund leaned down and whispered in the boy's ear, just loud enough for David to hear standing next to him, "So do I."

It began to rain.

CHAPTER 38
Arondight and Galatine

IT CAME AS MORE OF A drizzle, really, and no one seemed particularly bothered.

Four men carried into the enclosure—with what appeared considerable difficulty and care—a large stone disc, atop which gleamed two long curving implements. They grunted as they hoisted the disc onto the heavy slab.

Edmund regarded the preparations with satisfaction. "Splendid. This way, if you please."

The guests followed Edmund to the exhibit. The storm clouds had funneled almost directly overhead, and this, along with the moon's trajectory, shrouded the morning in shadow. In the darkness, the exhibit shimmered in even more brilliant relief. The group shuffled into the enclosure and looked from table to table in wonder.

Donovan stared at the items on the slab.

Edmund placed a hand on his shoulder. "It speaks to you, does it not?"

Donovan slowly nodded.

David moved closer, eager to see what had called to Donovan, and which now, somehow, called to him.

They were beautiful. The two blades overlaid each other in perfect symmetry, breathtaking in their elegance.

Several other guests wandered over and stared, transfixed by the magnificent weapons of ancient lore.

Edmund smiled almost paternally. "Two of the most famous swords in all of history."

The boy with the book wormed his way to the front of the group, and whispered, "Excalibur."

Edmund patted him on the back. "No," he said gently. "That most hallowed of weapons resides with the Lady of the Lake, but in point of fact, the mighty Arondight is revered in nearly equal esteem, and is remarkably similar in power and design, its inscriptions carved by fairies, its immutable blade forged, it is said, by the stars. See how it glows, even now, all these centuries later. Bestowed upon Lancelot by the same fair lady who now guards Excalibur, its blade reflects the tranquility and magic of those waters."

The boy with the book smiled limply, as though lifted by each word to faraway places.

His mother made her way up to him, pursed her lips, and smiled unpleasantly. "In the story, sweetheart."

Edmund glanced at her, and she stepped back as though struck, but then he smiled and outstretched his arms toward the two shimmering blades. "The mighty Arondight! And behold the great weapon that rests beside it, a blade alongside which it has done battle, and against which it has dueled. I give you the indomitable Galatine."

David grimaced, but Edmund's smile deepened as the boy with the book flipped excitedly through his pages.

"Galatine," the boy said, as though to himself. "Galatine... here! Galatine was the favored sword of Sir Gawain."

Edmund's eyes blazed. "Again, correct. Galatine, given Gawain by the Lady of the Lake, was the true twin of Excalibur and considered by some its equal. The shadow to Excalibur's light, its storied history remains regrettably obscured by comparison. Well done, young man."

The boy with the book beamed.

Donovan edged closer to the slab.

"Knights of the Roundtable had many weapons of choice," Edmund continued, "and several swords each, but most harbored a favorite, that trusted blade that served them well in the most daunting of moments. As our impressive young scholar notes, Arondight for Lancelot, and Galatine for Gawain. And now—" He gestured skyward with both arms. "—I draw your attention to the beautiful phenomenon unfolding above us."

David, and each of the guests, looked up. The eclipse was nearly complete. A flock of gulls fluttered past, honking nervously, their silvery bodies ghostlike against the blackening sky. The guests were pressed in tightly together, murmuring in admiration at the eclipse, as well as the ancient artifacts.

Something compelled David to glance behind them, beyond the enclosure.

Several more people had assembled, definitely more than he had noticed before. Some of them appeared to be the manor staff who had erected the exhibit, but they numbered more than David had noticed previously. Others had joined them, including, to his great chagrin, the McAlister brothers along with their hounds. Maybe twenty men in all now stood there, and their positioning had in essence formed an enclosure around the enclosure itself. They stood with vigilant postures, their expressions severe.

David could see why Edmund treasured his possessions so deeply—the swords *were* beautiful, and whether or not they carried with them more than just the power of legend, they had succeeded in mesmerizing each of the guests. Yet the demeanor of Edmund's men seemed excessive. Certainly his guests posed no threat.

"Can we hold them?" Donovan asked

Edmund's eyes glinted. "I was rather hoping you would ask."

Donovan's mouth slowly curled into a grin, and he turned to David. "Come on."

David's dad stepped forward. "Hold on." He looked at Kathy, who had been staring vacantly at the swords but now looked down.

They'd spoken privately for several minutes after the hunt, and while David had been unable to make out their conversation, things had seemed icy between them ever since. David was not displeased.

His dad turned to him. "Do you want to?"

David answered without realizing. "Yes."

Donovan's grin became triumphant.

"Okay." David's dad still sounded uncertain. "But be very, very careful."

Edmund addressed his guests. "Our two brave warriors dare enter the battlefield." Some of the guests chuckled, but David's dad did not. "And we are obliged to give them their space. To appreciate the power of these legendary weapons they must hold them, wield them, feel their weight and their history as they guide them through the air. I would not like for anyone to be caught by a pass of one of their blades." He motioned the group backward. "Now, if you'll be so kind."

Donovan stepped forward.

David cast a final glance back at the men who'd encircled the enclosure. They edged closer as Edmund gently herded the guests from the exhibit. Eventually, the groups had exchanged places, Edmund's men now standing between the guests and the enclosure.

David and Donovan now stood alone.

David's dad lingered on the periphery of the ring of guests. "I'd like to stay somewhat close."

Kathy placed one hand on his shoulder and pointed behind him. "Rachel."

David stood on his toes and peered through the darkness. Rachel had wandered from the group and was proceeding straight toward the far edge of the plateau. He began to head for her, but his dad saw too and had already broken into a sprint.

"Rachel!" his dad cried.

His sister stopped and looked back, and now — his eyes having adjusted to the darkness — David spotted what had stolen her attention: a deer — small, a fawn — stood at the periphery of the plateau, nibbling at tufts of grass along the rocky ledge. It looked up at the commotion and peered about before returning its attention to its snack. David exhaled as their dad arrived by Rachel's side.

Edmund, satisfied that everything was all right, returned his attention to the boys. "Gentlemen." He gestured to the hallowed blades.

David nudged Donovan. "Which would you —"

"This one." Donovan's hands flew around the magnificent hilt of Galatine, sword of Gawain, and as they did, he jolted upright as though electrified. Tension rippled through his forearms, but after a moment, things seemed to ease.

Donovan exhaled deeply and looked at David. "Whoa." He hoisted the sword.

More honking sounded above—louder—as the flock of gulls zigzagged about in disoriented fashion. Outside the enclosure, the hounds paced uneasily, whimpering, their tails curled limply beneath their hindquarters.

David looked skyward once more. The moon had superimposed itself flawlessly upon the sun. The eclipse was complete.

"Beautiful," Edmund murmured.

Any lingering traces of illumination were swallowed up as the entire dome of the sky descended as a curtain of darkness. The world all around stood silently, as though listening. The animals stood as statues, and the sea below the cliffs fell still.

Then light....

At first only a pinprick, but as David watched, it expanded in intensity, blossoming around the dark ring on which it perched, like a diamond catching the light just right. Several of Kane's guests shielded their eyes against its brilliance, surreal to behold on this day-become-night, but David's attention roamed elsewhere, back to the slab upon which rested the other sword, Arondight.

It was calling to him.

He knew something of Lancelot but nothing of his blade. Yet, as he gazed at it, he felt himself falling in, as he had with Malea in the drainage tunnel all those months ago. He watched his hands, as if guided by some other force, extend toward and then close around the handle. The blade beckoned him once more, and though in his heart he knew he must answer, he paused as though at the gate of an unknown world.

He glanced at Donovan, who wielded Galatine with wide-eyed wonder, guiding the prodigious blade slowly to and fro, and then lifted his own weapon. He'd expected it to be heavy, but it was exceedingly so. It began to descend with alarming momentum toward his feet, but power surged through him, and he shifted his weight and forced the great sword skyward. It felt immediately more comfortable, and he guided it through the air as if he'd done so a thousand times.

He turned around to look for his family. Kane's men maintained their posts, and beyond them Edmund led the guests a bit farther away, pointing off toward distant points on the island. Rachel stood beside her dad, holding his hand and pointing toward the fawn. His dad nodded, but he'd apparently managed to coax Rachel away for now.

They turned back around toward the enclosure. Though a considerable distance still separated them, David could see, even through the darkness, his sister's face contorting. She raised a finger and pointed behind him precisely as a great rush of air whistled into his consciousness.

He ducked.

Rachel had saved his life....

CHAPTER 39
Awakening

...BUT ONLY FOR THE MOMENT.

Donovan had set upon him, his face snarled with contempt, his blade raised over his head in preparation for another strike.

Someone shouted, "They're awake!" and everything slowed down in that strange way it sometimes does when everything is happening so very fast.

The world around David disintegrated into chaos: figures darting this way and that, people yelling, and the still pervasive darkness rendering it near impossible to distinguish individuals. He could just make out his dad running frantically toward him, but couldn't tell whether Kane's men were trying to get out of the way or restrain him.

Each of these thoughts evaporated as quickly as they'd materialized, as Galatine sliced toward him. He reacted with impossible muscle memory, as though an ancient voice guided his movements. *Evade*, it instructed him. *Parry.*

He did. He ducked again but this time rolled, tucking Arondight beneath him before springing to his feet with an upward sweep of his blade. Steel rang against steel as a blaze of lightning unfurled from the heavens, fusing the two great swords together for the briefest of moments in a blinding confluence. It felt as though the strike had emanated from within him. His blood had become a boiling cauldron, and his body pulsed with electricity. He gripped Arondight with all his strength, and his eyes locked with Donovan's.

Donovan cried out and wrenched himself backward, and their swords burst apart with an ear-splitting *pop*.

David was thrown to the ground.

"David!" his dad's voice commanded. "Let me *through*!"

Out of the corner of his eye, David perceived a rolling tangle of people stumbling about in the darkness. His heart welled with pride, but for the moment it appeared he was on his own.

He got to his feet, aligned them shoulder-width apart, and with both hands raised Arondight above his head.

Donovan's eyes simmered with rage, rooted in an animosity David had sensed but never comprehended... until now. Donovan unleashed Galatine once more, carving the fog and rain with a lethality beyond anything Donovan alone could have possessed.

David met the assault, summoning strength and resolve from a reservoir he hadn't known resided within him.

Donovan was unrelenting, though, rushing him again and again. They fought, wielding the legendary blades as though they'd done so for a lifetime. Steel twisted, sliced, clanged, with neither boy gaining an advantage. When one would unleash a barrage of blows, the other would fend him off with an equally impressive flourish. Arondight and Galatine had come alive in their hands, gilded with fire from the heavens and tinged with the bluish hue of the ancient waters from which they'd been forged.

"I told you," hissed Donovan, "that it was not the end." He charged.

David sidestepped and, with a great cry, mounted his own attack, unleashing Arondight from every direction, wielding the great weapon with a swordsmanship not born of this lifetime. He didn't comprehend Donovan's assertion, and yet he did.

Donovan attacked with renewed vigor, driving him backward.

David's foot snagged in a small depression in the ground and he fell, his back thudding into the unforgiving earth. Arondight flew from his hands and clattered to the earth a few feet away.

Donovan smirked—here was his window, the moment of advantage that had until now eluded them both. He raised Galatine high above his head.

David rolled. As he did, he felt Galatine penetrate the ground mere inches away, where his head had lain a fraction of a second before. Arondight beckoned and he retrieved it, hoisting the now familiar blade as he sprang to his feet.

Donovan snorted angrily and ripped his own trusted blade from the soil. They circled one another, and Donovan's face contorted into a veil of hatred.

They charged.

Power surged like a current within him, but as the collision neared, David searched the tortured face of his rival and understood: if he tried to counter hate with hate, he would surely lose.

And so he fell.

He fell as Galatine sliced toward him, and this decision proved sage, as Gawain's hallowed weapon narrowly missed its mark. Upon impacting the ground, David rolled and flicked out a leg, sending Donovan tumbling to the ground. Galatine cartwheeled high into the air before diving downward and impaling the earth. Donovan scrambled and floundered toward it, but David was upon him, kicking him onto his back and pointing his blade toward Donovan's throat.

"No," he said.

As he stood over his fallen rival, the dark pall of the eclipse began to peel back. The moon edged ever so slowly from its docking with the sun, emancipated rays of light flaring across the sky and diffusing what, moments before, had been the prevailing curtain of night. As the illumination spread, something caught David's eye, far off, at the edge of the plateau near where they'd completed their arduous climb.

"Do it," Donovan spat. "You know you want to."

David looked back down at Donovan. "It didn't have to be this way, my friend." The words escaping his lips were his own... and not his own.

"It had to be this way, and no friend are you, nor were you ever."

And now, he knew. Instinct had roused first, muscle memory springing to life in the nick of time and resurrecting a swordsmanship centuries dormant, but now the fog was lifting, memories shaking off their slumber. They burst the dam of what had been his unawakened soul, and he clenched his eyes shut and steadied himself as they flooded over and through him, time unraveling inside him like a waterfall in reverse. Quick, blurring visions appeared, not stopping but roaring past, defying resolution, until at last they slowed, and images dropped into the picture as though from a thousand different skies, contorting, twisting, and then interlocking with other pieces until the puzzle was complete.

He opened his eyes. "Gawain."

"You utter my name as though we were brothers," Donovan hissed. "But who betrays a brother as you betrayed me?"

Donovan's face continued to simmer with rage, but now a different face materialized — incandescent and beautiful — in David's mind's eye. He thought at first it was Malea, and then Amanda — but no, this was different. *She* was different. It was her, and now he understood.

Where Donovan lay, so too had Gawain. Beyond them had loomed the great castle, towering and intact, beside them a shield, adorned with the face of the woman loved by both. Her beauty was otherworldly, breathtaking. Now he — Lancelot — watched his once brother — Gawain — take his final breath before channeling it up through the centuries to this moment, breathing vengeance and strength into Donovan.

"She made her own choice," David said. "If you loved her as you claimed, you would have honored it."

Immortality, he understood now, wasn't about living forever: it was, more than anything, about those who forever refused to let things die. He lurched unsteadily as this great portal, which connected time and place and people and souls, opened and filled him with a great many things.

Not only Lancelot filled him but more — many more — the images, the lives, the puzzle pieces that had surged past moments ago. He was young, old, of different cultures. He was a man, and at least once, he could see — *feel* — a woman. He saw each of them, *felt* them, and in this moment finally understood that he was at once many yet one. All that he'd ever seen, felt, and been now flowed through him. It filled him, empowered him, and weakened him. Each voice, each memory, each life awakened within him, demanding articulation.

The upward waterfall ceased, memories pooling in his mind like swirling eddies of understanding. Marcel had spoken of it as a gift, but also as the greatest of burdens. No wonder, for beneath the brimming exhilaration—the thrill of knowing he held at his fingertips scintillating powers of untold lifetimes— simmered the growing realization that along with the power came the pain. People dreamed of immortality, spoke of it wistfully, but what they couldn't know was that immortality, at its core, embodied the greatest frailties of the mortal world—fear, loss, vengeance, hate. So powerful did these sometimes become, that even as mortal flesh passed from this world, these ugliest elements of the human condition ceaselessly endured.

He had lived many times—lived, loved, and lost. He'd experienced life's greatest joys, suffered its greatest hurt, and as he awakened, so too did each of his slumbering souls, jagged pieces from each lifetime that carved into his consciousness and bled into him, pooling, converging, until finally reuniting as one.

Souls.

Now he remembered something else Marcel had told him long ago in the cemetery, back when disbelief had been a luxury.

Incipient soul.

He looked at Donovan, still maintaining the tapered, serrated tip of Arondight at Donovan's throat, but shook his head as he did so. Perhaps running his blade through would end this madness—maybe such were the rules of the game—but the part of him that was still him, the *most* him, refused. No longer could he deny that the door had been opened to a new and dangerous world, or that he was caught up in something he could scarcely comprehend. Marcel had told him, and now he knew, that there were dark forces at work—Kane, and perhaps many others—orchestrating the movements of whatever sinister plans had been set into motion.

But he would not be a puppet in their act.

He pulled his blade from Donovan's throat.

CHAPTER 40
Son of Benwick

"DAVID!"

His dad and Rachel now stood beside him — with Kathy beside Donovan — as time and motion wrestled their way back into their normal rhythms.

His dad threw his arms around him before glaring back at Donovan. "What the hell is wrong with you? You could have killed each other!"

Donovan, appearing dazed, didn't answer.

"How long," David gasped as his dad steadied him, "were we fighting?"

"I don't know. Not long — maybe thirty seconds? It was hard to see and everyone was bumping into each other and it was crazy. Are you okay?"

David stared in disbelief. *Thirty seconds?*

It had been much longer; he was sure of it. He raised his head, and as daylight continued its resurgence, things around them slowly returned to some semblance of normalcy.

Parents reassured children; manor staff — and Kane himself — reassured parents. At the edge of the plateau that exited back down onto the path, another of Kane's men, dressed like the others in hooded Kane Manor robes, stood unmoving.

David realized it was this figure who'd caught his eye a few minutes earlier.

Kane whirled and strode back into the enclosure.

David tensed. At the edge of the plateau, the figure moved forward, his movements halting and uncertain. From this distance, David could scarcely gain a sense of the man's features, and yet something was familiar....

There was no time to contemplate the matter, as Kane approached and knelt beside the still prone Donovan and retrieved Galatine, which lay a few feet away. David's eyes narrowed, as he was certain he saw Kane whisper to Donovan, "*You have failed.*"

Kane rose and walked toward David and his family, leaving Donovan and his mother stone-faced behind him.

David tensed, and his heart pounded as his eyes fixed on the great sword gripped in Kane's hand. He wrested free from his dad, shepherded Rachel behind him, and positioned Arondight into a defensive posture.

"David!" His dad moved before him, his eyes wide with astonishment. "What are you doing?"

"It's quite all right, sir. He just endured quite a trauma." Kane extended his empty hand toward David, smiling. "If you please. It would of course be prudent to return these to safekeeping in short order."

Though something tugged deep inside as he did so, David slowly presented Arondight to their host.

"It's not all right," his dad said to Kane. "He should not point a sword at you or at anyone, and you shouldn't allow these to be handled." He glanced over to where Kathy continued to tend to her son, his face full of anguish. "You never know when something crazy can happen. And I would like to know why the hell your men held me back."

David stood in the breach between his dad and Kane and stared as the two men locked eyes. His heart stirred with the resolve he observed in his dad's gaze, but paused on glimpsing the fire in Kane's.

Their host was clearly a man unused to being challenged, much less reprimanded, but after a moment the fire dimmed, Kane's face softened, and he addressed them in an apologetic tone. "You are, of course, quite right. Not once has something like this occurred, in all the times I granted the privilege to guests. But no excuses — I thought they were of age to handle the responsibility. I was mistaken. I beg your forgiveness. As for my men, they were only seeking to protect you. Commendable as your fatherly instinct was, rushing in like that almost certainly would have ended badly."

David boiled as he watched his dad's features ease slightly.

"Well," his dad said. "I appreciate your honesty."

David shut his eyes. Surely, after all that had happened, his dad could see what even his seven-year-old sister so readily could — that Kane was evil; that he had baited the trap for him and Donovan both, manipulating things back home for the past year, and who knows how much longer, to lead invariably to this day; that Kane had played a hand in whatever had become of David and Rachel's mother.

Yet his dad apparently could not see it, and as David slowly reopened his eyes, he saw that the battles that lay ahead would include some with the man whom he'd so desperately wished to spare further grief. For so long, he had debated whether to confide everything to his dad, and after what had just transpired with Donovan, he'd been certain that he would not have to do much convincing, that he could now share all that had been happening, everything that Marcel had told and taught him.

Marcel.

David whirled around, straining frantically to see past the meandering clusters of guests in hopes of spotting the man he was so certain he'd glimpsed just moments ago, and whom he desperately longed to see, but he didn't see him.

Was it yet another case of wishful thinking, or perhaps another trick of the mind?

He was certain it hadn't been.

Both his dad and Kane stared at him, doubtlessly wondering what or whom he was looking at. Maybe it had been Marcel, disguised in Kane Manor attire; if so, he likely didn't wish his identity revealed. A crazy notion, but the line between madness and reality seemed to be evaporating by the moment.

David stood shoulder to shoulder with his dad, but Kane's stare seemed to cut between them, as Arondight and Galatine had sliced through the sea-thickened air minutes before.

"My sincerest apologies to you both," he said. "A man of honor acknowledges his failures and takes measures to make things right. I assure you I shall do just that." He smiled down at Rachel, who latched onto her dad's leg.

She made a face and tucked her head into her chest.

Kane headed back toward the larger group. His staff had escorted a visibly shaken Donovan and Kathy back to the path to return to the castle, and the rest of the visitors and staff prepared to return as well.

"Dad," David whispered as his dad scooped up Rachel and prepared to follow the rest of the guests. "Don't you see what's happening?"

"What do you mean?"

David gestured all around them. "Everything: this place, the castle, the hunt, and now this—Donovan trying to kill me." He paused, wanting to spill everything, including the not incidental matter of his immortality, but he remained uncertain.

"I know." His dad placed a gentle hand on his shoulder. "I know. I am so sorry for all that has happened. You can be sure I will insist that Donovan and Kathy—or that we—stay elsewhere tonight. Donovan clearly needs help, and I hope he gets it, but I will not let him around you again." He offered a smile and began to turn away.

David grabbed his arm. "Dad, it's not just that! Don't you see? It's too many coincidences... everything that has been happening. Everything since Mom...." He couldn't go on.

Rachel looked down at him from her perch and nodded.

"David!" His dad's tone startled him. "I know you miss her. I do too. We all do. Terribly." He stepped closer to his son and placed a firm hand on his shoulder. "But you must let this go. Especially—" His voice fell to a whisper. "—in front of your sister."

With a cry, David wrenched free from his dad's grip and ran. He raced across the plateau, in the direction opposite of where the guests had begun their climb back down the path, the sound of his sister's voice echoing after him. He hated to upset her further, but something in him compelled him onward, fueled with an adrenaline he was surprised to still possess following everything that had just occurred.

He recalled the plateau dropped sharply and dangerously in spots, and this route down to the beach—he could immediately observe—would take him over large, sloping boulders. From his vantage point, it appeared that stone stairs had once descended to the shore, but erosion had all but washed them away. The patch of land immediately before him burst with brush and wildflowers, and he tore through it, nearly falling several times as thickets reached and twisted around his ankles and gravity intensified owing to the considerable decline. When he reached the boulders, they were smooth and slick, but he didn't slow, cascading over them like water. A strip of sand separated the base of the large hill from the lapping waters of the sea, and it wound toward the line of caves they'd observed during their ascent. When he finally reached the shore, heart pounding, his momentum propelled him forward, stumbling toward the surf. He turned and continued running, this time toward the caves.

It seemed ages ago, but David recalled Kane explaining to the boy with the book that one of the caves was named for Merlin. He couldn't remember which, and he didn't care; he ran for the nearest, largest opening, splashing in past the mouth of the cave but halting abruptly, surprised by how much colder and darker it had immediately become.

It took a moment for his eyes to adjust, but when they did, he observed that the sea wound its way through into far recesses of the cave—perhaps all the way through it—like an underground river. Something in him seemed to be crying out in alarm, as if warning him away from this place, but other voices welled up within him too, urging him onward. This immortality thing, for all its wonder, would not be easy to master. Several voices—pieces of things, pieces of *him*—

clamored within him, and they were not of one mind. Inside his head, it felt like a radio set to several simultaneous frequencies.

As he moved forward, the world outside disappeared with every step, until only stone and water and darkness remained.

He stopped.

Up ahead, perhaps fifteen feet away, where the cave narrowed into a funnel of black, he perceived a disturbance in the water—a soft rippling sound, growing more pronounced by the moment. He took a step back. What looked to be a small whirlpool swirled before him, spiraling downward and fanning out in concentric rings.

Despite everything that had been happening—so much of which, until the very moment of their occurrence, David would have considered impossible—he was not prepared for what came next.

The boy with the book had spoken in awestruck tones of the mythical wizard for whom this place was named, and most of David's recollections of the legend cast the ancient mentor of Arthur in a noble light. Now, as David squinted into the dark cauldron and beheld that which slowly materialized from its depths, it became clear that most of the versions had gotten it terribly wrong.

It wasn't the prospect that Merlin was evil that most unnerved him; it was that there was a Merlin at all.

Aren't legends — even if based on kernels of truth — but fanciful embellishments, if not utter fiction?

As he stared, paralyzed, at the terrible thing taking shape before him—taking shape and *moving toward him*—the answer became obvious.

Not always.

Opposing instincts collided within him: run, or stay and fight.

Fight? How?

Whatever epiphany had just been confirmed in the duel with Donovan—whatever powers of lives past he might possess—he could hardly claim mastery over any of them. Besides, which of these powers could conceivably be called upon to counter those of the sinister figure that now waded toward him?

The instinct of flight prevailed, and he stumbled backward through the knee-high waters, but his eyes remained riveted on those of the approaching entity. They seemed to sear into him—fiery crimson orbs sunken into the skull of the dark sorcerer. It occurred to him, as he watched the hooded figure withdraw a long tapered weapon from his cloak, that legends were not always conjured tales of an imagined past but, in some cases, pieces of truth too unsettling to accept.

He continued his awkward, splashing retreat until his back thudded against the jutting far wall of the cave, startling him, but he didn't remove his gaze from the now sparking tip of the wizard's wand. A terrible sadness welled up within him—far greater than his fear—at the realization that his life was apparently at an end. His heart broke for what it would do to Rachel and their dad—and their mother too, if she was still out there.

He remained more convinced than ever that she was, but now he would never learn the truth. Now he would never find her.

The fabled conjurer was nearly upon him, twenty feet away. The waters separating them began to roil, as something else was emerging—minions, perhaps, from the same dark world as the great wizard.

Wait.

He recognized her before her glistening torso had even fully breached the surface of the murky waters — the creature from the drainage tunnel, the one Marcel had called Malea. He recognized her despite the fact that she was clothed quite differently from that first encounter, the day of his fifteenth year. On that day, she'd appeared to him in a beautiful white gown, her golden locks nestled beneath a flowery crown. Now, as she burst from the waters, it was apparent that she was... well, not clothed at all.

David gasped; she was beyond stunning. Beads of water flew in ellipses from her flowing hair as she whipped around toward their adversary. For the briefest of moments, her eyes locked with David's — emerald, as he so vividly recalled, but blazing as she readied for battle. Her unclad figure was sculpted, taut, perfect; her hue a dark and exquisite blue in the twilight of Merlin's cave. From her shoulder blades protruded two small but distinct fins, and between her slender fingers stretched shimmering slips of webbing.

Merlin recognized her too. "You!" he bellowed, and directed his weapon in her direction.

Everything happened fast, and not in that way where fast-moving things seem to slow down into a momentary picture of clarity, as David had experienced several times of late. This was just fast, lightning fast, blinding. Incandescent silver slashes of lightning pulsed from the tip of Merlin's wand, as if a raging thunderstorm had somehow alighted within the cave's gloom. Malea evaded the point-blank strikes with contortions so nimble as to resemble one of those rapid-flip picture books. David could only gain a fleeting sense of her darting figure, a shadowy impression vanishing and rematerializing within the fiery constellation of the sorcerer's assault.

David flinched as a glowing rope from Merlin's wand whistled past. A spot on the wall just above him rained down fragments of exploded stone. He scampered to a nearby stalagmite, not as tall as him but wider, and crouched behind it.

"Son of Benwick!" Merlin's call was haunting and accusatory as it reverberated off the cave walls, along with the fiery eruptions from his magical weapon.

David didn't recognize the name; he could only assume it referred to one of possibly several aliases of Lancelot. Of *him*. All that mattered was that Merlin intended to kill him.

Malea seemed just as determined to stop him. David peeked out from behind the boulder and stared as her movements seemed somehow to grow even faster—so fast, in fact, that her fading imprint lingered momentarily in spots she'd just been, like the tail of a comet. He began to gain a sense of her movements, and she appeared to be no longer merely evading but rather closing in. Her speed escalated to otherworldly levels.

Merlin continued to expel blast after blast at her, as though firing into an approaching cyclone. "You will not stop me, nymph!"

The nymph had other ideas. The cyclone thickened, with the charges from Merlin's wand encircling madly within, giving the appearance of a fiery lasso.

David rose up from his hiding spot, it having dawned on him that Malea's life was, at this moment, endangered as well.

Has she been struck? Is she injured? Should I, could I, intervene?

No time to contemplate: an explosion sounded as a geyser erupted from where the two beings had come together in the swirling waters. A wall of rain pelted down on David, and when it cleared, he could see neither Merlin nor Malea. The place in the water where they had converged churned, and David scampered forward from behind the rock.

"David?"

He froze, his dad's voice echoing unmistakably through the cavern as the waters before him calmed. Perhaps the two ancient figures would reappear, and his dad would at last witness a piece of this new world into which his son had been thrust. Perhaps now he would know that nothing was as it seemed, including, surely, what had happened to the mother of his children.

"I'm here, Dad!" He looked to his left. Faint streaks of light from the mouth of the cave infiltrated the gloom, through which his dad approached. Turning back quickly, he eyed the depths into which Merlin and Malea had descended. The waters undulated lightly, no more than they might on any occasion, depending on the behavior of the sea that fed them.

"David." His dad had reached him. "I know you're upset, but you can't run off like that... not in a place like this. You can get hurt in here. The tide can come in quickly. People drown in places like this."

David's eyes widened. "Rachel... where is she?"

"It's okay. She's with Sydney and her parents. I couldn't risk taking her down here."

"But Donovan... and Kane! The swords!"

His dad placed his hands on David's shoulders. "It's all right. Donovan and Kathy were taken away. I made clear that either they or we needed to stay elsewhere tonight, and Edmund agreed. And the swords were taken back to the castle. Rachel is okay, but probably worried about you, so let's get out of here, shall we?"

He gently began to steer his son back toward the entrance of the cave, but David paused and glanced back one more time to where the two unearthly figures had, moments ago, done battle before his very eyes. The dark waters breathed softly, calmly, as though nothing out of the ordinary had occurred.

"David."

He turned back to his dad.

"David, what is it?"

David eyed the waters a final time. "Nothing."

CHAPTER 41
A Walk in the Moonlight

ONCE BACK AT THE CASTLE, THEY confirmed Donovan and Kathy had vacated the premises, headed — they were told — home, where they would seek psychiatric help for Donovan. After getting something to eat, David went to his quarters, where all of Donovan's belongings were indeed gone, and collapsed onto the bed and fell quickly and deeply asleep.

It was the first time in a long time that he did not dream.

He awoke at dinner time, and though many of the remaining guests, and even Kane, stopped by to check on him and express their concern, he didn't much feel like company, so the manor staff were kind enough to bring him his meal in his room. After what happened — not just the attempt on his life, but his awakening and first reconnections with lives past — he longed to be alone.

He nibbled at his food, but didn't have much of an appetite. Then, finally, it hit him, and he couldn't help but smile when the words escaped his lips.

"Holy shit."

His dad probably would have admonished him; then again, in light of all that had happened, perhaps not. No matter, because they were honest words, and they fit, and he laughed at the relief of having, at long last, a normal reaction to the extraordinary occurrences of the past eighteen months. Some of what he'd found most worrisome in all of this had been how many things he'd been able to take in stride. He'd just learned he was one of the most legendary knights in history, and had been attacked in the shadow of an eclipse by a rival from centuries ago; that, and the little matter of a beautiful water nymph saving him from a certain wizard of ancient lore.

Holy shit indeed.

He found a small measure of comfort in how discombobulating it all was. It helped him believe he was still at least a little bit *him*, as opposed to having stepped aside and vacated himself to make room for another — or many others — no matter how cool some of those others might be.

Later that evening, the three of them went for a walk in the moonlight, beneath the stars. Rachel tired quickly and their dad carried her, and soon she fell asleep in his arms. Their dad said they'd better turn back so he could put her to bed, but David asked if he could stay out a little bit longer, explaining that after all that had happened, he just needed a little time alone. Donovan was gone, so there wasn't anything to worry about. After reminding him not to be long, and not to wander from the walking paths, his dad headed back inside with Rachel.

Kane had warned them on their first day that, at night, the moors thickened with fog, and more than a few unfortunate individuals had become disoriented and stumbled into a bog or one of the many meandering streams. Nonetheless, David walked just beyond the crest of one of the bedrock outcrops.

In the darkness, a light flickered. David smiled and broke into a run straight toward it. When he got there, a figure leaned out from the shadows.

"I knew it was you," David said.

"Master Rose." Marcel stepped from the tree line and drew on his pipe, igniting another orange glow before expelling a tight plume of smoke into the heavy mist.

David threw his arms around him.

"There now." Marcel patted him on the back. When David straightened back up, Marcel looked him in the eyes. "Are you all right?"

"I guess. I mean, all things considered."

Marcel managed a smile. "A fair point. Donovan has left the castle?"

"Yeah, my dad insisted on it. They're going home. Kathy is taking him to some sort of hospital, they said, to get help. Dad said it was either that or he would involve the police."

"I see." Marcel exhaled another set of spiraling rings.

"Do you think that was a mistake? Do you think we should call the police? He did try to kill me."

"No. What matters is that you are safe, but the involvement of the authorities in this matter would not, unfortunately, be helpful. Nor, I'm afraid, shall any hospital provide to him the kind of help he may need."

David frowned. "It almost sounds like you feel sorry for him."

"In a way." Marcel inserted a thin implement into the bowl of his pipe and stamped out the burning embers. "A fragrance that carries a long way, I fear. Best that I not chance giving us away. Some people take to drink to soothe the nerves, but this—" He nodded toward the pipe. "—is one of my primary weaknesses, for better or worse."

David nodded. "What about Donovan?"

"Ah, yes... I do sympathize somewhat, difficult as that may be for you to hear. He has been preyed upon in much the same way as have you, compelled by unseen forces centuries old, and only now, like you, having awakened into an entirely new world."

A mushroom of smoke lifted from the extinguished embers in the bowl of the pipe and drifted lazily upward. Beyond the low-clinging mist the sky was clear, cloudless, and the moon, which had hours earlier taken center stage, bathed the night in its glow.

David looked at Marcel. "Why did you leave school?"

Marcel nodded, as though approving the question. "I am most sorry for that. I was removed, shall we say. I had failed in my assigned duty to prompt your awakening."

David's eyes grew wide, and he felt suddenly ill. "You work for Kane?"

"So he believed. This required no small effort on my part. I infiltrated his ranks long ago, ensured I would become a counselor at your school. I knew what he wanted, and I knew I would stall as long as was possible, but after your fifteenth birthday—the required age—he grew impatient. I was removed from my post, much like poor Cheswick. By this point, his suspicions of me had grown sufficient that I dared not linger or try to contact you."

"Kane needed me to awaken." A statement.

"Yes, and as he failed again and again, I knew he would bring you here, where your incipient soul would have no choice but to rouse. I knew when he would play his hand."

Understanding and then anger rose within David. "Then why didn't you tell me?" he demanded, louder than intended. "Why didn't you stop things before we picked up the swords?"

"You think too much of me, I'm afraid. Remember what I told you all along. I would seek to delay things, to protect you, as long as I possibly could, but in the end I am beholden to the same rules as the rest—as Donovan, Kane, you—part of the same world. There are those who would contend I have already interfered far more than is permitted, that I continue to do so now."

David shook his head. "But I saw you, today, after I fought Donovan, when Kane started to come toward me. You started to come toward us too."

"You are remarkably observant, and you are also correct. There are some destinies that are immutable and before which I dare not intercede. You and Donovan, your incipient souls—it was a confrontation that had no choice but to play out. But Kane—" Marcel's eyes glinted with an intensity David hadn't before observed. "—is another matter. He is permitted no more a right to interfere than I, though I would argue he has abused his rights egregiously. I did not think he would risk exposing the secrets he safeguarded for centuries by attempting to harm you himself. He knows the rules, but I had to be here, just in case."

"I saw Merlin today," David said, almost as an afterthought. "In the cave."

"I know. Malea discharged her duty honorably."

"You knew?"

"I knew."

"I thought you couldn't interfere."

Marcel's eyes twinkled. "I didn't."

"She said something about assembling. Not today, but back then, first time I saw her. A great assembling."

Marcel nodded. "She spoke true, premature though she was to do so. Yes, the Great Assembling is upon us, here in the year of the eclipse. The stars are aligned, as they say. A battle nears in our immortal world."

"What will happen with Donovan?"

Marcel smiled. "Today you survived a plot centuries in the making. You have experienced your awakening, a trauma endured by precious few. Yet here you are concerned with the life of the person who tried to take your own." Marcel's eyes gleamed in the moonlight. "Untold powers are soon to be conferred upon you—countless traits from lives and ages gone by—but pray you never lose sight of this one." He placed a hand over David's heart. "As for your question, I fear I do not know. Donovan is beholden to the same pull of fate as are you. Now that he is awakened, it will be up to him to decide which path to follow. For now, it is good you two shall be separated. Kane will not, of course, acknowledge orchestrating the chain of events that culminated here today, but now that his plan is foiled, I believe him too smart to try something similar, at least anytime soon." Marcel inhaled deeply and looked toward the heavens. "Besides, I have reason to believe his attention has been drawn elsewhere."

The gravity of Marcel's words was not lost on him, but something more urgent welled up within David now, the thing that had, beneath everything, consumed him for more than a year. "My mom... it's tied to all this, isn't it?"

"Yes."

Something caught in David's throat, and his legs began to fail him.

Marcel caught him under his arms and gripped him tightly.

"Is she...." David's voice left him.

"I believe she is alive. I cannot promise it, but there is reason to believe it."

David dabbed his eyes with his shirt sleeve. "Do you know where she is?"

Marcel shook his head. A wave of despair began to rush over David, but Marcel gripped him by the shoulders and said, "But I believe *they* do."

A great sob escaped from deep within David's soul, and he fell into Marcel's arms and gripped him tightly. For a year and half, he'd somehow managed to hold things together, but now the dam burst, and he gritted his teeth but couldn't hold back the torrent. The tears fell in fear of what his mother might be enduring at the hands of her captors. They fell in relief that she was — as he'd believed all along — quite possibly still alive. They fell in hope that now, somehow, someway, he might find her and bring her home. They fell most of all for Rachel, to whom he'd made the most solemn of vows. So many times he'd cursed everything else that had been happening — the strange encounters, newfound abilities, immortality itself — for, remarkable though these things were, they had so often served to distract him from the one thing that mattered most: fulfilling his promise to his sister.

He looked at his watch, paying no mind to the time. The hands had continued their faithful revolutions ever since that day at the stream; his heart thrummed palpably, as though keeping time with them.

"Why do you believe it?" He looked up, hopeful. It occurred to him that, in that moment, Marcel might be conflicted in much the same way David often was with Rachel, afraid of raising false hope. Rachel was beyond hopeful—she brimmed with certainty—that their mother was out there, somewhere, and she retained this conviction on faith alone; David needed something more, something concrete and tangible. Perhaps, at long last, Marcel possessed it.

"The Lightkeepers," Marcel said.

David's shoulders fell slightly. More inclined though he might now be toward accepting the truth of these new and dark and immortal worlds, it was not what he'd hoped to hear.

"Throughout time, each Lightkeeper had a vigilant, a protector."

David inhaled deeply and looked up at the moon, as though expecting in its light some indication of the answers he sought. "My mother."

Marcel nodded slowly. "It would stand to reason. Their path to you would be easier with her out of the way."

David's throat went thick. "I thought you said you think she's alive."

"I do. I believe they detained her on that terrible winter night. I believe they have her still. It was in their interest that you believe her dead, as pain and grief so often succumb to anger, and together they would— they hoped—hasten your awakening. But if the legends are to be believed, they would know well that her life must for now be preserved. I believe they have taken her not to harm her but rather to see that no harm becomes her."

David wobbled where he stood, exhausted beneath burdens both physical and otherwise. It felt increasingly unavoidable that those answers resided somewhere in the infinite gulf of things behind him, and things ahead, yet he felt no closer to either.

Marcel reached out to steady him.

When after a few moments things eased, he straightened up and turned with moonlit eyes toward the vast blackness of the moors. "I don't understand. If they want her out of the way, why keep her safe? What do the legends say?"

Marcel now gazed toward the heavens, as though likewise seeking counsel. "I have lived a long time, as by now you have surely imagined. Centuries. I have seen many things, but the origins of the immortals and the first days of the Lightkeepers precede even me, to say the least. Legends evolve, fade, and rise again, but one truth has been accepted by our kind from the beginning: that in the end, if those malevolent agents succeed in extinguishing all immortals of noble spirit, and then the last of the Lightkeepers, the world shall be plunged into an eternity of darkness more infernal than purgatory itself."

David nodded. "I know. You told me. I am the last. They will come for me again."

"Yes, but that is not all. You may resist them, defeat them, as you gallantly accomplished today. You may emerge victorious time and time again, for centuries hereafter. But again, they will come and pursue you centuries more. So it is written, and so it has been."

"Then how can I stop it? End it once and for all? Other than being killed."

Marcel spoke gravely. "Your mother.... The ancients foretold of the Time of Sacrifice, that moment when at the end of all things, The Guardian shall give over her own life for that of the Lightkeeper, and in so doing—in that most selfless of actions, which repudiates by its very essence everything those forces of darkness seek to impose upon the world—save the world from that damnable fate."

Marcel paused and looked into David's eyes as though regarding each and every soul that had ever resided within him. "The ancients believed that the soul of the Lightkeeper shall, in that moment, fuse with heavenly illumination, and that light shall vanquish darkness for all time, and the world shall enter the most blessed of times—the time of Angels."

David shook his head. "Okay. I don't understand all that, and I don't know if it is true. I just want to find my mom. Why take her now? Are we at that moment? Are we at the end of all things?"

"Not quite yet." Marcel stared out at the unfathomable gloom of the moors, as if seeing through it and far beyond. "There is something they seek. Until then, they must preserve your protector—your mother—at all costs. Should she perish before they find their treasure—and before they visit you again—then that time they have feared for millennia shall be evoked."

With each beat of his heart, David felt his blood coursing through him, and as it coursed, it seemed to whisper to him as many voices, each of them attesting to the gospel that Marcel had shared. The ancients, they murmured, were right. That moment in time will come.

But in this moment, there was only one thing. He met Marcel's gaze. "Do you know where she is?"

"No, but I know where Kane heads next, and your mother is a prize to him, like any of his treasures. I should expect that where we next find him, we may find her."

"I want to look for her."

Marcel nodded, his expression now more kindred than paternal. "And so you shall, but I fear even more patience is now required, unfair as that may seem. You are now awakened — part of a world and a war that can be vengeful and unforgiving. Where we go, others shall follow, and yet others shall await us. Everything is at stake. It is essential that you be trained."

"Dueling?"

"Dueling, yes, but that is but a part. I shall teach you to commune with and channel the greatest powers of your lives gone by."

"David!" His dad's voice echoed through the darkness, urgent and concerned.

"Will you meet him?" A million thoughts flooded David's mind. "We can tell him about Mom, about Kane, everything. And then—"

"David." Marcel's voice was quiet but resolute. "No."

The voice of his dad trumpeted once more into the night.

"No one must know I am here. It would jeopardize you and your family, as well as my ability to attend to things I must, and to provide whatever support I can to you moving forward. It is, as ever, up to you whether you choose to tell him, but I am afraid I must now take my leave."

David stared helplessly as Marcel retreated back into the shadow of the woods. "I'm scared," he called.

"I should expect so," Marcel replied from beyond the tree line. "Why so many people ascribe shameful connotations to such a normal human condition is beyond me. I get scared too, my boy, even at my, shall we say, considerable age."

David lowered his head. "Kane did all this. I fell right into it, into everything. All I've wanted to do was find my mom. I promised Rachel, you know? But all this time, I've been a pawn in his game."

"Listen to me. They have conducted up to this point, but now, I dare say, you have struck a chord — a shot across the bow. You have been heroic, regardless of immortality or great powers or dark forces. You held your family together, and have been a beacon of light for your sister. You have not failed her. You have saved her."

David did not bother this time to blot his eyes. "She has saved me," he whispered.

His dad's voice echoed again on the wings of the evening breeze.

"I must leave you," said Marcel.

"What do I do now?"

"For now, try to live as normally as possible, crazy as that may sound. Return to school. See your friends. But soon will come a choice. When it is safe, I will return to you, and we will train."

David's heart accelerated. "But can they kill me? I mean, Donovan couldn't, and remember what you told me about what happened to me in the stream way back then? You said I drowned, but if I did, obviously, I came back to life."

Marcel had reappeared from the tree line. "I am afraid so. You survived death that day because you were one day short of the required age. But at fifteen, souls may be awakened, destinies may be fulfilled, and forces of light and darkness resume their conflict."

His dad's call issued forth once more, close now.

Marcel moved quickly toward David and pressed something into his hands. "I almost forgot to give this to you. Hide it now, keep it safe. Be sure it makes it home with you. When the time is right, its purpose shall be revealed." He pulled David into a final embrace. "Goodbye, Master Rose, and Godspeed."

And with that, he withdrew once more into the woods and vanished.

David closed his eyes for a spell, and when he opened them, he peered at the object in his hands, brows arched, and jammed it into his pocket.

He then turned and headed back toward the castle, toward his father's voice.

CHAPTER 42
Home

WHEN IT CAME TIME TO LEAVE the castle the next morning, the same driver in the same sleek limousine awaited them.

A few of Kane's staff loaded their bags, and Kane himself escorted them to the vehicle. He extended a hand to David's dad. "Once again, sir, my humblest apologies for the tribulations your family endured here. I hope, despite everything, it was a memorable trip."

David's dad took his hand. "A bit more than tribulations, but I realize you couldn't foresee it. Hopefully, Donovan receives the help he needs, but my only concern is my family."

"As it should be, sir. As it should be."

Rachel yawned as her dad buckled her into her seat, then took his own place in the vehicle.

David and Kane faced each other, the mist-wrapped castle looming over them. Alone in the dark of his quarters the previous evening, David had envisioned countless variations of how this moment might unfold, including scenarios in which he would draw Kane out in a grand battle of wits—like Chester at the chess board—exposing him for the liar and fraud and villain they both knew him to be. Then, at last, his dad would see. But in each instance, reality eventually intruded with the sobering reminder that Kane was

THE AWAKENING OF DAVID ROSE

good, too good for him just yet, and such an attempt would only backfire, and upset his dad and impose an even greater wedge between them.

A different scenario, quieter but still critical, had settled into his mind before he'd finally drifted off. It was unfolding this very moment.

"It was nice to meet you." He extended a hand to the man who'd orchestrated an attempt on his life. "Thank you for everything. It was all so impressive." A surge of exhilaration coursed through him as he observed a moment of uncertainty in their host — slight, fleeting, but there.

Kane took his hand. "A pleasure, to be sure, and I dare say the most impressive thing here was you." Their eyes locked as Kane maintained his grip on David's hand. "Until we meet again."

David maintained his gaze. "I look forward to that."

After David had settled into his seat, Kane closed the door, and David's heart pounded as the limo crept slowly forward. He'd wondered — in the scenarios that had played out in his mind — if Lancelot or any of his past personas would make an appearance during this last encounter with Kane, instilling in him, perhaps, some great measure of confidence and resolve from ages past. They had not. It had just been him, and he'd been scared to death the entire short-lived exchange.

Now, as the vehicle eased away in the direction of the rising sun, leaving Kane and his castle and every secret it possessed behind, a smile begged at the corner of David's lips. Scared or not, he had, in Marcel's words, fired a shot across the bow.

He didn't look back.

***

They remained quiet most of the flight home, still exhausted, still in a state of disbelief, yet, at the same time one of dawning realization—an awakening for each of them. There would be time to talk about all of it once they returned home, which they were each desperate to do. The flight was quiet and peaceful. At various intervals, they slept.

***

Though the flight to New York was long and followed by a second flight from New York to home, as soon as they arrived and unpacked, David called Amanda. Since they'd gained five hours on their return, lingering traces of daylight remained.

Rachel was, of course, exhausted, and fell asleep on her dad's lap on the couch.

"Please, David." His dad sounded more than exhausted himself. "Don't be long."

They road their bikes and met at Moreland Farms, at the stretch of road that looked out over the propane tanks, across the property to the old farmer's home, and beyond that, his fields. The fields—lush now—rolled out like emerald waves to the far horizon, beneath a darkening sky streaked blue and orange.

They sat quietly a while, but at length he told her everything, and she listened, her demeanor solemn and empathetic.

When he finished, they both fell silent again, as if letting things settle along with the fading sun. Everything was pretty around them, peaceful. When another day broke tomorrow, they understood, their world would be anything but.

Amanda's voice at last dissolved the silence. "So all that strange stuff at school... it was all about you — all the focus on feuds and violence, Cerratus. It was all to try to get you to awaken?"

"Yeah."

"That was why Mr. Cheswick left. He must not have cooperated. They must have really scared him."

David nodded. "I think he stood up to them, but Kane is too powerful."

"And the real estate contest to win the vacation... all to lure you guys out there?"

"He was behind everything."

Amanda's eyes grew wide as she tried to work things out. "The note...." Her voice dropped. "The note about the milk... it was from Donovan's mom?"

"Yeah. Chester helped me to see it. Kane set all that up too. He made us think Mom was dead, got Kathy to get closer and closer to my dad, to cause more conflict and bring Donovan and me together."

Amanda shook her head. "Your poor father, with what happened with your mom, and then Kathy, and all that has happened to you. He still doesn't believe it all, though?"

"Kane is good." David caught himself and added, "Well, not *good*, but you know what I mean."

"What do you suppose will happen to them? To Donovan and his mom?"

David's eyes narrowed. "I don't know. They say he's getting help. Kane told him he'd failed. Marcel says, in a way, Donovan has been used by them almost as much as I have."

"Marcel is a good man."

David nodded. His lips moved as if conjuring a response, but no words came.

"It's all pretty amazing," Amanda said. "You say you two were reliving a feud from medieval times, and maybe I was the maiden you dueled over all those centuries ago?"

"We seemed to think so, anyway."

Amanda nodded, her gaze still fixed on the horizon. Her eyes glinted. "That's pretty wild—hard to believe as it still is—and maybe even a bit sweet." She turned her head and regarded him. "Maybe you fought over me, and maybe you didn't, and maybe you have all these ancient powers now, but you need to remember something, and Donovan too, wherever he is: I'm nobody's prize."

***

Though his dad told him he didn't need to go back to school immediately, David was adamant that he would. Nothing would ever be the same again, but returning to school felt like an invaluable—if unsteady—anchor, tethering his two worlds together. He wasn't leaving one world for another, but rather embarking upon the most formidable of balancing acts between the two.

Even school felt different, to each of them— Amanda, Robert, and Chester too. He'd shared with them every detail, and now that he understood it was only the beginning, David knew he would need them more than ever. After a few days, they slipped back into the routine of things as best they could, but even so, each carried a burden only the other three could hope to understand. Their other friends and classmates went about their lives as usual—and why wouldn't they?—comfortably unaware that not only was there more to their worlds than they could possibly imagine, but there were more worlds too.

Some bright spots did emerge. Mr. Cheswick had returned, and Rendicott and Cerratus had gone. The lessons seemed to have gone back to normal, and there was no hint of Kane, no sightings of strange visitors in long dark coats. It was as though an ill wind had passed through their town but, at long last, dissipated, replaced by the carefree gusts of spring.

They rode bikes, with Chester's wheelchair whirring alongside them. They played ball and studied for final exams. David pushed Rachel on her tire swing, and with each revolution, her hair poofed up, and she giggled, and it seemed as if all their worries were borne away on the same jaunty breeze.

Soon would come summer and sixteenth birthdays and driver's tests—and adventures and danger likely to eclipse all that they now imagined. What was certain—and this seemed to David the most crucial anchor of all—was that whatever they faced, they would do so together.

CHAPTER 43
Close to Her Heart

DAVID PUT RACHEL TO BED THAT night, as always. When he asked what she wanted him to read, she said, "A Frosty poem."

He retrieved the book of poems. He knew which one he would read her, and wasn't exactly sure why he hadn't chosen it before.

"Scootch." He gently nudged her over so he could sit.

She'd already climbed under her covers, and wriggled to make a bit of room for her brother. "A rhyming one?" She pulled herself up slightly to get a better look.

"Yes, it rhymes a bit."

Pleased, Rachel rested her head on his shoulder and waited for him to begin.

"Stopping by Woods on a Snowy Evening." He eased his voice to just louder than a whisper.

> *"Whose woods these are I think I know.*
> *His house is in the village though;*
> *He will not see me stopping here*
> *To watch his woods fill up with snow.*
> *My little horse must think it queer*
> *To stop without a farmhouse near*
> *Between the woods and frozen lake*
> *The darkest evening of the year.*
> *He gives his harness bells a shake*

To ask if there is some mistake.
The only other sound's the sweep
Of the easy wind and downy flake.
The woods are lovely, dark, and deep,
But I have promises to keep,
And miles to go before I sleep,
And miles to go before I sleep."

He looked down at Rachel to see if she'd liked it, but her eyes were closed, her lips settled into a smile.

David smiled too, even though his mind raced with many considerations, not all of them happy ones. He thought of his mother, and when he looked back down at Rachel, he noticed a note clutched in her hands — the first one their mother had given her when she'd learned to read.

You are an angel from Heaven. Love always, Momma.

The paper rested securely in her little hands, atop her chest, close to her heart.

Watching her drift off to sleep, with a smile on her face, was about the most peaceful thing David could imagine. At least for the moment, it made everything seem right with the world.

EPILOGUE

HALFWAY AROUND THE WORLD, TWO MEN stood side by side, struggling to catch their breath in the suffocating heat and dust. A sprawling excavation tent enclosed the dig site, yet, despite providing shade, it seemed to trap the oppressive heat all the more. They had toiled throughout the blistering day, parched and exhausted, but quickly dusted themselves off and stood at attention as an ominous-looking figure strode into the tent.

The stranger, tall and imposing, wore a long dark coat. He didn't appear to be perspiring.

"Such sloth," the man said in ancient Akkadian tongue, and the two dig laborers stared at him, unknowing. The man, noticing their blank stares, addressed them in Iraqi Arabic instead. "Why have you stopped?"

The two laborers looked at one another incredulously.

"Sir," one of them said. "We work all day and grow weary. We do this every day and know not why. Can you please tell us, why do we dig?"

The man in the dark coat regarded the men, who shifted uneasily, dust wafting up from their shuffling feet. He began to pace slowly back and forth before them. "We stand here in ancient Babylonia. Mesopotamia. Many have visited here. Many have made pilgrimage." He paused and grinned at the staring men. "Babylon was excavated in 1811, and countless times since. Brilliant scholars and historians pierced this land with their spades. Why did *they* dig?"

The men listened in fearful silence.

"Much perished when a raft containing over forty crates of artifacts sank into the Tigris. A major excavation was conducted on behalf of the British Museum. There was widespread looting at the site. There were many finds, but the brutish methods of excavation, so common then, caused considerable damage." The man moved closer to the laborers and placed a hand on the shoulder of each.

They startled at his touch, then attempted to steady themselves.

"Worry not, my friends. You are doing a noble service and are therefore useful to me. There are the laborers, like you, and there are the visionaries, like me. Most recently, digging resumed here in 1987. The work concentrated on the area surrounding the Ishara and Ninurta temples in the Shu-Anna city-quarter. *This* area."

The man in the dark coat looked once more at the men. "And so now, my friends, does it start to dawn upon you, the significance of this place?"

The laborers glanced nervously at each other, and the one who'd spoken up earlier did so once again. "Sir, yes. Your expertise of this site is impressive. Clearly, many harbor interest, but...." The worker stopped and looked down uncertainly.

"Continue."

The laborer gulped before looking back up at their strange visitor. "Sir, I still ask, with respect, *why* were they interested? Why do we dig? What do you seek?"

The man in the dark coat nodded, as if validating the merits of the inquiry, and commenced his slow pacing once more. "What do I seek?" he asked, as if to himself. "Must you know? It is indeed difficult to suppress. Seems I've borne the onus for time in memoriam." He reached into the folds of his coat and moved directly in front of the men. "I seek the greatest power the world has ever known."

Summoning the men to bow their heads closer, he unburdened himself and watched their eyes grow wide.

"Yes, yes," the stranger said. "Now you see."

The laborers had not time to catch their breath before the man plunged a dagger swiftly, brutally, first into the chest of one and then the other, before either could react or comprehend what had occurred.

The man turned around as his victims slumped to their knees, clutching at their mortal wounds. They pitched forward into the sand as the strange visitor strolled from the site.

He paused at the edge of the tent, smiling into the blinding sun. "And now you know, my friends," he said, without looking back. "I can feel it. We are close."

THE END

Acknowledgements

For David and Rachel, who — groan as they might upon reading this now — demonstrated from the first a bond which stands immutably as the genesis for and heartbeat of this story. And for Daniel, who arrived after this tale was conceived, and whose irrepressible spirit has breathed new life into the project, and into me.

For Linda, who brought them into the world — countless were the occasions I slipped away after dinner and on weekends to write, missing my children but soothed by the invaluable knowledge they were in the care of the finest mother one could wish for his children.

And for Marjorie Stelmach, brilliant poet, generous soul, my favorite teacher, and the one who told me more than three decades ago that she expected to see my name on book covers one day. That day arrives a touch later than perhaps I reckoned, but I vowed upon hearing those words to remember them in my dedication when it finally did. Thank you, truly.

About the Author

From childhood I kindled three dreams: to one day become a father, a writer, and a baseball player.

Two of three ain't bad. (I shall neither confirm nor deny holding out deluded hope for the third.) Most of what I write is fiction, but not all. I write the occasional article and guest post, and conduct some interviews. I'm an English major, have a masters in social work, and have been a nonprofit leader for many years. I am crazy for sports and animals, am helplessly in love with the written word, and am eternally grateful for my family, who make me luckier than I could ever deserve.

For more, please visit Daryl Rothman online at:
Website: www.DarylRothman.com
Goodreads: Daryl Rothman
Twitter: @DRothmanWrites
Facebook: @AuthorDarylRothman

What's Next?

Be sure to check out the second book in this "David Rose" series, which is now available.

David Rose and the Forbidden Tournament

It's one thing to discover a whole new world, but quite another to survive it. David Rose discovers that, on top of everything else, immortality can kill you.

It's been less than a year since his fateful 15th birthday, but for David Rose, everything has changed. He's learned of his immortality, discovered a sinister plot centuries in the making, survived an attempt on his life at a medieval castle in England, and through it all, he's more convinced than ever that his mother is alive.

David has been awakened to a wondrous new world, yet one fraught with peril. Despite all his new powers and potential, David feels more vulnerable than ever. His awakening has served as a beacon to other immortals, some of whom view him as a threat to be dispatched.

Strange things are happening with Rachel, their father has withdrawn again, and David worries they are no closer to finding their mother. Just as he's learning how to channel the greatest powers of his past lives, he's abducted by a rogue syndicate bent on exploiting immortals and pitting them against each other in battles to the death.

More from Evolved Publishing

We offer great books across multiple genres, featuring high-quality editing (which we believe is second-to-none) and fantastic covers.

As a hybrid small press, your support as loyal readers is so important to us, and we have strived, with tireless dedication and sheer determination, to deliver on the promise of our motto:
QUALITY IS PRIORITY #1!

Please check out all of our great books, which you can find at this link:
www.EvolvedPub.com/Catalog/

Thank you!